Dear Mystery Read

DEAD LETTER newcomer Molly Brown has won considerable praise for her first novel INVITATION TO A FUNERAL. Everyone from *Library Journal* to *Time Out UK* (who named it Historical Crime Novel of the Year) have applauded Brown's thoroughly entertaining tale of life, and death, in Restoration London.

Aphra Behn is a playwright whose plays are the hottest ticket in all of London. While in the midst of rehearsal for her latest play, Aphra receives word that her father's great friend, Matthew Cavell, is penniless and dying. When Aphra goes to comfort him, he's already dead, in the cold confines of a London's Good House shelter. Not long after Matthew's death, his brother Elias turns up dead in Aphra's outhouse. Unable to figure out why anyone would want these two destitute brothers dead, Aphra goes looking for answers. Answers that will send shock waves all the way to King Charles's majestic throne.

With stunning historical detail, ferocious humor and the ambitious Aphra, INVITATION TO A FUNERAL is a mystery lover's dream. Enjoy!

Yours in crime,

Joe Veltre
Associate Editor
St. Martin's Press Dead Letter Paperback Mysteries

Other titles from St. Martin's **Dead Letter** Mysteries

Dead Letter is also proud to present these
mystery classics by Ngaio Marsh

INVITATION TO A FUNERAL

MOLLY BROWN

St. Martin's Paperbacks

To Margretta Brown, and also to the memories of Paul Dorrell and Erna Wachtel, good friends whom I will always miss.

Special thanks to Brandon Butterworth for countless cups of tea. Thanks also to Chris Amies, Ben Jeapes and Gus Smith for taking the time to read a rough draft of this on disk.

Author's Note

A lot of what follows is based on actual events, though I have taken liberties with some of the dates. For example, Doctor Alexander Bendo's office opened for business in the summer of 1674, but I could not resist including him.

Previously published in Great Britain by Victor Gollancz.

INVITATION TO A FUNERAL

Library of Congress Catalog Card Number: 98-12772

ISBN: 0-312-97094-3

Printed in the United States of America

St. Martin's Press hardcover edition/May 1998
St. Martin's Paperbacks edition/July 1999

10 9 8 7 6 5 4 3 2 1

Prologue: 1667

He crawled, naked and bleeding, along a windswept beach. Sand blew in his eyes, scoured his skin, ground his wounds. The wind was cold and harsh; it slapped his long black hair across his face and whistled past his ears. He stopped and raised one hand to shield himself. He kept the other tightly balled into a fist.

The wind carried a deafening cacophony of sounds: the crash of waves, the shrieks of gulls, the cries and groans of other men like him — the wounded and the sick — stripped of their clothing and abandoned.

Black clouds moved across the grey sky. He climbed on to a rock and looked out to sea. His ship had disappeared over the horizon. He opened his fist and stared at the worthless ticket he still clutched, given in lieu of pay.

Chapter One

It was nearly ten of the clock when the playwright Aphra Behn came downstairs and found three bodies on her parlour floor. She lifted her full skirts and stepped carefully over the first two. The third one she kicked. It opened one bloodshot eye. It closed it again as she threw back the shutters, flooding the room with light. 'S'nails,' she said, 'it's raining.' Then she turned to survey the room, her head throbbing.

The screen she used to protect her face from the reddening effects of heat – a metal stand hung with a small fringed square of thick green cloth embroidered with gold – had been knocked over and was lying face-down in the grate. The cloth alone had cost her thirty shillings. Luckily the fire had gone out hours ago and the grate was cold, so her beloved screen wasn't burnt. But it was covered in ashes, and that was infuriating enough. She shook it out of the window before putting it back in its usual place, in front of an upholstered stool a few feet away from the fireplace.

The stool's upholstery was dotted with wine stains. So was her carpet. Her desk top was covered in lumps of wax – the remains of candles left to burn themselves out. A small table had been placed upside down, the tablecloth carefully draped across the legs to make a little tent. And, she noted, every single picture and tapestry on the walls was now hanging slightly askew: each tilted to the right by about two inches. How witty of them.

9

'God's my life,' said the third body, 'my poor head feels about to burst.' He touched the spot, just below his ribs, where she had kicked him. 'And I have a fierce pain in my side, just here.'

'God's nails, Hoyle! What are you still doing here?'

'Sleeping, my dearest. Or at least I was.' The man sat up, yawning and rubbing his eyes, then rose to his feet. He was in his late thirties, only a year or two older than Aphra. His clothing was expensive: a green silk coat edged with lace, satin breeches, silk stockings – but badly wrinkled and in need of cleaning. His leather shoes had gold buckles, but they were streaked with dried mud. His close-cropped dark hair was caked with white powder. A long brown periwig, elegantly curled, lay on the floor behind him. Beside the wig lay a sword. Beside the sword lay several empty bottles and an empty jug.

The other two men began to stir. Their clothes were equally expensive, and equally dishevelled. One straightened his wig and stood up, farting loudly. 'I beg your pardon, dear lady,' he murmured, bowing.

The one remaining on the floor grasped first the leg, then one arm, and finally the back of a carved wooden chair as he slowly pulled himself up into a standing position. 'I am your servant,' he said, gulping. 'Your most obedient servant.'

Hoyle began to laugh. He stopped when he saw the look on Aphra's face. 'Sweet soul,' he said, lowering his voice to a soothing murmur, 'why look so grim? Is something the matter?'

'Is something the matter?' she repeated, incredulous. 'Is something the matter? Many, many things are the matter, John Hoyle. And not least of these is that you and your friends persist in using my house as an inn!'

'An inn would have given us a bed,' muttered the one clinging to a chair for support. Aphra turned, her face a mask of fury. The man who had farted left the room hurriedly, explaining he had desperate need of her house of office.

'What did you say?' Aphra screeched, crossing the room in two large steps.

The man quickly manoeuvred himself around the back of the chair as if he meant to use it as a shield. Aphra felt a stabbing pain in her right temple. Her tongue seemed coated in dust. She took a deep breath and forced her voice back down to a normal level. 'Pray repeat yourself, good sir,' she said, struggling to remain calm, 'I did not hear you.'

'I said nothing of importance, dear lady. It was a jest — merely a very poor jest.'

She turned back to John Hoyle. 'Leave my house this minute, or I will fetch the constable.'

'The constable!' John Hoyle exclaimed, laughing and slapping his thigh. 'Madam, I am a gentleman and an attorney; no constable would dare touch me.'

Aphra reached up and grabbed him by the collar of his green silk coat, pulling him down until his face was only inches away from hers. She could feel the heat of his breath on her skin. 'If the constable will not dare touch you, then I will.'

He bent down even further, brushing his lips against her ear. 'Please, madam. Do.'

She let go of him, blushing crimson. 'Damn you, Hoyle,' she said, 'I have no time for this.'

The man who had rushed out to her house of office returned from the garden.

'Goodbye,' she said, ushering the men into the street.

Aphra hated rehearsals, and the rehearsal she hated most of all was the first one. The first rehearsal of a new play was always chaos. It didn't matter that when the play had been accepted by the manager it had been read out loud to the entire company; not one of the actors would remember a single line from it or even what it was about. They never did.

Young Mr Davenant had the cast already assembled on stage, waiting for her. She was fifteen minutes late, thanks to Hoyle and his friends, and though she only lived around the corner from the Dorset Garden Theatre, the rain was so heavy she was soaked through. Her brown hair, in perfect ringlets only minutes before, now hung lankly down her back. She took off her dripping wet cloak and cast it to one side, cursing to herself.

The cast sat on benches carried up from the pit, in almost total silence. There were nearly twenty-five of them. Why, oh why, had she written a play with so many characters, and all those crowd scenes? A few of the younger girls were giggling together in one corner, but the majority were badly hung-over and more asleep than awake. Exactly the way she felt, thanks again to John Hoyle and his friends. Why had she ever opened the door to them in the first place? And how much wine had she drunk? All she knew was her house was a mess and her head felt like it was trapped in a vice. Damn that Hoyle, damn him.

The fact that the actors hated these morning rehearsals even more than she did usually gave her a perverse sense of consolation, but not this time. Looking over the assembled group, she suddenly realized she had more to worry about than just getting through the first reading with eyes that refused to focus and a mouth that tasted like old boots; her leading actress was nowhere to be seen.

She took Mr Davenant to one side. 'I don't see Mrs Decker.'

'That's because she isn't here,' he stated matter-of-factly.

'Where is she?'

'I have no idea.'

Aphra felt her jaw tightening; she was struggling not to scream. The fact that Mr Davenant was so calm only made her want to scream louder. She was late, the cast were obviously in no fit state for a rehearsal, and the leading lady was missing. His late father would have been shouting and punching the scenery by now; you knew where you stood with a man like that. But this young Charles Davenant was a total mystery to her. He had warned her not to cast Elizabeth Decker. But Aphra had ignored him and cast the woman anyway, sight unseen – as a favour to a friend. And now that Decker hadn't shown up young Davenant *wasn't* raving or throwing things. He wasn't even taking the opportunity to remind Aphra that he had told her so. Young Davenant was not a normal man.

'Shouldn't we begin?' he asked her gently. He didn't even remind her it was her fault they were running late. It was maddening.

'Yes.' She picked up her copy of the script and sat on a stool, facing the actors. 'I'll read Mrs Decker's part for now,' she told them. Each had been given a roll of paper with their own lines and cues written out; only Mr Davenant, Aphra and the prompter had copies of the entire play.

A shiver ran down Aphra's spine; she always hated this bit. 'Act one, scene one,' she began, 'opens to reveal an empty street...'

She was reading the heroine's speech from the fourth act when the doors at the back of the theatre flew open, and John Wilmot, Earl of Rochester, entered, leading the nineteen-year-old Elizabeth Decker by the hand. Aphra turned around, stopping in the middle of a sentence.

The earl wore a coat and breeches of blinding yellow trimmed with scarlet ribbons, high-heeled leather riding boots, leather gloves and a wide-brimmed yellow hat with a bright red feather. His wig was the colour of molten gold, falling in deep waves past his shoulders. He was not yet thirty, and with his large blue eyes, full lips and prominent cheekbones, his face could easily have belonged to a beautiful woman – a beautiful woman who hadn't slept for a week. He made his way unsteadily through the pit, kicking benches aside, practically dragging the young actress behind him.

She was tall and slender and her plain clothing contrasted sharply with that of her ostentatious companion. Her dress was brown, with an unfashionably high neckline. Her dark hair had been pulled back from her face and pinned into a neat bun. No curls, no powder, no jewellery. She had no need for them; her eyes were large and round, with an expression of almost

13

childlike innocence. Her skin was perfect: clear and smooth with a natural hint of pink to her cheeks. She didn't seem the least bit bothered about the fact she was being pulled along like a puppy on a leash by a man who was obviously drunk, her pretty face looking slightly vacant, as if her mind was somewhere else.

'Divine Astrea, beauteous poet,' the earl said, noticeably slurring his words. He removed his hat with a flourish and bowed low, swaying slightly to one side. He released his grip on the actress to take one of Aphra's hands and press it to his lips. He kept it there too long; she finally pulled her hand away. 'Sweet lady, I beg your forgiveness most humbly on behalf of my friend. It was I who caused her to be late; I was ... coaching her.'

Several of the actors burst out laughing. 'Coaching her?' one of the men said, 'First time I ever heard it called that!'

Rochester swung around wildly. 'What villain dares insult this lady? Apologize, sir, or die!' He pulled out his sword and fell backwards into the pit.

The actor apologized.

Mr Davenant helped Rochester backstage. Aphra suggested they read the play through again, from the beginning.

The theatre was empty and everyone had gone to a tavern for lunch. Everyone except Aphra – she couldn't stand the thought of a crowded tavern full of chattering actors, not today. And Elizabeth Decker, who said she was going back to her lodgings to study her lines. And Rochester. He was still around somewhere.

Aphra found him in the props room, asleep on a couch. Someone had thrown a fake tiger-skin rug across him as a blanket. The end with the tiger's head was draped over his feet. It had yellow glass eyes and an open mouth full of pointed teeth, the tips painted to resemble dripping blood. Aphra thought for a moment, then carefully lifted the rug, turning it around so that the tiger's open mouth was barely an inch from the earl's nose.

She tapped him on the shoulder and stepped back.

Rochester opened his eyes, screamed, grabbed the tiger by the throat and spent a long, horrible moment wrestling with a rug. Then he saw Aphra, standing only a foot away and laughing so hard she was bent over double.

'What pleasure it is to wake and find I have female company,' he said, tossing the rug aside with a forced nonchalance. 'Is your rehearsal finished already?' He arched his back, stretching like a cat. 'How time flies when a man is sleeping.' Still lying down, he shifted to one side, patting a spot on the couch beside him. 'Pray have a seat.'

'What? Having seen you overcome that fierce beast of the jungle and then discard it? What guarantee do I have you would not overcome and then discard me?'

'I wouldn't dream of attempting it, madam. I know you are fiercer than any tiger.'

'I'm happy where I am, thank you.'

Rochester rolled his eyes and sighed. He bent his arms behind his neck, resting his head on his hands. Then he slowly and deliberately crossed his legs. 'There,' he said. 'You need have no fear of compromise; all offending parts have been secured. So please sit down.'

Aphra sat on the edge of the couch with her arms crossed.

'Fair Astrea, I am concerned for you; you look tired.'

'I *am* tired.'

He smiled a mischievous smile, his eyes twinkling. 'And who's been keeping you awake at night?'

She frowned at the floor, saying nothing.

'Not that John Hoyle again? You said you were finished with him.'

'I was.' She paused, looking uncertain. 'I am.'

Rochester shook his head with an exaggerated sigh. 'Drop him, Aphra, drop him. The man has all my bad points with none of my charm.'

15

'Charm?' Aphra repeated. 'Charm? You burst into the theatre drunk, waving a sword and threatening the actors, and you dare speak of charm?'

He shrugged. 'I might have been much drunker and waved a pistol.'

'I didn't wake you to talk about John Hoyle – or your supposed charm – but to talk about your friend Mrs Decker.'

'I'd much rather talk about my charm.'

'I'm going t⊔ replace her.'

'Replace E⊔⊔⊔ Rochester sat upright. 'Why?'

'Because sh⊔⊔⊔⊔⊔⊔ will ruin my play. It will be a disaster, closi⊔⊔⊔⊔⊔⊔e.'

'You think s⊔⊔⊔⊔⊔⊔⊔Aren't you being a little unfair to her?'

'Unfair to *her*⊔⊔⊔⊔⊔e play doesn't run for at least three perfo⊔⊔⊔⊔⊔rthing. You know that! My last play only⊔⊔⊔⊔ord another failure.'

'But you can't ⊔⊔⊔⊔must be in your play, and she must overw⊔⊔⊔h her talent.'

'Rochester, I don't ⊔⊔⊔⊔veryone knows Elizabeth Decker is your mis⊔⊔⊔⊔u give her large sums of your wife's money to live ⊔⊔en who take an actress as their mistress would insist she leave the stage. Yet you insist the opposite. Why?'

'Where is Elizabeth now?' he whispered, looking around.

'She's gone to her lodgings.'

'And the others?'

'They'll be back soon, but we are quite alone for the moment.'

Rochester sighed and leaned forward. 'The reason Elizabeth must be in your play is that I made a wager with Lord Buckingham that, given six months, I could make her the best actress on the London stage. That was five months ago.'

'God's night-shirt! You'll never win this ridiculous wager. She's the worst actress I've ever seen!'

'We have an entire month before your play opens – you've

no idea how much she's improving; she gets better every day. I'll split my winnings with you, Aphra; I'll give you a quarter.'

'Ha! You think I would settle for less than half?'

'All right, half.'

'How much did you bet?'

Rochester paused a moment, then shrugged, staring at his fingernails. 'Five hundred pounds.'

Aphra jumped up, waving her arms. 'Five hundred pounds! Are you mad?' She took a deep breath and shook her head. 'No, I cannot risk it. I am in debt already; I am behind in my rent, and I owe fifty pounds to a money-lender. If this play does not succeed I shall be destitute.'

'What's the most you're likely to get from the third night's benefit? Maybe one hundred pounds, if the theatre is full to overflowing. With the way attendances have been falling this last year, more likely seventy or eighty pounds. Shall we be optimistic and say you'll get eighty? How much will be left once you've paid your money-lender? I know the rates these usurers charge. You will have to write another play immediately, and maybe you'll get something from it and maybe you won't. Either way, you'll find yourself in debt again soon enough; you always do. Why do this, Aphra, when you can equal the receipts of three or four plays in just one night? All you have to do is keep Elizabeth Decker in the cast, and leave me to do the rest.'

He was right, of course. Despite the fact that the average third night's benefit for a new play was more than most people earned in a lifetime, Aphra always managed to spend more money than she earned. She reminded herself that this was largely because she found it almost impossible to say no to anyone, no matter what their request. She knew she should say no now.

'No,' Aphra said.

'What?'

'No,' she said again, inwardly wincing. She was perfectly

17

aware that even though she was saying no, it wasn't the right no. Not the no that meant she would have nothing to do with another of his foolish schemes, but only the no that meant if she was going to involve herself in a foolish scheme, she would at least do it properly. 'I shall not leave this matter to you. If Elizabeth Decker is to win our bet for us, we need someone to train her who knows what they are doing! I know just the person; I will send a message immediately.'

Rochester laughed. 'So it's *our* bet now, is it?'

The rain had stopped, but the sky was still overcast and the streets far from dry. Rochester's coach raced down the Strand, splashing water and mud in all directions, then turned north into Lincoln's Inn Fields.

The coach slowed down in the southernmost field of Lincoln's Inn, Ficket's Field, where an audience stood watching a dancing bear. The sight of an elderly and unhealthy looking bear in chains, rearing up on its hind legs to move in clumsy circles, held little interest, so the coach did not stop. It did stop for a moment in one section of Cup Field, where a wrestling match was in progress – teams of butchers versus tanners – and stopped again further down, near a mob cheering a pack of dogs being set on an ox. Someone demanded threepence each for a ticket, and the coach moved on.

The coach stopped again in Purse Field, near Holborn. 'What is it this time?' Aphra muttered.

Rochester shushed her and stuck his head out of the window. A few yards away a crowd was gathered around a small platform on which a bearded man in long embroidered robes stood, holding up a bottle of dark green liquid. 'This liquor I guarantee,' he told the crowd, 'to act as remedy to all distempers, whether colic or consumption, fistula or flux, gangrene or griping guts, palsy, pox, or the purples, rupture, rickets or rising of the lights, sleeplessness, sciatica, scurvy, wind or worms. All these may be cured by one drop of this miraculous essence. And yet miracle this is not, but *science*, taught to me by a great master of healing arts.'

'How much for your physic?' Rochester shouted.

'A paltry one and six is all I ask for this blend of finest quality herbs, imported at great expense from the mysterious East. For one shilling more I may divine your future by palm or stars.'

'I'll leave the stars for another time,' said Rochester, tossing some coins on to the stage, 'but I'll try anything in a bottle.' A boy dressed in a dark frock and apron rushed to scoop up the coins. He counted them carefully before bringing a bottle of the green liquid over to Rochester's coach and handing it up through the window.

'Rochester, what are you doing? The man is an obvious charlatan,' Aphra whispered fiercely.

'I know that. Yet look how the rabble push forward to give him their money.'

Aphra looked towards the stage. It was true; the man could barely be seen for the rush of people moving forward to purchase his remedy.

'So these people are gullible fools, taken in by a mountebank. Does that mean you must give him your money, too?'

'I have my reasons,' Rochester said, smiling mysteriously.

Another coach approached the stage from the other direction. It was huge in size and scarlet in colour, trimmed with gold and rubies, and drawn by eight horses in feather head-dresses and jewelled bridles. It came to a halt directly opposite them, on the far side of the stage. The coach window opened and the bearded mountebank rushed over, leaving his assistant to deal with the crowds.

Rochester slid down in his seat, hiding. 'Do you recognize the occupant of that coach?'

Aphra leaned towards the window; he sharply ordered her back.

'Don't look,' he hissed.

'How am I to see who it is if you will not let me look?'

Rochester pulled his hat down low over his eyes, then slowly slid back up again, carefully peering out of the window from behind the frame. 'I'll tell you who it is. It's only the most ambitious of all His Majesty's bastards: James Scott, Duke of Monmouth.'

'Monmouth? What's he doing conversing with a mountebank?'

'Perhaps he is asking him if he will ever be king. His Majesty's eldest son is a great believer in astrology and even magic.' Rochester turned to her, raising one eyebrow. 'Or perhaps he needs a remedy for the purples.'

'Well, aren't you going to speak to him?'

'No. I prefer to watch him from a distance. The actions of this young bastard duke always hold a certain fascination; he is so lacking in subtlety.'

'He holds no fascination for me,' Aphra said. 'He is foolish and arrogant, and I thought we were going to have lunch.'

'Very well,' Rochester sighed. 'He's leaving anyway.' He tapped the roof to signal his driver. The coach hadn't moved many yards when it came to another stop. A group of beggars was blocking the path.

Aphra didn't need to look to know they were there; she could smell them. She looked anyway. Their clothes were little better than rags, still wet from the rain. The dampness of their clothing only intensified the odours of filth and vomit and stale perspiration. Many of them were on crutches, some were missing a limb, others had skin covered in oozing sores. She covered her nose with a scented handkerchief, but it wasn't enough to block out the stench of decay.

It was the smell that brought it all back to her. She only had to take one breath and she was back in chains, part of a mass of bodies on a bed of filthy straw.

Outside the coach there was a chorus of voices: 'Please my lord, bless you my lord, I was a soldier, I was a sailor, I lost my arm fighting for the king, my leg fighting for the king, my health fighting for the king, my family, my fortune, fighting for the king, fighting for the king, fighting for the king ...'

Aphra remembered the sound of her own voice, echoing off the walls of a cell nine years earlier: 'I should not be here! I am a servant of the king!' She saw herself weeks later, cheeks pale and hollow, hair alive with lice, blinking eyes unaccustomed to light, chained to other prisoners like herself, who had no money to pay for their keep. A gaoler's rough hands shoved her from behind, causing her to stumble. Another guard walked ahead holding one end of the massive chain, pulling her and the others along like cattle. Forcing them into the street to beg for bread.

'Aphra, are you all right?' Rochester asked, placing a gloved hand on her shoulder.

'Please give them something,' she whispered, 'they are hungry.'

'I intend to,' he assured her. 'I am always remarkably generous with my wife's money.' He threw a large handful of coins out of the window. The coins scattered in all directions, as did the men chasing them.

Rochester was reaching up to tap the roof again when a voice said, 'Mistress Johnson? Mistress Aphra Johnson?'

A toothless man stood at the window on Aphra's side of the coach, looking at her questioningly. Grey hair hung in strings around a grime-streaked, ravaged face. 'It is Mistress Johnson, isn't it? Mistress Johnson that sailed on the *Guiana* to Surinam?'

'Dare you molest this lady? Begone, villain, before I slice you in two!' Rochester shouted, reaching for his sword.

'Wait,' Aphra said. She turned to the man, trying not to wrinkle her nose; the smell coming from him was overpowering. 'I was once known as Johnson, and I have been to Surinam on the ship you mention. How do you know this?'

'I travelled on that same ship. Perhaps you remember me? Elias Cavell. My brother and I were going to join our uncle on his plantation.'

'Elias Cavell,' Aphra repeated, trying to hide her shock. 'I remember you.' She remembered a man in fine clothes. Someone with an arrogant expression, thick black hair and the beginnings of a middle-aged paunch, not this toothless skeleton standing before her now. 'God's death, Elias, what's happened to you?'

'The war, Mistress Johnson, that's what happened to me, as it did to so many others. I lost everything when the Dutch took Surinam.'

'And your brother? What became of Matthew?'

'So you haven't forgotten *him*, Mistress Johnson,' the man said quietly.

Matthew was younger than Elias, without his arrogance or his paunch. His eyes had been large and brown, his voice deep and soft, his touch gentle. 'No, I haven't forgotten him. How could I? And please,' she added, 'I have not been Mistress Johnson for many years; Mistress Johnson brings back too many memories. I am Mrs Behn.'

'Mrs Behn?' the beggar said, his eyes widening. 'Not the famous Mrs Behn of Whitefriars, the poet they call "The Divine Astrea"? That isn't you?'

'Well, I don't know that I'm famous,' Aphra said modestly. Rochester muttered something about the correct word being infamous, but she ignored him.

'To think I knew you when you were a shy and dutiful daughter,' Elias said excitedly. 'Who would have thought you'd become the scandal of London?' Aphra's expression hardened, and he quickly changed his tack. 'Of course it was a terribly sad voyage for you, Mistress Johnson ... I mean Mrs Behn. And for a woman left in your position, to make your own way in the world the way you have ... well, you'll hear no criticism from me, that I'll tell you. I only regret I personally was not more help to you in your sorrow, but my brother was always better gifted to handle problems of a delicate nature than I was.'

It was true that Matthew, though younger, was the more

practical one. When the terrible event had happened and her life had been shattered – only the first of many times her life would be shattered, as she would come to discover – it was Matthew who had comforted her, taking the time to listen to her woes and complaints. Elias had been sympathetic, but Matthew was the one who'd taken charge. Neither she nor her grief-stricken mother had to lift a finger; Matthew handled everything. And it was Matthew she had never forgotten.

'You both offered me much comfort, for which I am still grateful,' she said. 'And yes, your brother was a great help to me and my poor mother. But where is Matthew now? With his kind heart and practical nature, can he not help you in your present...' She paused, fumbling for the right word. 'Misfortune?'

Elias hesitated before answering. 'Matthew can do nothing for anyone.' He lowered his eyes, shifting his weight from foot to foot. 'He was press-ganged on to the *Revenge*, then a Dutch cannon shot away his leg. Now he picks oakum for one shilling per hundredweight. But he does not complain...' His voice took on a wheedling tone. 'At least he has a food to eat and a roof above his head, while I have neither.'

'Oh, God. This news is so distressing it makes me sick to hear it.' Aphra wiped away a tear. 'Elias, I am short of funds ...' She turned to Rochester. He sat staring straight ahead with a bored expression on his face, restlessly drumming his fingers. 'Rochester, can you help this poor soul? I assure you he is no ordinary mumper, but was once a man of property.'

'If it means we can finally leave these wretched fields and find a tavern; I've been sober for nearly an hour.' He reached into his pocket for a coin.

'Is that Lord Rochester?' said Elias, poking his head inside the coach. A tiny black insect leapt from his scalp on to the seat; Aphra grimaced and crushed it. 'You were on the *Revenge* with my brother; he often spoke of you.'

'I don't remember him.'

'Of course not, my lord,' Elias said, taking the coin and moving back from the window.

Rochester reached up to signal his driver.

Aphra leaned out of the window. 'Where can I find Matthew?'

The colour seemed to drain from Elias's face. 'You don't want to find him,' he said. 'I must admit that though I am grateful for your and my lord's generosity, I now wish I had not made myself known to you.'

'Why not?'

He looked down, shuffling his feet. 'Because I am ashamed of what I have become. I am not the man you once knew, and neither is my brother. At least do him the honour of remembering him as he was.'

'If you do not tell me where he is this moment, you may be certain I will find out anyway.'

Elias raised his head, a strange half-smile on his face. 'If you wish to find my brother, look for him at Gospel House, Deptford.'

The early autumn air was cold on the river, and soon it would be dark. A man with massive shoulders rowed silently, avoiding Aphra's eyes. She'd borrowed ten shillings from Rochester – an advance against her winnings – and this trip to Deptford and back would cost her at least two of them, depending on how long the boatman had to wait for her. She pulled her cloak tight around her shoulders, watching the scenery drift past as the little boat moved further and further east. And she wondered what she was doing. And why.

She had known Matthew Cavell only briefly. She hadn't seen him or heard from him for almost fourteen years, but she remembered the last time she saw him as clearly as if it was yesterday. His brother had said Matthew was a different person from the one she had known. Well, she was different too. She had known a young man with a bright future as a prosperous colonial planter before him. He had known a sheltered virgin in her early twenties: a quiet girl allowed no further ambition than to make a good marriage. Well, maybe not *quiet*, she thought, making an ironic face.

She realized the boatman was looking at her; his eyes had gone quite round. She pulled up her hood and spent the rest of the journey with her head down.

When she'd told Rochester she was going to Deptford to see Matthew, he'd said, 'What? You wish to rekindle an old romance with a one-legged man who picks oakum?' She'd told him he didn't understand, it wasn't like that at all. Matthew Cavell had once done her a great service, for which she had never repaid him. Rochester managed to make several obscene innuendoes from her use of the word 'service' – nothing unusual for him once he'd had a few drinks. She had left him alone in a tavern and made her way to the river on foot.

Gospel House turned out to be an almshouse run by a charity for 'sick and decayed seamen'; an adjoining building housed seamen's widows. The door was answered by a maid who looked about twelve. She led Aphra into a large room lit by flickering rushlights. About a dozen people – men and women both in identical light blue gowns, not one of them looking a day under sixty – sat on wooden benches, picking bundles of old rope into pieces. They looked up when she walked in.

Aphra curtsied and nodded as her eyes scanned the room, searching for a familiar face in the shadows.

'Is Mr Cavell here?' the kitchen maid asked.

'He be upstairs,' said one of the old women, regarding Aphra with undisguised curiosity. 'I reckon he's tired. You be the third person come asking for him today.'

'Oh, a lot of people come to visit him, do they?' Aphra said, smiling politely.

'It would seem so,' said the old woman. 'All men, of course. And now there's you.'

'I'll tell him you're here,' said the young maid. 'What was your name again?'

'Johnson,' Aphra said, giving the name Matthew had known her by all those years before. 'Aphra Johnson.'

The old woman patted her bench. 'Come sit you down, Mrs Johnson. He'll be some time coming downstairs – poor man's only got one leg, you see.'

'I never meant to inconvenience him,' Aphra protested. 'I can go upstairs to him.'

The woman clucked in disapproval. 'Wouldn't be seemly. The men sleeps up there, you see.'

'I see.' Aphra sat down.

'Be you some relation to Mr Cavell?'

Aphra shook her head. 'He is an old friend.'

The woman narrowed her eyes. 'That's what them others said, said they was old friends. He's a lucky one, to have so many friends.'

'Have you lived here a long time?' Aphra asked her, changing the subject.

'Long enough. I'm Virtue.'

'Pardon?'

'I'm Virtue. Virtue Hawkins. My husband were gunner on the – ' She was interrupted by a high-pitched scream.

There was general chaos as those who heard the scream struggled to get to their feet while those more hard of hearing cupped their hands to their ears, loudly demanding to know what was going on. Several tables were knocked over by people reaching frantically for crutches. The rope they'd been working on spilled, turning the floor into a slippery obstacle course. More than one fell down. Aphra ran into the hall and up the stairs in the direction of the scream, followed by a hobbling surge in matching gowns.

In a long room lined with rows of cots, she found the maid with her head buried in her hands, shaking convulsively. On the cot directly in front of the girl a bald-headed man with one

26

leg lay with his arms outstretched, a woollen shawl stuffed into his mouth. He'd been stabbed several times. Aphra instinctively threw her arms around the girl, pressing the sobbing child's head against her chest and gently stroking her hair. She looked over the girl's shoulder at the body on the bed. It looked nothing like the Matthew Cavell she had known. Could time — or even death — change a man that much?

Virtue came up from behind Aphra and took the serving girl by the hand. 'Here, child, come with me.'

One of the men stepped forward and closed the corpse's eyes. 'You shouldn't have done that,' said another. 'We might have seen the murderer in them eyes.'

'That's right,' said a third man. 'They say dead men's eyes reflects the last thing they seen while they was alive.'

Aphra stared unbelieving at the lifeless body sprawled in front of her, the body of someone old and ill, with translucent skin and bones as fragile as glass. Wiping away a tear, she closed her eyes, trying desperately to do what Elias had requested of her: to remember Matthew as he was. But she couldn't do it; the ghastly image of an old man with a shawl stuffed down his throat would be with her for ever.

A woman's voice boomed from the doorway. 'What's going on here?'

Aphra turned and saw an aproned woman as broad as she was tall — and she was one of the tallest people Aphra had ever seen — with hair and eyes the colour of lead. She covered the distance from the doorway to the cot in three long strides, taking in the situation with a glance. A boy of about ten remained cowering in the doorway.

'Boy,' the woman bellowed, 'run and fetch the constable. Now!' The boy ran. The woman turned her attention to Aphra, regarding her with a look of combined distaste and suspicion. 'And who are you?' she demanded in a voice that shook the walls.

Chapter Two

'Squintabella fainted when she heard the news!' Nell Gwyn announced for the twentieth time that day as she strolled through St James's Park arm in arm with George Villiers, Duke of Buckingham, once one of the most devastatingly handsome men at court – now nearly fifty with a bloated face and body decaying almost as rapidly as his dark brown teeth. 'Right in the middle of the Stone Gallery,' she added, triumphantly flicking her chestnut curls as they made their way down the path leading to the duck pond.

'Squintabella?'

'Louise,' Nell explained, rolling her eyes impatiently.

'Ah,' said Buckingham, enlightened. Nell loved devising new names to taunt her enemies with, and the woman she had dubbed Squintabella – Louise de Kéroualle, Duchess of Portsmouth – had been her avowed enemy for five years. Ever since the king had left the then heavily pregnant Nell behind at Newmarket so he could seduce Louise de Kéroualle at Euston.

Buckingham chuckled to himself. The morning's incident signalled the start of another skirmish in the never-ending war between the king's two favourite mistresses: one a former orange-seller and actress, the other a French aristocrat the king had met while negotiating a treaty at Dover. And now there was the introduction of a third – dangerous, and beautiful – combatant. The king had given Hortense Mancini, Duchess of Mazarin, her own suite of rooms inside Whitehall Palace: an apartment once occupied by another dangerous beauty, the now-discarded Barbara Castlemaine, Duchess of Cleveland.

Hortense, a tall Italian with waist-length black hair and eyes said to be an intoxicating mixture of green and hazel, was moving into the palace today. This was the news that had caused the Duchess of Portsmouth to collapse. 'I think Louise chose an excellent place to faint,' he said, steering Nell around a puddle left from the morning's rain. 'There's always someone around to catch you.'

'Unfortunately there was,' she said, looking up at him. At less than four foot ten, with feet rumoured to be the tiniest in the kingdom, she had to look up at most people. 'Arlington was standing right next to her.'

'Arlington! I've been practising Arlington.' Buckingham took a strip of black plaster from his pocket, slapped it across his large, purple-tinged nose and began to strut in a circle, waving his arms in all directions. 'Just as Cromwell sought to separate king from country,' he said, imitating the Earl of Arlington's shrill, self-important way of speaking, 'so Roundhead sabre sought to separate nose from skull. This is no ordinary plaster I wear, but a symbol of devotion to my king.'

Nell laughed and clapped her hands. 'Give me the plaster!' Buckingham handed it to her, and she stuck it across her own nose. 'I ask you,' she said, mimicking Arlington's pompous voice, 'what man hath greater love for his king, but he would risk his nose?'

'Oh, excellent! You should have been with us last week,' Buckingham told her, 'I think it was Wednesday. Rochester, Buckhurst, Charles Sedley and I marched up and down the corridor outside Arlington's apartments, wearing Spanish capes and with our faces covered in plasters! Rochester must have worn at least seven — on his forehead, his cheeks, his chin. Unfortunately Arlington didn't see us because he'd gone out, but he must have heard of it upon his return because he hasn't spoken to any of us since.'

'If I'd known it was that easy to silence Arlington, I would have marched past his rooms wearing plasters a long time ago.

But enough about him. You must stop and listen for a moment. I am trying to tell you something important, and you haven't heard the good part yet!'

Buckingham reached down and peeled the plaster from her nose. 'Sorry, I can't concentrate with that thing on your face. Now tell me, what is the good part?'

'*This* is the good part: when the king was informed that the Duchess of Portsmouth had collapsed and been carried to her bed on a pallet, do you know what he did? He yawned!' She became a picture of exaggerated innocence: all wide-open eyes, puckered lips and apple cheeks. To heighten the effect, she raised one finger to her mouth and batted her eyelashes. 'Isn't that the most wonderful news you ever heard?'

Buckingham pursed his lips. 'Perhaps,' he said carefully. He looked around to make sure no one was nearby before continuing, 'I have no love for the Catholic Lady Portsmouth, I know she is merely a tool of France, but why should the Lady Mazarin be any different? She is not only a Papist, she is niece to Jules Mazarin, the late cardinal. Mazarin was one of the most powerful men in France; there can be no doubting where the lady's sympathies must lie. I promise you, Nelly, there are those of us at court – loyal Protestants – who feel cause for much disquiet.'

Nell stamped her foot. 'I am sick of hearing of Papist spies and plots, George. It's nothing to do with me.'

'But surely this news about the Duchess of Mazarin must affect your position, too?'

Nell took a deep breath and threw back her shoulders, assuming a posture and look of cool disdain calculated to make her seem much taller than she actually was. 'Pray, why should my position be affected? I am still in favour with the king. I have recently been the recipient of his ...' she paused, lowering her gaze, '... attention.' She looked up again, smiling. '*Very* recently, I might add, while everyone knows the king has not visited Squintabella for at least two months. You tell me who has most to fear from this Mazarin.'

'Certainly not you, Nelly. I can't imagine you fearing anyone.'

She laughed, playfully twirling a strand of her hair.

'Except me,' Buckingham added. 'In your bedchamber. In the dark.'

Nell looked at Buckingham sadly, remembering the blond gallant who had broken so many hearts. She reached up and patted him on the cheek. 'Behave yourself, George, or I shall box your ears!'

Louise de Kéroualle, Duchess of Portsmouth, stood in one of the many corridors of Whitehall Palace, watching a procession of goods being carried past her into the apartment beyond, by a procession of liveried servants. There were dozens of trunks, probably filled with dresses and jewels. There were statues, paintings, birds in cages, dogs, squirrels. A monkey in a hat and collar. Swords, daggers, pistols and rifles. A crossbow. An enormous gun with a stand and a five-foot-long barrel.

The servant carrying the long gun was obviously struggling. Another put down the trunk he was carrying and rushed to his aid, helping him guide the barrel through the door. The rest of them were already inside. Keeping one eye on the doorway, Louise knelt beside the abandoned trunk, and reached for the latch.

'Up from your bed of pain already, Louise?' asked a woman's voice.

The Duchess of Portsmouth jumped, clasping one hand to her chest, and turned to face Nell Gwyn. At twenty-seven, the duchess was one year older than Nell, a few inches taller and several pounds heavier, especially around the face and neck. The king often teased her about her chubby cheeks, which she tried to disguise by parting her dark hair down the middle and arranging it in ringlets close to her face.

'What's the matter, Louise? Did I frighten you?'

31

Louise straightened up and took several deep breaths in order to compose herself. 'No, of course not, Nelly. *You* couldn't frighten me if you tried. But *mon dieu*, your dress! It's enough to startle anyone. How much do they pay you to wear it?'

Nell's face creased in mock concern. 'Oh, poor Louise. They told me you were ill, but I had no idea it was so bad. How I envy your courage, and your complete lack of vanity, to allow yourself to be seen looking the way you do.'

'How I envy *you*, Nell, to be behind that face rather than have to look at it.'

Nell slapped her hands to her cheeks in amazement. 'What a coincidence! I envy you for exactly the same reason!' She filled her mouth with air, blowing her cheeks out as far as they would go in an exaggerated impression of Louise's round face.

The Frenchwoman sighed. 'Why can't you just go away? Nobody wants you here, you know.'

Nell tapped both sides of her face, emptying her cheeks with a little pop, before putting on her haughty, nose-in-the-air expression. 'I was invited.'

'The fact that you came only shows you have nothing better to do.'

'The fact that you open another's trunk only shows you own nothing better yourself.'

Louise shrugged, her lips drawn into a thin, mirthless smile. 'I was merely curious. So much unusual baggage, no?'

Nell laughed. 'And that's just for overnight. Imagine if she was planning to stay a while.'

Hortense Mancini, Duchess of Mazarin, appeared in the doorway, dressed in a man's coat and breeches. 'Nelly! Come in. And the lady Portsmouth.' She raised one eyebrow. 'Up so soon? I heard you were ill.'

They entered a vast room piled high with the Italian duchess's possessions. A team of servants was busily unpacking. She led them down a long corridor, past several doors, towards the rear of the apartment. She was much taller than either of them, and in her breeches and man's shoes she was able to take such long strides that Nell and Louise had to pick up their skirts and run to keep up with her. 'The first thing I did was to set up the table,' she said, keeping several steps ahead of them. 'Otherwise I'd be so bored, and I hate to be bored, don't you?' She stopped and waited for the other two. 'Here we are.'

'How many rooms do you have?' Nell asked, out of breath.

'I haven't counted them yet.'

'I have twenty-four,' Louise sniffed.

'No one asked you,' said Nell.

Hortense pushed through a pair of double doors, entering a room furnished only with a round table and several wooden chairs. A sixteen-year-old girl sat at the table, shuffling a pack of cards.

It was dark and Nell was seven hundred pounds poorer when she finally stepped into a sedan chair to be carried around the corner to her house in Pall Mall.

To lose all that money to a sixteen-year-old girl, that was humiliating. Her one consolation was that Louise had lost even more – nearly a thousand guineas. Maybe Louise would have to pawn some of her jewels, and Louise would hate that. Especially once Nell made sure that everyone in Whitehall had heard all about it.

She wondered if the king knew that the Duchess of Mazarin had been teaching his daughter Anne to cheat at cards. Was it worth saying anything to him? No, she thought. Not yet, anyway.

Hortense had several points in her favour, as far as Nell was concerned. The main one being that Hortense could be a powerful ally against Squintabella, the Duchess of Portsmouth. Hortense had completely displaced Louise in the king's affections, and Louise despised her for it. Generally speaking, anyone Louise hated was all right with Nell. And if they happened to hate Louise back, as Hortense certainly did, that was even better.

Nell and Hortense were going to be great friends.

Nell's maid greeted her with the news that her new dress from Paris had arrived that afternoon. Then she handed her a letter, which had also arrived that afternoon.

Nell stared at the note for several moments, frowning. The tutor she'd recently engaged for her elder son had agreed to give her some lessons as well – in reading, and even a little bit of writing – but the hastily scrawled marks on the page in front of her were indecipherable, nothing like the immaculate penmanship of the boy's tutor, Bevil Cane. She handed the letter back to the maid, and asked her if she could make it out.

The maid squinted at the letter, holding it a few inches from her face, and cleared her throat. 'Dearest Nell,' she began, 'I am in desperate need of your assistance . . .'

Chapter Three

Aphra sat up in bed, groaning. Someone was pounding on her front door. She stumbled over to the window and opened the shutter. The sunlight was blinding; she couldn't see a thing. 'Who's there?' she shouted, shielding her eyes.

'S'teeth!' a woman's voice called from a pink and white coach in the street below. 'It's nearly eight of the clock! Still abed, Aphra?'

'Nelly!' She threw on a dressing gown and hurried down the stairs. She opened the door just as Nell's driver, who'd been the one knocking, returned to the coach to help his mistress step down, which she seemed to be doing with some difficulty. Nell eventually managed to get out of the coach and on to the street. Aphra couldn't help thinking that with her Cupid's bow lips, heart-shaped face and chestnut ringlets, she looked more like an exquisitely carved porcelain doll than a full grown, flesh and blood woman. 'Are you quite well?' Aphra asked her once she was inside.

'Of course I am,' Nell said, following her into the parlour.

'But you had such trouble getting out of your coach.'

'Oh, that was my new dress.'

'I don't understand.'

'Feel it,' said Nell.

Aphra touched one of the sleeves. 'Nell, your dress is stiff as a board.'

Nell tried to shrug, then grimaced in pain. 'Only the top half. I am quite comfortable as long as I don't try to raise my arms any higher than this.' She bent her elbows. 'Don't look at me

35

like that! It's the latest fashion from France. Everyone at court is wearing them.'

'You know what I think about the court and its fashions. Are you able to sit down in that thing?'

'Don't be foolish.' She flopped on to an oaken settle, landing with a thud. 'They tell me it gets easier with practice.'

'And who is this actress I'm meant to instruct?' Nell asked later, over a breakfast of beer and caudle.

'Her name is Elizabeth Decker.'

'Decker! God's flesh, you haven't cast Elizabeth Decker! The last time she appeared on stage everyone said a plank of wood could have played the role with more feeling.'

'I know, I know. But it is imperative that Mrs Decker stars in my play and that she is not just good, but brilliant.'

'Why, Aphra? In heaven's name, why?'

Aphra told her about the bet.

Nell frowned, momentarily puzzled. 'Five hundred pounds? Is that what Rochester told you?'

'Yes. Why?'

'Nothing,' Nell said. She tried to cross her arms, but couldn't manage it. 'You've been borrowing money again, haven't you?'

Aphra stared at the floor.

'How much?'

'Fifty pounds from a moneylender. Ten shillings from Rochester. At least *he* will not expect interest.'

'Oh, you fool! Why didn't you come to me?'

'I've taken advantage of your generosity so many times in the past ... and now there's worse.'

'Worse? What could be worse?'

'Last night a man was murdered and I said I would pay for his funeral.'

'What?' Nell shook her head as if she was trying to clear it. 'You'd better start from the beginning.'

*

At the age of twenty-three, Aphra Johnson was terrified she would be an old maid. As the daughter of a genteel family whose Royalist leanings had caused them to lose everything under Cromwell, she had no dowry and no prospects. She would inherit nothing, and everyone knew that a woman without means was 'over the hill at twenty-four, old and insufferable at thirty'.

As an unmarried woman, she had few respectable options. She might work seven days a week spinning cloth for two shillings and four pence without food, or six pence per week if food and drink were provided. If she was extremely fortunate, she might get a position as a ladies' maid in a fine house, and earn up to seven pounds a year.

Then, suddenly, everything changed.

With the restoration of the monarchy and the intervention of a powerful friend, her family was given a chance to start again in the New World. Her father was appointed Lieutenant General of the colony of Surinam, on the coast of South America. There, he told her, he would make his fortune. As the daughter of such an important official, she would have an exalted position in colonial society. She would be provided with a proper dowry. She would marry a man of substance and spend the rest of her days as a gracious society hostess.

They sailed from England with approximately sixty other passengers. She heard her father say that some were political or religious dissidents, and others were criminals escaping justice. Her mother said that most were just younger sons without an inheritance, sent abroad to make their own way.

Aphra was not permitted to speak to any of them.

The voyage seemed to take for ever. She stood on the gently rocking deck, hour after hour, day after day, week after week, gazing at nothing but endless sea. One evening – six weeks into the voyage, still nearly four weeks away from Surinam – her father became ill, complaining of a pain in his stomach. The next morning he was dead.

Passengers and crew gathered on deck, watching in respectful silence as the wrapped body of Aphra's father was slowly lowered into the ocean to the accompaniment of a sailor's horn and her mother's sobs. 'We are finished,' her mother whispered, 'finished.'

One evening, on deck, a tall dark-haired man approached her to offer his condolences, and before she knew it she had told him her whole life story, which up until that time had *not* been very interesting. And she told him what she'd been hearing all day, until she could no longer stand it: her mother's non-stop wailing. 'Do you know what she says she finds most distressing? It's not the poverty, she says. Not the fact that we are stranded far from home, in the middle of an ocean. What my mother finds unbearable is the thought that my father did not have what she considers a proper funeral. She asks me over and over again, how can his soul rest easy while his body is devoured by fish? How is she to mourn him without a marker on which to lay flowers? How is he to reap his final reward without a blessing from the church? And how is she, a penniless widow, to pay for this blessing? This is what I have been hearing today, and will hear tomorrow, and the day after that and the day after that.' She stopped suddenly, raising her hand to her mouth. 'Oh good sir, please forgive me. I did not mean to prate on so.'

She hadn't meant to speak to him at all. Her father had always forbidden her to speak to men unchaperoned. He would have slapped her if he had come upon them now, standing alone beneath a darkened sky. But her father was dead and there was something about this man that made her feel she could tell him anything, and he would understand, or at least *listen*.

Suddenly she realized: no one had ever really listened to her before. She had been lectured by her father, worried over by her mother, instructed by a succession of tutors, but not one of them had ever listened to a word she said.

For the next three weeks Aphra talked and Matthew Cavell listened. And when the ship finally landed in Surinam, he proved that he really had been listening. Within a week of their arrival, he arranged and paid for a spectacular funeral for her father, with printed invitations and music and mourners. He and his brother Elias acted as pallbearers, carrying a beautifully carved empty coffin through the streets of the colony's main town, then laying it to rest beneath the centre aisle of the town's only church. Aphra's mother had wept for joy. 'At last my mind can rest at ease. Your father is with the angels now,' she'd whispered to Aphra as they watched nearly two hundred guests help themselves to ham and biscuits and burnt claret, also paid for by Matthew Cavell.

'I never saw him after that. His uncle's plantation was a three-day journey upriver, and he rarely came into town. We returned to England, the Dutch captured Surinam, and I heard nothing more of Mr Cavell. Until yesterday.'

Nell's mouth dropped open. 'Why did he do it? Were you his mistress?'

'There was never a hint of intrigue between us. Though I doubt I would have been unwilling.' She paused, thinking. 'No, I have often wondered about this myself. It was my mother who was so concerned with the need for ceremony and display, not I. So why should he go to such trouble and expense to soothe my mother's grief? He never knew us before the voyage, and he made no attempt to contact us after we left. I must admit it is a total mystery to me, Nelly. Though it would seem there is little mystery regarding his death.'

'Why?'

'Several people said they heard Matthew and another inmate of the house, a Mr Josiah Mullen, arguing that afternoon. By the time I arrived at the almshouse last night, Matthew was dead and Mr Mullen had disappeared. It's all rather obvious, isn't it? Matthew was murdered by Josiah Mullen. But this Mullen is not my concern, he will be arrested soon enough. My concern is with an obligation I dare not deny. I owe a debt – of more than money – which I must repay.'

'If only I had known of this yesterday, I would not have been so reckless.'

'What do you mean?'

'I am almost completely without funds. I lost seven hundred pounds at basset to the king's daughter Anne.'

Aphra wrinkled her forehead, puzzled. 'Do you mean Barbara Castlemaine's daughter, Anne of Sussex? But she's only a child, isn't she?'

'Some child! She's been married nearly a year. She has the physical stamina of her father along with the morals of her mother, and I can think of no worse combination. It seems she has abandoned her husband to spend every waking moment in the company of her inseparable friend, Mazarin, who now occupies the very rooms in which Anne spent her infancy.'

'But the Duchess of Mazarin is nearly thirty. Does it not seem strange she should spend her time with such a young girl?'

'They have a lot in common,' said Nell, struggling to rise. 'They both have husbands they prefer to keep at a distance.'

'I suspect that many women have that in common,' Aphra said, pulling Nell up by the shoulders. 'I'm sorry to have mentioned this other business to you. Please don't give it another thought. I shall manage somehow.'

'I only said I had no money. I never said I wouldn't help you. Don't worry, Aphra. It will be a splendid funeral. I have a plan.'

Once again, Aphra was fifteen minutes late for rehearsal. This time, however, they had started without her. Elizabeth Decker was already on stage with another actress, reading through the first scene. Nell stopped half-way down the aisle, a look of disbelief on her face. 'Come, Nell,' Aphra whispered, 'she's not that bad.'

The other actress began a long speech. Nell and Aphra watched in amazement as Elizabeth Decker stood listening to the other woman with a look of intense concentration, her lips noticeably moving in unison with the other's speech.

Nell turned to Aphra, raising a sceptical eyebrow.

'Well, maybe she is,' Aphra conceded.

Rochester was up in the Royal Box, leaning back with his hat pulled down over his face. While Aphra spoke to Mr Davenant, Nell excused herself, made her way up the stairs to the box and snatched the hat. 'Good morning, John!'

'Wha'?' He yawned and rubbed his eyes. 'Nelly! Are you to be our acting coach? Elizabeth could not be more fortunate!'

'Whether I am to be a coach or not is yet to be determined,' Nell whispered furiously.

'What do you mean? Surely you wish to help Aphra? Is she not your loyal friend?'

'She is. But I have other friends as well, such as my dear Lord Buckingham.'

'Ah,' said Rochester. He raised one finger, as if something had just occurred to him. 'But you must agree that poor Aphra needs the money more.'

'She told me you promised her two hundred and fifty pounds, which she seems to believe equals half your winnings.'

Beads of sweat appeared on Rochester's upper lip. 'That is correct.'

'Buckingham mentioned this bet to me quite some time ago, and he was under the impression you had wagered a thousand pounds. Now, I am surely no scholar, but the one thing every orange-seller learns is how to add and subtract,' Nell told him. 'Perhaps the figuring of sums was not part of your education?'

Rochester sighed, resigned. 'How much do you want?'

After rehearsal, Nell returned home to change from her new dress into one which allowed her to move her arms.

Aphra said she would wait in the coach.

Once she had changed into something more flexible, Nell inspected the rest of the gowns in her wardrobe. There was nothing that would do. She told her maid to write a letter to her dressmaker, ordering a plain black dress with matching hat and veil to be delivered no later than noon tomorrow.

'Has someone died, mistress?' the maid asked, taking a sheet of paper from a drawer.

Nell nodded.

'Oh, mistress, I am sorry.'

'Don't be. I never even met the man.'

'Mistress?' the maid said, puzzled.

Nell told her how Aphra's chance meeting in Lincoln's Inn Fields led to her promise to pay for a burial.

The maid shook her head, looking even more confused.

'I still don't understand how you got the money,' Aphra said later, as Nell's pink and white coach retraced the path Rochester's coach had taken the day before, through Lincoln's Inn Fields.

'What does it matter how I did it? Just be satisfied with what is done. You shall have your funeral.'

'But the coffin you ordered has solid gold handles and only this morning you didn't have a penny. How –'

'How, how, how!' Nell interrupted, rolling her eyes in exasperation. 'Ask me how one more time and I shall lock you in a room with the Duchess of Portsmouth, and leave you 'til only one comes out alive!'

Aphra assured her she would not ask her 'how' again. Instead she concentrated on what she had returned to the Fields to do: locate Elias Cavell and tell him the tragic news. They rode up, down and across the Fields, scattering pennies and questioning beggars from behind scented handkerchiefs. There was no sign of Elias, and no one they spoke to had seen him since the previous day. No one had any idea where he might be. 'When you see him, tell him to contact Mrs Behn of Dorset Street immediately,' Aphra found herself repeating again and again.

'Look,' Nell said, pointing at a scarlet jewel-studded coach in the distance. 'Catch him!' she shouted to her driver.

Aphra was thrown back in her seat as the horses broke into a gallop. Nell laughed and whooped throughout the chase, applauding as they drew up beside the other coach. .

'Hello, my little prince!' she called out of the window.

The Duke of Monmouth turned to face them. Aphra's mouth dropped open. She had never seen the king's eldest son up close before, and she had no idea he was so attractive. He had his father's black hair, dark flashing eyes and full lips, but unlike his father he was only twenty-nine years old and his features were straight and even. Even Nell had to agree that the king could never be termed conventionally handsome, but his son could be termed handsome and more.

'Nelly, I meant to call on you, but I have been very busy.'

'So I can imagine,' Nell teased him, raising one eyebrow. 'Though I doubt you shall find what you like to keep you busy in a place such as this. May I suggest a better location?'

The Duke looked confused for a moment, then he blushed. 'Mrs Gwyn,' he said imperiously, 'sometimes I find you quite shocking.'

'No more shocking than your own mother,' Nell retorted, reminding him of his status as a bastard. 'Do come and visit your little brothers sometime,' she added, referring to her own two sons by the king. 'They are quite fond of you, you know.'

'And I am fond of them,' he replied, his face softening. 'Now you must excuse me, madam, for I am abroad on a matter of great urgency.'

'Farewell, Prince Perkin,' Nell said, waving.

The Duke of Monmouth's face turned as red as his coach. Then he was gone.

Nell turned to Aphra, looking as if she would explode with mirth. 'He *hates* it when I call him that! He just hates it!' She

43

composed herself with a deep breath and added more calmly, 'And now back to our own urgent business.'

Eventually they found someone who told them that whenever Elias had money he went to stay with a Mrs Adams, at an address in St Giles. Aphra gave the man a groat and told Nell's driver to take them there.

'But the printer closes in half an hour,' Nell reminded her, 'and what about Rochester and Mrs Decker? They will be knocking at your door any moment now.'

'No need to worry about Rochester,' Aphra said. 'I've given him my key and told him where I've hidden a jug of sack. He won't mind waiting, but you are right about the printer. We'll stop there first.'

Aphra examined the fifty identical cards she had ordered earlier. The words *'Memento Mori'* were inscribed across an illustration of a coffin, with a skeleton standing on one side and the hooded figure of death, holding a scythe, on the other. Below that were the printed words: *'You are Invited to accompany the Corpse of MATTHEW CAVELL from Gospel House Deptford to the Parish Church of St Mary's Deptford this Wednesday at Seven of the Clock in the Evening Precisely and Bring this Ticket with you.'* Below that was another illustration, of a coffin being carried down a street by night, accompanied by a procession of mourners holding flaming torches.

'These will do nicely, don't you think?' she said as Nell handed over the money.

Nell nodded and patted her on the arm. 'If only your friend could see them, he would be very pleased.' Her eyes began to sparkle the way they always did when she had mischief in mind. 'In fact, while we're here, I think I shall order some cards myself – for someone who definitely will see them, and will be anything *but* pleased.'

*

Mrs Adams lived down an alley too narrow for Nell's coach. She and Aphra got down from the coach, and over the objections of Nell's driver – who insisted it wasn't safe, only to be reminded by Nell that she had been raised in a worse alley than this one – proceeded the rest of the way on foot, surrounded by barefoot children in rags, touching the women's clothing with filthy hands. Nell had to slap more than one little hand that she found reaching not for her dress, but for her purse. She only managed to disperse them by tossing a handful of farthings into the air and letting them scatter. The children abruptly abandoned the women to chase the coins. Nell watched them for a moment and then turned to Aphra, looking more solemn and serious than she had ever seen her. 'Look at them, Aphra. I was just like them once: my father in prison, my mother too poor to feed us. This is where I came from, and I shall never allow myself to forget.'

They navigated their way down the narrow passage, avoiding piles of stinking rubbish and excrement – both human and animal – only to be splashed with the contents of a chamber pot tossed from an upstairs window. Aphra grimaced and swore under her breath. Nell swore louder, and then she laughed. 'Fear not, Aphra. I'll wager you none round here will comment on the smell.'

They found the house at the dead end of the alley. It was tiny, with no upper floor. More like a hut than a house. The door was opened by a man with bloodshot eyes almost as red as the hair hanging greasily to his shoulders. Aphra nearly choked; the stench coming at her from the inside of the house was worse than anything in the street. It made her eyes water. She raised her handkerchief to her nose, unable to speak. Nell was more subtle; she lifted her own handkerchief with a delicate, pretended sneeze. 'Is Mrs Adams at home?' she asked, smiling.

The man stared at them as if he could not believe his eyes. 'Please come inside,' he said finally, with an awkward attempt at a bow.

The windowless room was dark and it took a few moments for Aphra's eyes to adjust. Then she saw at least one cause of the stench she found so offensive: in the middle of the straw-covered dirt floor a sow was nursing half a dozen squealing piglets. The room also contained three beds, five adults, two children and a scattering of chickens.

Before anyone else could say anything, an elderly man blurted out, 'Damn me for the son of a whore, if it isn't little Nell herself!'

Nell peered at the man a moment, obviously confused.

'Don't you remember me, Nelly?' the old man asked her. 'Back in the days when you used to help your mother behind the bar ... It's me, Toby.'

'Toby Rainbeard!' Nell exclaimed. 'I can scarce believe it! What joy it is to see you.'

While Toby excitedly explained to the others just who their visitor was, Aphra managed to give Nell a discreet nudge. 'You know this man?' she whispered.

'An old friend of my mother's,' Nell whispered back. 'I haven't seen him since I was a child.'

A grey-haired woman with sharp features approached them. Gripping the rough material of her dress with a pair of blue-veined, twisted hands, she curtsied and stammered that their presence was a greater honour than she had ever dared dream of.

Behind her the room was plunged into a frenzy of activity, with much sweeping and rearranging of furniture. One of the children ran out of the door, returning a moment later with two wooden stools, apparently borrowed from a neighbour. This was confirmed a moment later, when the neighbour himself arrived, dressed in his best frock and bearing a jug of beer. Mrs Adams introduced him as her dear, dear friend, Meldrick Bridger.

Nell and Aphra were seated on the stools with great ceremony, and offered beer in earthen mugs. As the introductions were exchanged, it seemed that Toby was not the only man present to have known Nell's mother. Nell was soon reminiscing about the old days in Coal Alley, when at the age of seven she'd got a job pouring drinks in a bawdy house. She was on her third mug of beer and seemed to have settled in for the evening when Aphra reminded her of the reason for their visit. 'Oh, yes,' Nell said. 'My friend would like to ask you some questions.'

'I am looking for someone. Elias Cavell. Do you know him?'

The only sound in the room was the grunting of the pigs.

'He is a tall, thin man in his early fifties, with grey hair and no teeth. A mumper in Lincoln's Inn Fields told me he sometimes comes here,' Aphra persisted.

There was still no answer.

'The mumper told me Elias comes here when he has money for a bed. I know he had some money yesterday. I thought perhaps he may have come here last night.' One of the children started to say something, but was quickly silenced.

They obviously knew him; perhaps they thought they were protecting him. Of course, Aphra thought, for all they know I am here to have him arrested; I might have a dozen constables lurking outside. She had to convince them she meant him no harm. She took a deep breath and tried again. 'I am a friend of his. I knew him many years ago, and I only wish to give him some important news regarding a member of his family.'

Finally, Toby Rainbeard spoke. 'I do not know this man, but since you are a friend of little Nelly's, if ever I should meet this man ... pray, what was his name again?'

'Elias Cavell,' she repeated, unable to control the edge of exasperation creeping into her voice.

'Though it is doubtful our paths should cross, if I should meet this Elias Cavell, I might perhaps give him a message.'

'I would be most grateful to you, Mr Rainbeard, if you would be so kind as to do that,' Aphra replied. 'Please, if you should encounter Mr Cavell, ask him to contact Mrs Behn immediately.

That's Mrs Aphra Behn, of Dorset Street, Whitefriars.' She stopped and waited for their reaction. There wasn't one. 'If I am not at home, I can usually be found at the Dorset Garden Theatre,' she added, certain that the mention of the Duke of York's theatre would make them realize just who they were talking to. They didn't. She realized with a sinking heart that not one of them had ever heard of her.

'If I should meet this man, I will tell him,' Toby assured her.

'Perhaps you should leave a card with Toby,' Nell suggested. 'So there shall be no doubt as to your motives.'

'But I wanted to tell Elias the news in person, gently,' Aphra protested. 'I thought that would be kinder.'

'That may be, but I fear the time grows short.'

'You are right,' Aphra said. She reached into her purse and handed Toby one of the illustrated cards. Even if he could not read, he would know what it was.

Toby examined the card for a moment, turning it over and over in his gloved hands before he finally spoke. 'I believe I may have met this Elias after all. I will do what I can.'

After the incident with the chamber pot, Nell insisted on stopping off in Pall Mall to change her dress again. Once again, Aphra waited in the coach.

Rochester and Mrs Decker had let themselves in and were sitting in front of the fire when Aphra finally arrived home, nearly an hour late. Aphra left Nell in the parlour with the others while she retired upstairs to change her own soiled clothing.

She was down to her smock and bodice before she noticed the package on the bed. It was a small cloth bag of sugar sops, tied with ribbon. A card on the mattress beside it read: 'To Hermia from her Lysander. Always.'

She sat down on the bed, shaking. Damn the nerve of that John Hoyle, sneaking into her bedchamber while she was out! He had handed back her key a long time ago – he must have made a copy, the duplicitous rakehell! Why couldn't he just leave her alone? It was he who had been unfaithful, not her. *And not just once.* He was the one who'd said it would be best if they never saw each other again. She'd thought her heart would break, but she'd agreed and carried on with her life. Now he wanted her back because the one thing he could not stand was the fact that she could carry on without him. *Would* carry on without him. She added a change of locks to her mental list of necessary expenditures.

She ate a handful of the sugar sops, wondering what might have happened if she had been home when Hoyle had come calling. What if he'd been sober, and repentant. If he'd told her he loved her and couldn't live without her. If he'd reminded her of the way they were in the beginning, and said he wanted it to be like that again. What would she have done then? She didn't know.

She held a small looking glass up to her face. She didn't remember looking that old. Where had those lines around her eyes come from? And when had the flesh beneath her chin started to sag like that? She tried to tell herself it was nothing a good night's sleep wouldn't cure. If only she could sleep, she would be all right.

But there were people in the house and there was work to be done. It was that or debtor's prison, and that was the one thing she had sworn upon pain of death: she would never go back to prison. She stood up and got dressed.

It took some time before she felt presentable enough to face her guests once more. She must have rearranged her hair a dozen times, and it seemed to her that she couldn't get the stink of that St Giles alley out of her nostrils, no matter how much perfume and and powder she applied. Still far from satisfied, she finally came to the conclusion that she had done all she could do.

She returned to the parlour to find all her furniture shoved to one side and Nell playing the heroine's part opposite

Rochester. Elizabeth sat on the settle, holding the script and silently mouthing the words along with them.

'Oh my daughter, my only daughter,' said Rochester. 'What woe has befallen this household!'

'What is the next line?' Nell asked Elizabeth.

'"Good heavens, sir. Is she dead?"' Elizabeth read from the page.

'Good heavens, sir,' Nell said, all wide-eyed innocence. 'Is she dead?'

'I would she were,' said Rochester. 'For there would be less dishonour in it.'

Nell turned back to Elizabeth. 'What does she say next?'

'"Pray sir, I fail to understand you."'

Nell placed one finger on her lip and tilted her head to one side, looking puzzled. 'Pray sir, I fail to understand you.' She walked over to Elizabeth and took the script from her hands. 'Now you.'

Elizabeth took a deep breath. Then she tilted her head to one side, looking genuinely puzzled. 'Pray sir, I fail to understand you.'

'Brilliant!' said Rochester, applauding.

Nell turned to face him, crossing her arms. 'Mrs Decker has managed to say one line with the appropriate facial expression. Let us see if she can manage two, or even three, such lines – preferably in a row – before we declare her brilliance.'

'Did I do something wrong?' Elizabeth asked.

'You were very good,' said Rochester. He crossed the room to sit next to her. 'Very good indeed,' he told her, gently patting her hand.

Nell and Aphra exchanged ironic glances. Nell picked up a candle and excused herself to 'go and pick a rose'. She walked through the kitchen and out into the garden, and then she came running back. 'Aphra!' she shouted, 'There's a man in your house of office!'

Rochester leapt up, drawing his sword.

'No, no,' Nell said, waving the sword away, 'you don't understand! He's dead!'

Rochester raced into the garden with his sword drawn, followed by Aphra, Nell and Elizabeth, each shielding a lit candle.

Aphra held her breath as Rochester opened the door to the outhouse at the bottom of her garden; Elizabeth and Nell each raised a hand to cover their mouths and noses. 'I've been meaning to have the night men round,' Aphra mumbled apologetically.

Rochester took the candle from Aphra's hand and thrust it through the open doorway, revealing a ragged figure, half-sitting, half-lying across the wooden bench inside. He prodded him with his sword. There was no movement, no sign of life. He moved in closer, holding the candle up to the dead man's face.

'God save us,' Aphra gasped. 'It's Elias!'

'Elias?' said Nell.

'Oh law,' said Elizabeth. 'I feel most unwell. Most unwell.'

'Come inside,' Nell said, gripping Elizabeth firmly by the arm. She led her back into the parlour and poured her a drink of sack before going out the front door into the street where her coach was waiting. 'Find the watch,' she told her driver, 'and be quick about it.' The coachman nodded and drove off. She looked up and down the unlit street; there didn't seem to be anyone about. Lifting her skirts, she squatted down over a gutter.

She returned to the parlour to find Elizabeth bent forward with both her hands clasped over her mouth. 'S'death,' Nell muttered, thinking of Aphra's carpet, 'let's get you back outside.'

Nell stood in the street, holding Elizabeth by the shoulders while she heaved and retched without result. 'By the mass,

Elizabeth! If you would be ill, then be ill. If not, let us go back inside; Aphra will be needing me.'

Elizabeth straightened up and nodded weakly. 'I am better,' she said, shaking off Nell's grip.

Nell's coach reappeared at the end of the street, the seat beside her driver occupied by an elderly man clutching a squirming black dog with a snout like a barrel. The dog leapt from the old man's lap as the coach pulled to a halt. It ran towards Elizabeth, barking furiously.

'Spike!' the man shouted after the dog. 'Spike, get away from her, you wretched cur!'

The dog bared its teeth and growled.

Elizabeth clutched at Nell, her face turning deathly white. 'Oh law,' she said, vomiting on to the dog's head. It squealed and ran back towards its master.

'Aye, missus,' the old man said, laughing, 'that's taught old Spike his lesson!'

Elizabeth sank her head into Nell's shoulder, making a little whimpering sound. She was several inches taller than Nell, and quite a bit heavier. 'God's flesh,' Nell muttered, struggling to keep her balance.

The old man slowly stepped down from the coach. Nell was certain she could hear his joints creaking, even over the whining of his dog. He had to be at least seventy. He was almost completely bald beneath his large-brimmed hat, with blackened teeth and mottled, loose-hanging skin. He wore a knee-length frock, exposing stockinged legs like twisted kindling. In one gnarled, blue-veined hand he grasped a lantern. Nell's driver handed him his catchpole, which he balanced precariously over one shoulder, and then his bell.

The dog began to shake itself dry, splattering the old man's stockings. 'Stop that,' he said, giving the dog a little kick. The dog yelped and shook itself more furiously than before. The watchman stepped away from the dog, and bowed to the two women. 'Now, ladies, what be the trouble here?'

Chapter Four

The Stone Gallery was crowded as usual. Thomas Alcock moved unnoticed among the chattering throng. He was about twenty-five, of medium height and slender build. His coat and breeches were of the finest silk, bedecked with flowing ribbons. He wore a waist-length elaborately curled blond wig, face paint and a little heart-shaped velvet patch on his right cheek. But in such a fashionable company as this – the courtiers of Whitehall Palace – his appearance was so unremarkable as to render him invisible. Passing by a fop in earnest conversation with an elegant lady whose low-cut dress exposed an admirable pair of nipples, he paused briefly to comb his wig and listen, but heard nothing of interest. The fop was a man of no influence, his companion a woman of little importance. Alcock kept walking and left the gallery, having spoken to no one.

From the Stone Gallery he made his way along a long corridor that, if he continued on his present course, would eventually lead him to His Majesty's private apartments. This corridor, like the Stone Gallery, was lined with handsome people in expensive clothing, adopting elegant poses. He strolled past them slowly, listening unobtrusively to various snatches of conversation, making mental notes as to who was present and who was not, and who was speaking to whom.

The evening's census accomplished, he left the chatterers behind, turning right down one corridor, left down another and then right again. It amused him to think of the hallways of Whitehall as an endless maze, lined with doors.

And behind every door, he thought, lips curling into a smile, lies intrigue.

He came to a seemingly deserted corner, lit by a couple of sputtering candles. He glanced about to assure himself that no one was nearby, took one of the candles from its holder, pressed his hand against a panel in the wall and stepped through to an unlit stairwell. He made his way up the narrow, twisting stairs, shielding the candle against draughts; its fragile flame was the only thing that stood between him and impenetrable darkness.

The queen no longer resided in Whitehall Palace. She had moved down the river to Somerset House some time ago, taking only the most pious of her ladies with her, and Alcock found the remaining not-so-pious ladies to be an excellent source of useful information for his master. The ladies were unaware of this, of course.

Alcock stopped at the next landing, pressing his ear against the wall. A woman's voice came from the other side: 'Your grace, please!' Then he heard a man laughing, a deep, evil laugh.

Alcock knelt down, holding the candle up to the wall in front of him, looking for the small circle that was his spyhole. He found it and placed the candle on the floor beside him, marking the hole's location with his finger. Then, using a small twig, he gently nudged aside the bottom corner of a tapestry hanging on the other side of the wall.

Neither the lady nor the gentleman with her noticed the almost imperceptible movement of the tapestry. No one ever did. Alcock didn't recognize the lady. She was young and her pale green gown revealed a good enough figure, but in Alcock's considered opinion – and he had come to view himself as quite an expert in these matters – her face left much to be desired. Her eyes were too small, her chin too pointed, her forehead too wide. And she did not seem pleased with her companion's attentions, swatting his hand away from her breasts. 'No, your grace.'

'Come, Winnifred,' the man said, pulling her towards him. With one hand, he grasped her firmly around the waist. With the other, he lifted her skirts. Alcock couldn't see the man's face; his back was towards him. But the voice sounded familiar.

'I said no!' The woman slapped him hard across the face.

The man released his grip. 'Your servant, madam,' he said, bowing. He turned to leave, raising one hand to his reddening cheek.

Alcock finally saw the man's face, and it was all he could do not to laugh out loud. The Duke of Buckingham rejected by the homeliest of all the queen's maids – this was exactly the sort of news he was paid to gather. His master would be very pleased, perhaps even pay him a bonus.

The woman Buckingham had addressed as Winnifred spent a moment collecting herself, then disappeared behind a door further down the corridor. Alcock remained where he was was, kneeling alone behind the wall, waiting.

He was used to waiting. It was how he spent most of his time: waiting unseen for something – anything – to happen. And it usually did. This part of the palace was a favoured destination for court gallants in search of intrigue. All that was required of him was patience.

He didn't mind these long periods of nothing happening. They gave him time to think. And to dream. Mostly dreams of powdered, perfumed women whispering secrets to him and him alone. He had fallen, half sleeping, into one of these pleasant reveries when he was jolted awake by the sound of footsteps and women's laughter.

He leaned forward, pressing his eye close to the spyhole, then froze at the approach of another set of footsteps, this time behind him. He extinguished the candle with his fingers, plunging himself into blackness.

He turned, careful not to make a sound, and saw the light of two candles on a landing below. He heard two voices, both male, but one much louder and higher-pitched than the other.

'Fool!' the one with the higher voice was saying. 'Don't you understand this could mean the ruination of us all?'

The other muttered something Alcock couldn't hear, which caused the first speaker to respond, 'No! There is no choice in this matter. There's nothing for it, but someone must go back and search the house.'

Alcock craned his neck forward, trying to see their faces, but it was impossible; looking down at them from above, all he could see was the movement of two small flickering lights, followed by a couple of indistinguishable shadows. Then he realized to his horror that the lights were getting closer. He had to get away quickly. It was one thing to roam the corridors of the palace listening to gossip, quite another to be caught spying in a secret passage.

He glanced through the spyhole; there were two women talking on the other side of the wall. He could hardly push his way through a secret panel while they were standing there.

The two men were close enough now for Alcock to hear the quieter voice. 'But my lord, are you sure this course is wise?'

'Dare you question me? Impudent dog!'

'I meant no disrespect, my lord.'

Alcock rose from his kneeling position, stuffed the still-warm candle into his pocket, and moved away from the landing. The only way to go was up.

Alcock had never been this high up in the palace; the stairs here were even narrower and steeper, and more slippery, than those below. And there were no windows to these back stairs, no sources of light anywhere. Unable to use his eyes, he relied on his sense of touch, reaching ahead into the blackness, locating each subsequent step with the tips of his fingers, pulling himself up and forward.

He had no idea how high he'd climbed; he thought he must be nearly at the roof, when suddenly, up ahead, he saw the light of another candle. He made out the outlines of three men huddled around it, talking in hushed tones, their faces rendered

56

grotesque and unrecognizable by flickering shadows. He pressed his back against the wall and held his breath.

'Lord Arlington must surely be informed,' one of the men said, his voice barely above a whisper.

Alcock's ears pricked up at the mention of the Lord Chancellor's name. Henry Bennet, Earl of Arlington, was also head of His Majesty's Secret Service. His master would be most interested in news of any intrigue concerning Lord Arlington.

'Arlington knows already,' said another. 'Of that you may be certain. To seize our advantage we must act quickly. That is why I offered the man my protection and agreed to meet him again this Thursday.'

'But how do we know that we may trust this man?' said the first.

'We don't,' said the second. 'I only pay once I am convinced of the item's value. Are we agreed?'

'We are agreed,' the other two replied in unison.

'Then let us waste no time.'

With that, the three men vanished from sight, apparently through the wall. Alcock felt his way up after them, curious to see who they were and where they went. If he could identify them, perhaps he might make sense of their baffling conversation, or at least determine its importance. His master once told him that content meant little, what mattered was who did the speaking.

By the time he reached the landing where they had stood, located the hidden panel by touch and stepped through into the corridor beyond, it was too late. The men were gone.

He hurried along the full length of the corridor, pausing at every corner to look up and down each intersecting passage. No sign of anyone.

He turned to go, and then he heard a woman crying. He glanced up and down the hall – still no one about – then knelt beside the nearest door, placing one eye to the keyhole.

In the room beyond, a woman lay sobbing on a velvet couch.

The awkward, narrow shape of the keyhole severely restricted Alcock's vision. All he could see of the reclining lady were her skirts – brilliant blue satin, studded with jewels – and her shoes, the same jewel-studded satin as her dress. He shifted position several times, but the lady's head and torso stubbornly remained out of view.

A small, dark-haired man walked briefly into Alcock's line of sight, crossing in front of the lady. He was about forty, impeccably dressed in lace and silk – both immaculate – and had a closely trimmed, thin black moustache. Alcock recognized him instantly as Honoré Courtin, ambassador of the court of King Louis.

The woman sat up and shouted something in French, throwing down a handkerchief, and Alcock finally saw the swollen, tear-streaked face of Louise de Kéroualle, Duchess of Portsmouth. A uniformed servant rushed forward to replace her handkerchief with a fresh one, then hurriedly backed away, out of sight.

Courtin and the duchess began to speak in French: Courtin soothing, the duchess angry and fretful, occasionally bursting into tears. Alcock smiled to himself; here was a situation he could understand, with participants he could recognize.

He didn't speak French, but in this case he didn't need to. There was only one thing they could be talking about.

In another part of the palace, Hortense Mancini, Duchess of Mazarin, stood in the middle of a large room cleared of all carpets and furniture, wearing a doublet and loose-fitting breeches, her body in the 'on guard' position: left arm raised into a V-shape behind her, right arm at chest height in front, elbow bent, hand grasping an imaginary sword. The sixteen-year-old Countess of Sussex adopted a similar pose, and the two women began to move in a silent, wary circle, foreheads creased in concentration. A dark-skinned adolescent in page's livery stood beside the fireplace, looking bored.

'Ha!' Anne shouted, lunging forward. 'Take that!'

Hortense leapt back, swinging her imaginary sword around to block the other's thrust.

'And that!' Anne shouted, lunging again, only to be blocked once more.

'Keep your knees bent,' Hortense told her, stepping sideways.

'They *are* bent,' Anne said, glancing down to check.

Hortense jabbed her in the ribs, exaggeratedly pushing her invisible blade in to the hilt, then twisting. Anne clutched at her side, dropped her invisible sword and crumpled to the floor. Hortense nudged her with her foot. 'How many times must I tell you? Never look away in the middle of a fight! *Watch* your opponent, learn to read their thoughts, anticipate their every movement!'

'But you said – '

'I've just killed you,' Hortense interrupted. 'The dead mustn't speak to the living.' She turned to the boy standing by the fire. 'Mustapha, help me dispose of the body.'

'My lady?' he said.

She rolled her eyes in mock disgust; slaves had no sense of humour. 'Must I do everything myself?' A door swung open behind her and a dozen spaniels ran yapping into the room, rushing to lick the face of Anne of Sussex. The Duchess of Mazarin knew whose arrival those dogs heralded. She turned and curtsied, tugging at the sides of her breeches as if they were a skirt. 'Your Majesty honours us with his presence.'

Anne pushed the yapping dogs away and scrambled to her feet.

King Charles II walked into the room, taking in her bare surroundings. 'I pray the furniture did not displease you, madam?'

Furnishings restored, Hortense, the king, and his eldest daughter sat laughing around a table as a stream of servants rushed into the room carrying jugs of wine and silver platters laden with food. Then Anne launched into another one of her stories. Hortense tossed some meat to the dogs gathered begging around her feet, only half listening as Anne went on and on about something that had happened when she was ten. The king raised a leg of mutton to his mouth, not even pretending to listen.

Anne's story was interrupted when a servant hurried into the room to hand the king a note.

Charles glanced at the seal and put down his mutton, scowling. He tore the letter open and read it, blowing out his cheeks. He looked thoughtful for a moment, then stood, carefully folding the letter. He walked over to the grate and threw it on to the fire.

'Is something amiss, sire?' Hortense asked, breaking the silence.

'I must attend to some urgent business,' he said, walking back to the table. Hortense rose to accompany him to the door. 'Dawn,' he whispered in her ear before he left, 'the usual place.'

The Duchess of Portsmouth was on her feet now, pacing back and forth, in and out of Alcock's range of vision. Still shouting in French.

Watching this prolonged fit of temper seemed a pointless exercise. He could be better employed elsewhere.

Alcock pulled back from the keyhole and rose to his feet. He turned just in time to see the bottom corner of a tapestry swing back into place.

Chapter Five

Two men lifted Elias's body on to a pallet and carried it through the house and out into the street. The watchman stood waiting beside a cart, holding up his lantern to light their way. Aphra followed the men outside, accompanied by Nell and Wellman Gue, the parish constable. Aphra already knew Mr Gue from his daytime occupation as a baker; she sometimes bought cakes from his shop. The watchman's dog bared its teeth and growled at their approach. The old man kicked it, and it ran beneath the cart, hiding behind a wheel.

Aphra stood beside the cart as the men loaded Elias on to the back. His eyes were closed now. The watchman had finally allowed her to press them shut after he and the constable had each taken a turn looking, without success, for the murderer's reflection.

She looked down at the lifeless body, ragged clothing caked with blood, throat slit from side to side, and shook her head in disbelief. Two men she hadn't seen for almost fourteen years had suddenly come back into her life, both changed beyond recognition. And now both were dead.

She closed her eyes and saw her father's funeral procession once again: Matthew and Elias solemnly bearing the empty coffin through the streets, then lowering it into the grave themselves. Though the church employed someone specially for this purpose, Matthew and Elias insisted they be allowed to perform this humble task as a mark of their deep personal regard for the dead man and his family. Aphra's mother had burst into tears and whispered that no gesture would ever move her more.

It was true that Matthew had been the one Aphra spent more time with, and who had – as far as she knew – handled the practical details of the ceremony, but as she relived the events of that day in her mind, she recalled the look of anguish on Elias's face as he bore the coffin into the church, the tear that glistened on his cheek as he covered it with a shovelful of earth. She owed Elias as much as she owed his brother.

'What will you do with him?' she asked the constable.

'He will be examined by the searcher, and then he will be buried on the parish.'

'No.' She could not abandon Elias to lie in a mass grave, unmarked and unmourned. 'He must be taken to Deptford to be buried in St Mary's Church beside his brother.'

'Aphra,' Nell said.

The constable asked who would pay.

'I will,' Aphra said, wincing at Nell's discreet elbow jab to her ribs.

'Aphra,' Nell repeated.

'I will make the necessary arrangements,' Aphra told the constable.

Rochester was still where they'd left him: sitting on the settle beside the parlour window, drinking sack straight from the jug. He'd fallen into a temper soon after the body had been discovered, nearly throwing the jug at the constable for daring to ask what time he'd entered the house that evening. He was a peer of the realm, he'd reminded the upstart, and would not be questioned by a baker.

He leaned back against the wall, eyes half closed, one hand balancing the jug on his knee. He was noticeably calmer now the watchman and the others were gone, and noticeably drunker.

'Aphra has just promised to pay for another funeral,' Nell told him.

'What?' He nearly dropped the jug. 'Is one funeral not enough for her?'

'Given the funds, I fear she would she bury all London.'

Aphra turned to leave the room, tired of being talked about as if she wasn't there. 'I will see if Mrs Decker needs anything.'

Aphra opened her bedchamber door and saw the top of Elizabeth's head peeking out from a pile of blankets. She was snoring. Aphra sighed. Seeing Elizabeth asleep reminded her how tired she was. She felt like crawling in beside her, but there were still people in the house, and much that needed to be done. She had to order another coffin and send messages to both Gospel House and St Mary's, telling them to make room for another body.

Then there were the occupants of the house in St Giles – they should be informed of their friend's death. As she doubted any of them could read, she would have to tell them in person. But that, she decided, could wait until morning.

She started to pull the door shut. The hinges creaked, and Elizabeth woke with a start.

'What? Who?'

'I didn't mean to wake you,' Aphra said from the doorway. 'Go back to sleep.'

'Sleep? Oh no, I couldn't sleep,' Elizabeth protested. 'Not after all that has happened.'

Aphra might have mentioned that she had never known anyone to snore while they were awake – but she lacked the energy for an argument. 'How are you feeling?' she asked instead, struggling to hold back a yawn. 'Are you any better?'

'I am sorry I was unwell,' Elizabeth said. 'It was the blood. I never saw so much blood.'

Aphra crossed the room and sat down on the bed beside her. 'I know.' She took hold of Elizabeth's hand and gave it a comforting squeeze.

'And the smell.'

Aphra dropped the hand and stood up, feeling a need to change the subject. 'Can I get you anything?'

'No, I must return to my lodgings; it's getting late.'

Aphra felt a wave of relief at the sight of Elizabeth finally getting out of her bed. She wanted her out of the house. She wanted everyone out of the house. Then maybe, at last, she could sleep. Maybe at last she could forget everything that had happened, if only for a little while.

Elizabeth gestured towards the little bag on the bedside table. 'May I?'

Aphra tensed, suddenly wide awake. In the shock of finding Elias's body, she had forgotten all about John Hoyle and his sugar sops. The constable said that Elias had most likely surprised a burglar, and everyone had agreed. He'd gone on to say she was fortunate not to have been robbed before, living as near as she did to the 'lawless sanctuary of Alsatia'. But there was nothing missing and no sign of forced entry. And Hoyle had definitely been in the house today, while she was out.

The only way into her garden was through the house. Might John Hoyle have let Elias in? And what if he had? That still didn't explain why Elias was murdered, or by whom.

'Have as many as you like,' she said.

'You're very kind.' Elizabeth reached for the bag, knocking Hoyle's card to the floor. 'Sorry,' she said, bending down to pick it up.

'Leave it,' Aphra said.

Elizabeth straightened up, holding the card. 'It was on the bed when I first came upstairs. "To Hermia from her Lysander. Always." They were the lovers in *A Midsummer Night's Dream*, weren't they?'

'One pair of them, yes,' Aphra said, snatching the card from her.

Elizabeth giggled. 'If you are Hermia, then pray tell me, who is Lysander?'

'No one you know,' Aphra said, feeling her jaw tighten.

Elizabeth leaned forward, a mischievous expression on her face. 'Is your Lysander as handsome as mine?'

Aphra shrugged. 'I might have thought so ... once. You didn't mention this card to the constable, did you?'

'No. Why should I?'

Aphra cursed herself for being such a fool. Why, after all the hurt and deception, should she still feel the need to protect John Hoyle? Let him be questioned by constables and magistrates. Let him rot in prison. Let him hang, she told herself; it made no difference to her. 'No reason,' she said, crumpling the card into a ball.

There was a knock at the door. Nell entered, carrying a cloak which Aphra recognized as her own.

'What is this?' Aphra demanded.

'Rochester says that you should not remain alone tonight – after what has happened – and I agree with him, so we have decided you should stay with me.'

'You have decided? Have I no choice in this matter?'

Nell tied the cloak around Aphra's shoulders. 'All right, you would have a choice; I will give you a choice. You may come to my house in Pall Mall, or you may go home with Rochester. Which do you prefer?'

A boy walked ahead of Nell's pink and white coach, holding a torch to light the way. 'Make way for my lady!' he shouted at intervals. 'Make way!'

Aphra sat staring straight ahead, arms crossed, mouth drawn into a thin line. Saying nothing.

'It will be all right, Aphra,' Nell told her, thinking she was still upset about the coffin. Elias's coffin was to be much plainer – and considerably cheaper – than the one they had ordered for Matthew. The way expenses were mounting up, even the plainest coffin was more than they could afford.

But that wasn't what Aphra was worrying about. She tapped

the roof to stop the coach. 'Turn around,' she said. 'I must go to Gray's Inn immediately.'

'Gray's Inn? Whatever for?'

'Never mind,' Aphra said, reaching for the door handle. 'I shall walk.'

'You will do no such thing,' Nell said, grabbing hold of her arm. 'I will take you, if you insist. But first I must know why.'

Aphra hesitated before she answered. 'John Hoyle may have been inside my house today.'

Nell sighed and told her driver to turn around.

'I will not be long,' Aphra said, stepping down from the coach in front of Gray's Inn.

Nell climbed out after her. 'I'm going with you.'

'No! I will speak to him alone.'

'You would confront him without a witness?'

'I have no intention of confronting him. I shall ask a few subtle questions and note his reactions, remaining calm and detached throughout.' She leaned forward, lowering her voice. 'Perhaps you forget I have some experience of these matters.'

'I have not forgotten you were once a spy,' Nell said, 'but it seems you forget where your spying brought you.'

The street, the coach, Nell, the driver and the link boy, all vanished, to be replaced by a scene in Aphra's head. She was back in prison, listening helplessly to a woman sobbing over her dying child. 'You are wrong, Nell,' she said, driving the picture from her mind. 'That is one thing I will never forget.'

'And what if your suspicions are right? What will you do then?'

'Suspicions? Who said I had any suspicions?'

'But you said he was in the house.'

'That means nothing,' Aphra insisted. 'I suspect John Hoyle of nothing. This visit is merely to prove how *right* I am not to suspect him.'

'That much is obvious,' Nell said drily.

Aphra looked up at the building that housed her former

lover's chambers. She'd been there many times before, when things had been different. 'You think I'm mad, don't you?'

'You're not mad, you're upset, and what you need is rest.'

'Perhaps,' Aphra said, 'but how can I rest while even the slightest doubt lingers in my mind? Elias was murdered in my house, Nell. That makes it my responsibility.'

'No one believes that.'

'*I* believe it,' Aphra said, walking towards the entrance.

Aphra knocked on a door about halfway down a long corridor lined with doors identical to that one.

Hoyle's voice came from within, sounding thick and muffled, as if he'd been asleep. 'Who's there?'

Aphra opened the door, entering a square, wood-panelled room lined with bookshelves. In the centre stood a desk piled high with papers, surrounded by several chairs. Beyond the desk, in the dim glow of the last remaining embers in the grate, John Hoyle's head was just visible, peering out from the velvet curtains surrounding his bed. 'You're abed early, John.'

'My darling love!' he said, remaining behind the curtain. 'How ... unexpected.'

'My business with you will not take long.' Aphra stopped in the middle of the room, beside his desk. She wanted to keep a safe distance between them. 'I have come for my key.'

'Key? I don't know what key you mean, my little pigsnie.'

'Do not play the innocent with me, John Hoyle. And do not call me "pigsnie". You know perfectly well I mean the key to my house.'

'But I returned your key some time ago, sweet darling,' he insisted, curtains still wrapped about his shoulders. 'Surely you remember.'

'And kept a copy!' she shouted, her patience nearly exhausted.

'No, no dear creature, I promise you are wrong!' He shifted behind the curtain, made a sound as if he was choking, then began to cough, a violent, racking cough that shook his whole body.

'Are you all right, John?' Anger temporarily forgotten, she rushed to his bedside. 'Can I do anything for you?'

He raised one hand to stop her coming closer; the other clutched the curtains hard enough to turn the knuckles white. 'No, madam, please. It's only the effects of a recent trip south of the river, where everyone knows the air carries many ill humours. I am quite well, I assure you. Though perhaps it would be best if I were left alone to rest.'

Aphra felt the muscles in her neck tighten. He had left a love note on her bed, and now he was trying to get rid of her. Well, that was fine with her. She had no intention of staying. 'Just hand me the key, Hoyle, and I will go.'

'But charming sibyl, I have told you I have not got it!'

'Then how did you come into my bedchamber today?'

Hoyle's eyes went round with surprise. 'What?'

'You entered my house while I was out, leaving a card and a bag of sweets on my bed. Do not try to deny this!'

'But I must,' he protested. 'It's true I brought you a bag of sweets, but when no one answered my knock, I left them outside, on your step. By my life, I – ' He stopped mid-sentence, glaring at her. 'It would seem someone else visited your bedchamber, madam, not I.'

A chill ran down Aphra's spine. This was not what she wanted to hear. Though she hated to admit it, even to herself, what she really wanted him to say was yes, he had made a copy of the key because he had never stopped loving her, and couldn't carry on without her. *Then* – once that fact had been established – he was supposed to convince her he'd had nothing to do with Elias's death.

Though on the one hand she was relieved that Hoyle had so easily allayed the suspicions she'd so adamantly denied ever having, on the other she didn't want to consider the possibility that some unknown person had found his way into the room

68

where she slept, alone and vulnerable. 'You never entered my house today?'

'Never.'

'You're certain? You swear it?'

'I tire of this conversation, madam. Yes, I am certain and yes, I swear it!'

'You say you knocked on the door and no one answered. What time was it?'

'What?'

'What time?' What time did you come to my door?'

'I don't know! I went on to the theatre in Dorset Garden and arrived during the interval between the first and the second act.'

'That would have been about half past three,' Aphra said.

'I suppose so. What does it matter?'

'It matters because – ' She was interrupted by a sneeze, coming from behind the drapes. Hoyle immediately started sneezing, but this time she wasn't fooled. She reached for the curtain. Hoyle clung like death to the two pieces of velvet pressed together beneath his chin.. She crossed behind him, pulling the material around from the other side. All she could see in the semi-darkness was a few strands of hair escaping from a huge lump in the blanket, but that was enough. 'You never change, do you, Hoyle?'

'Dearest! This is not what it seems!'

'Damn you, John Hoyle! I warn you, never come near me again!' She ran from the room, slamming the door behind her.

Nell was waiting in the hall. Aphra stormed past her, muttering curses.

'Aphra, wait,' Nell said, picking up her skirts to hurry after her.

'What are you doing here? I told you to wait outside!'

'I thought it best someone listen at the door while you remained calm and detached.'

*

Soon after their arrival in Pall Mall, Nell left Aphra asleep in one of the bedchambers, took a deep breath and headed for the kitchen. The maid who'd answered the front door had warned her there was trouble brewing, and now she saw the maid was right. A stout woman in an apron and bonnet rushed to meet her, her face red with indignation.

'She won't let me in,' the woman complained. 'There I was, rolling out the pastry for a nice pigeon pie when she comes up behind me and says she'll do her own cooking, thank you very much, and I'm not to get in her way.'

'I'll speak to her,' Nell promised.

'She'd keep me out, but not that Mr Cane. He's in there now.'

Nell rolled her eyes at the thought of what she would find in the kitchen. 'I will speak to them both. As for tonight, you may retire to bed early.'

'But my pie—'

'Leave the pie for tomorrow,' Nell interrupted.

The cook stared at her sullenly.

'What can I do?' Nell asked her. 'She's my mother!'

The cook sighed and nodded. 'Yes, mistress.'

Nell opened the kitchen door; it was exactly as she had feared. Her mother and her son's tutor sat bleary-eyed at opposite ends of an oaken table, a row of empty bottles between them. Her mother looked up at her approach, grey hair dishevelled, nose a brilliant shade of purple. She burped. 'Nelly, my little duck! Come and join us.'

'Mother, you've upset the cook again.'

Madam Gwyn waved a dismissive hand. 'Fie! Am I one to be fussed over by servants?'

'But why must you sit in the kitchen? Why not use the withdrawing room or the parlour, and let my cook get on with her work?'

'A pox on your withdrawing room and parlour! I am

comfortable in the kitchen.' She gestured towards the young man sitting across from her. 'And you, Mr Cane? Are you comfortable?'

'Quite comfortable, mother,' he said. From the day she had turned up on the doorstep with her trunk, Madam Gwyn had insisted that Bevil Cane call her 'mother'. He only did it when he was drunk.

Nell looked at her mother, planted solidly in her chair, then at the tutor, swaying in his, and resigned herself to the fact that neither had any intention of moving.

'How went your rehearsal?' Mr Cane asked her, patting the seat next to his.

Nell crossed the room and sat down beside him, resting her head on the table. 'Not well.'

Her mother made a little clucking sound, then poured her a glass of wine.

'I hope you gave my regards to the divine Mrs Decker?' Mr Cane asked. 'Did she ask about me? Did you tell her about my play?'

Nell twisted her head to look up at Bevil Cane, who was looking hopefully down at her. He was twenty-two years old, and not unattractive, with thick dark hair and an open, friendly face. But he was an impoverished scholar with aspirations to be a poet; did he really think he stood the slightest chance against an earl? She sat up and gulped down her wine, emptying the glass. 'I'm sorry, Bevil. There was no time to speak of your play; there was hardly time to speak of anything. A man was murdered tonight, his throat slit straight across. It was I who found the body.'

'Poor duck!' Nell's mother said, suddenly sober. 'Tell me everything that happened.'

'Crimine!' the old woman muttered as Nell finished her story. 'Foolish child! Have you lost the sense you were born with?'

Nell looked at her mother, puzzled. 'Foolish? Why?'

71

'You say the dead man was a mumper, and most likely a thief. Who knows what enemies such a man might have? Yet you and your friend go about Lincoln's Inn Fields giving out her address, so that any who wish him harm may know exactly where to find him.'

'S'death,' Nell said, 'I never thought – '

'You never thought! And who do you choose to confide in next? None other than that lying scoundrel, Toby Rainbeard! God's lugs, child! Are you mad?'

'I don't understand. I thought Toby was your friend.'

'Friend? Ha! He was a good customer, in the days when I sold strong waters, but he was never my friend. I promise you, daughter, he is not a man to be trusted.'

Chapter Six

Louise de Kéroualle rose from her bed, unable to sleep. One of her maids lay asleep on a small bed in the corner. The maid rolled over, muttering something, but did not wake up.

Louise crossed the room to sit beside the window, cradling a small telescope in her arms. It was a gift from the king, a reminder of happier times when her only rival for His Majesty's affection was a low-born orange girl turned actress.

A few years ago, Nell had pretended an interest in chemistry in order to impress the king. Nell, who couldn't even read or write, had actually requested she be allowed to enter His Majesty's laboratory to observe his chemical experiments, which she claimed to find fascinating. Louise immediately countered this by declaring she had always been a keen student of astronomy and hoped His Majesty might join her in stargazing. Charles finally resolved the matter by presenting Nell with a collection of glass tubes and Louise with a hand-held telescope, saying he hoped that each would now pursue her scientific studies independently.

It was true the king often dallied with Nell, for whatever small amusement she afforded him, but it was always Louise he came to when he wanted intelligent conversation in refined surroundings. It was always Louise for fine food and wine – everyone knew she employed the best chefs in Whitehall. And it was always Louise when he'd had a difficult day, and only wanted someone to rub his temples and murmur something soothing.

Always, she thought, until recently.

Nell had been a constant annoyance, but never a serious threat. Not like the Duchess of Mazarin. Everything had changed with her arrival. The king had been angry with Louise once or twice before, but he had never *ignored* her like this. He had never abandoned her to pine away, forgotten.

At least she had found a use for her telescope, now there was nothing for her to do but stare out of the window all day and night. She wondered what use if any Nell found for her glass tubes.

She bent her head forward, choking back a tear. The next thing she knew it was light and the telescope was on the floor; she must have fallen asleep. She rolled her head from side to side, shrugging her shoulders. God, her neck was stiff! And the room was freezing; the fire had gone out hours ago.

She stood up, yawning and rubbing her neck, intending to go back to bed; it was barely five of the clock and there was no reason for her to rise early. She leaned forward to draw the curtains and saw several figures moving about on the riverbank below the palace.

Charles was standing beside the Thames, surrounded as usual by yapping dogs and obsequious courtiers. The men removed the king's wig, followed by his coat, shirt, shoes and stockings. Then Charles strode down to the water, wearing nothing but a short pair of breeches, and dived in, leaving his courtiers to shiver on the bank.

This morning swim was a ritual of his; he did it every day, regardless of the weather. He used to come to Louise afterwards, laughing at how soft the men of his court were, that not one of them had the courage to follow him into the water on a chilly morning, not for a thousand guineas.

Louise watched him swim upriver for several minutes, growing smaller as he vanished into the distance. Then she saw someone leap into the water to join him. She reached for her telescope. After a great deal of pushing and pulling at the sliding tubes that held the lenses, she finally managed to focus on the other person's face. It was the Duchess of Mazarin.

'I hope you drown!' she shouted as the king splashed over to meet the duchess.

Her outburst woke the maid. 'Yes, my lady?'

Louise stepped away from the window, hiding the telescope behind her back; servants were such gossips. 'Go to the kitchen,' she said, anxious to get the girl out of the room, 'and tell them I would like an early breakfast.' She waited until the maid was gone before returning to the window.

She searched up and down the river, but the king and Mazarin were nowhere to be seen. She looked down at the bank below the palace. The dogs and courtiers were gone. She lowered her telescope, muttering a curse in French. She could imagine where the king and Hortense were now, and what they were doing.

She spent another moment at the window, staring straight ahead, wondering if she ought to go back to bed. The maid would bring her breakfast in a minute, but she would tell the maid to take it away; she didn't want it.

Of course, she thought, the instant she sent back her breakfast, the rumours would begin: the Duchess of Portsmouth refuses to eat, she is starving herself for love, she is a pitiful skeleton hovering on the brink of death.

That would show the king.

She was about to turn back to her bed, when she caught a glimpse of something moving on the opposite bank of the river. Curious, she picked up her spyglass.

She focused in, and saw a man looking up at the palace through a little telescope just like hers.

Aphra woke in a gigantic bed, not sure where she was or how she'd got there. When she saw that the sheets were pink satin, it all came back to her.

She leapt from the bed, dressing quickly. She gathered up

the few overnight things she'd brought with her, and headed for the door. There was so much to be done, and so little time in which to do it. She opened the door and stepped out into the hall, nearly tripping over a parcel tied with rope. On the floor beside it was a note addressed to: 'The Most Admirable Mrs Behn'.

It was from Bevil Cane, asking if she would do him the honour of reading his play, 'Aleister and Dorinda, a tragical romance in rhyming quatrains and couplets', which he had taken the liberty of enclosing. Then perhaps she might have a word with Mr Davenant about producing it at Dorset Garden. There was no hurry, Mr Cane went on to assure her, but since he had given her his only copy he would be very grateful if he could please have it back before Saturday.

As Nell's coach pulled away from Pall Mall, Aphra began to wonder when she would ever be able to stop all this rushing about. But the funeral was tonight, less than twelve hours away. If she could just get through this day, she told herself, then life would return to normal.

Or almost normal. There was still the play to worry about, and Elizabeth's performance. And Rochester's bet.

She felt like screaming. What had she got herself into?

'Are you all right?' Nell asked her.

Aphra looked down at her hands. They were clenched into fists. 'I'm fine,' she said, unclenching them.

It was a little after eight when Aphra climbed down from the coach at the top of the St Giles alley, clutching a stack of invitation cards with the words: 'and his brother, Elias', written in the margin. She was surprised to see Nell climb down after her. 'There's no need to come with me; this will only take a moment.'

'I would like a word with Toby,' Nell told her.

They made their way arm in arm down the alley, carefully

avoiding piles of stinking rubbish and excrement. This time Aphra had come prepared for the horde of grasping children, purposely bringing along her bag of sugar sops. And this time both women kept a wary eye out for chamber pots in upstairs windows.

Aphra knocked on Mrs Adams's door and waited. No answer.

She knocked again, calling Mrs Adams's name. Still no reply.

'Is it locked?' Nell asked her.

Aphra shrugged and turned the knob. The door swung open. She stepped inside, raising her handkerchief to her nose. The stench of sweat and livestock was more appalling than ever, but the people and animals were gone.

The furniture was gone, too. So were the clothes and plates and mugs, and anything else that might indicate anyone had ever lived there.

Chapter Seven

Monsieur Honoré Courtin sat at his desk, staring down at a blank sheet of paper. The situation at the English court was a delicate one; he needed to handle it with care.

He took a deep breath as he picked up his pen, aware that his sovereign, King Louis of France, would not be pleased with his latest news.

Your Majesty, his report began. *I regret I must inform you that the influence of Mademoiselle de Kéroualle has come to an end. The English king persistently ignores her in favour of the Duchess of Mazarin.*

I shall of course continue in my efforts to win the new lady to our cause, but thus far my every entreaty has been in vain. Whenever I seek to remind the duchess of her family connection to France, and to the only true faith, she replies that she cares nothing for family, and even less for religion: a shocking profession from the niece of a cardinal. Even offers of money seem to hold little interest for her, an attitude I find baffling in one so dedicated to the pursuit of pleasure. Still, given time, I am certain to convince her.

As for the other matter, I despair to inform you that the document is still missing.

The Duchess of Mazarin sat in front of a gold-framed looking glass, watching a maid comb and curl her hair.

Behind her Anne of Sussex sat up in bed, scowling at the sheet of paper in her hands.

'Another letter from France?' Hortense asked Anne's reflection.

'I have had three such letters in as many days. My mother writes that she is scandalized to hear of my behaviour, and insists yet again that my place is at my husband's side.'

Barbara Castlemaine? Scandalized? The thought of it made Hortense laugh out loud. 'If your mother had remained by her husband's side, you would never have been born, my dear!'

'She says she has written to the king, demanding I be sent away from court immediately.'

Hortense turned to face her. 'Charles would never do that,' she said. 'I wouldn't let him.'

'And this sloppily written communication,' Anne held up another sheet, 'is from my husband, wishing to know when to expect me.'

Hortense got up, waving away the maid and her comb, and crossed the room to sit beside Anne on the bed. 'Don't worry,' she said, plucking the letter from Anne's hand. 'I'll take care of it.'

'What will you do?' Anne asked her.

'This,' she said, ripping the letter in two.

Aphra and Nell sat on the same stools they had occupied the day before as Meldrick Bridger's daughter poured them each a mug of beer. Mr Bridger's house was not much different from that of his neighbour, Mrs Adams; it was a rudely constructed hovel, with a dirt floor, covered in straw. But Mr Bridger had built an interior wall, dividing it into two rooms, and added a couple of small windows to let in light and air. A girl of about four or five lay sniffling and coughing in a cot beneath one of the windows.

'Mrs Adams was arrested last night,' Mr Bridger told them. 'About eight of the clock.'

'Arrested by whom? And why?' Aphra asked him.

Mr Bridger shrugged. 'There were six or seven men; I don't know who they were. They said they were taking her for debt.'

A chill ran down Aphra's spine. 'Do you know where they took her?'

'To the Fleet.'

'And her children?'

'Taken to the Fleet as well.' Mr Bridger bent over the cot where the child lay coughing. He placed a hand on her cheek. 'My granddaughter sickens; her face is much too hot. She had an elder brother, but he died of a swelling in his throat.' He looked up at Nell and Aphra. 'I gave Mrs Adams what I could for her garnish, so the children would not starve for bread, but I am a poor man and could spare but a few pennies. Now I wish I had not spared even that; the little one grows worse, and I have no money for a physic.'

Aphra doubted Mr Bridger's claim to have given his neighbour money – that was an obvious ploy to gain her sympathy – but the little girl *was* ill. She reached into her purse and took out two shillings: enough to buy a bottle of medicine. 'What has become of the others who lived with Mrs Adams?' she asked, holding up the coins so Mr Bridger could see them.

'They went to find other lodgings, I suppose; I don't know where.'

'What about Toby Rainbeard?' Nell broke in. 'Do you know where he has gone?'

Mr Bridger shook his head. 'Toby Rainbeard?'

'The grey-haired man Aphra gave the card to.'

'He wasn't there when Mrs Adams was arrested. He left soon after you.'

Nell and Aphra exchanged a look of surprise. 'Did he say where he was going?'

'No, he left with another man.'

'What man?' Nell persisted.

'I do not know his name.'

'What did he look like?'

'A dark-haired man, very agitated in manner. Alas, I could not see his face; it was dark and he wore a large hat. He said he must speak to Mr Rainbeard urgently. The old man seemed to know him well; they went outside together, and did not come back.'

Zooks, Aphra thought, so Toby left with a dark-haired man in a hat: a description that might fit half the men in England. She gave Nell a little nudge with her elbow, signalling they had done all they could and it was time to go. 'Thank you, Mr Bridger, but Mistress Gwyn and I have pressing business elsewhere.' Aphra stood, handing the coins to the child's mother. 'I pray your little girl is better soon.'

'Tell her about the other man, father,' Mr Bridger's daughter prompted him, her eyes on the coins in her hand.

'What other?' Aphra asked her.

'The gentleman that came round nearly midnight, asking if we knew a Mrs Behn.'

Once again Aphra was late for rehearsal, and once again they had started without her. Elizabeth was on stage, reading through a scene with one of the actors. Mr Davenant was standing in the pit, massaging his forehead as if he had a headache; he seemed quite relieved when Aphra suggested that Nell take over as director. Rochester waved to her from the front row of the Royal Box, and she went up to join him.

'Rochester, I would speak with you. Did you enter my bedchamber yesterday?'

'When I enter a lady's bedchamber, I pray she never need ask whether I was there.' He rubbed his hands together, licking his lips. 'Perhaps you had a dream about me, Aphra? Pray sit down and tell me every detail.'

'You flatter yourself,' she said, sinking into the seat beside him. She placed the parcel containing Mr Cane's manuscript on the empty seat beside hers. 'There was a package left on my bed last night. I merely wondered if you brought it inside.'

'I have never even seen your bed, which strikes me as a terrible omission, as I so like to know where my friends sleep.'

Aphra gave him a look designed to make it clear she had no wish to discuss her sleeping arrangements any further. 'What time did you and Elizabeth arrive at my house yesterday?'

Rochester threw up his hands. 'You said to come at six of the clock; I assume we arrived about that time.'

'And there was no package on the step when you arrived?'

He shook his head. 'No. Why?'

'No reason.'

Rochester nodded towards the seat beyond hers. 'Is that the mysterious package you refer to?'

'No, that is a play by Bevil Cane.'

'Who?'

'A member of Nell's household.'

Rochester reached across her, picking up the manuscript. He glanced at the title and shook his head. 'A tragical romance? Where does Nell find these stray puppies?' He flicked through a few pages before tossing it over his shoulder. 'How long has this mongrel cur been living on Nell's generosity?'

Aphra shrugged. 'I don't know. A month or two.'

'I understand Nell's mother now resides with her as well.' Rochester leaned forward, whispering confidentially. 'They say the old woman was evicted from her lodgings.'

'And what if she was?' Aphra asked, exasperated. 'What concern is it of yours?'

'None,' Rochester said. 'I just thought it was amusing.'

'Well, it isn't.' Aphra sat with her arms crossed, trying to watch the rehearsal. Elizabeth was on stage with one of the actors, reading through the scene where the heroine pretends to be a Spanish princess. 'Ye Gods!' she muttered as Elizabeth declared her love for the hero. 'A parsnip might have said that line with more emotion.'

'It's only the third rehearsal, Aphra,' Rochester reminded her. 'Give her time; none of the cast have even learned their lines yet. Yet look how she remains still while the others speak, how she raises her hand to her face to convey surprise. She will justify your faith in her, Aphra, I swear it.'

'My faith? In Elizabeth? Ha!'

Rochester leaned back in his chair, feet on the gilt-adorned railing, lips pursed. 'Something troubles you, Aphra. I trust you haven't found another corpse?'

'No, I have not!' She hesitated before continuing, inwardly debating the wisdom of confiding in Rochester. He could be arrogant, inconsiderate and infuriating, but he had always been a friend to her, rising to her defence when others attacked her, praising and promoting her work while others condemned it – and her – as immodest and immoral. She finally decided that if she must speak to someone, it might as well be him. 'Though it is against all my better judgement to ask you,' she began, 'there are several things I find perplexing, and I wonder if I might bother you for your thoughts?'

'My thoughts I give freely, which may give some hint as to their value. Still, I will help if I can.'

She told him about her conversation with John Hoyle. The business with Hoyle and the sweets was still bothering her. If Rochester hadn't carried the bag of sweets inside, then who had? Perhaps Hoyle was lying about not having a key; he had certainly proved himself capable of lying about everything else.

Rochester agreed that seemed likely.

Then she told him about Toby Rainbeard, and how he had gone off with some stranger and never returned, and what Nell's mother had said about not trusting him.

Rochester shrugged. 'I would advise you not to trust any of old Madam Gwyn's associates.'

Finally, she told him about Mrs Adams's arrest, and the man who had knocked on the neighbour's door at midnight.

Rochester put down his feet and sat upright. 'He asked for *you*?'

'He asked if they knew me, yes.'

'Who was this man?'

'I don't know!' she told him, her voice rising. 'If I knew, it would not be a cause for concern, now would it?'

Rochester placed a gloved hand on her arm. 'No need to shout, Aphra; I hear you quite perfectly.'

She shook the hand away. 'I am *not* shouting!'

'Mrs Behn, *please!*' Mr Davenant called from the stage.

Aphra glowered down at the stage, then turned back to Rochester, lowering her voice. 'They told me it was dark and he wore a riding cloak to obscure his face, but his straight posture led them to believe he might be young. They also said he was tall, and by his speech they knew him to be a gentleman.'

'What men do you know that might be described thus?'

'I can think of several,' Aphra said. 'You, for one.'

Rochester leaned closer towards her, eyes sparkling. 'Would you like to know where I was at midnight, and what I was doing? I'd be happy to tell you everything, in intimate detail, but I fear you might blush.'

'Spare me your confessions, John. I do not blush easily, and I so hate feeling obliged to try.'

He shrugged, smiling. 'You know not what you miss.' His facial expression became more serious. 'What about John Hoyle? He might well have come looking for you after what happened in his chambers, if only to deny it ever *did* happen. That's what I would do. Deny it, I mean.'

'But why look for me in St Giles? He knew nothing of my visit there.'

Rochester raised one eyebrow. 'Perhaps he got the address from Elias, when he encountered him in your house of office.'

Aphra clutched at the gilded railing across the box, cursing herself for being such a fool. In spite of everything, she had managed to convince herself Hoyle had nothing to do with Elias's death. Now she wasn't so sure. 'Is that what you think?' she asked Rochester. 'You think it was Hoyle killed Elias?'

'I might think that,' Rochester said carefully, 'if I could only

think of a reason for him to do so. But there's none I can see.'
He shrugged again. 'Jealousy? Surely Hoyle would not view a
toothless beggar as his rival.'

'What if he mistook Elias for a burglar?' Aphra said quietly.

'Then he would think himself a hero. He would want you to
know what he had done. He would brag of it.'

She loosened her grip on the railing, relieved. 'You may be
right.'

'In this one regard, at least, you may be certain I am right.
And though I am loathe to admit it, I fear your local baker is
probably right as well: Elias surprised a burglar. They say the
thieves of Alsatia have organized themselves into companies,
and go about boldly by light of day,' he reminded her. 'And
you live an easy distance from their sanctuary.'

'But nothing was stolen,' she protested.

'Because the burglar panicked and ran before he could take
anything,' Rochester told her. 'As for the man who asked after
you in St Giles, did these neighbours say nothing else that might
help determine this man's identity?'

'They only said he asked for Mrs Adams first, and then
Elias – '

'Oh fie on it, Aphra!' Rochester exclaimed. 'All this fuss over
nothing. The man was seeking that cursed mumper, not you!
How many people heard your name when you went searching
about the fields?'

Aphra sighed and nodded. 'That is what Nell said.'

'And she is right; the fact this man knew your name is
nothing for you to worry about.'

'But Elias was murdered in my – '

'Whoever asked for him in St Giles didn't kill him,' Rochester interrupted. 'If you murdered a man, would you then visit
his neighbours many hours later, to ask if they knew where you
might find him?'

Aphra thought for a moment before she answered. 'What
better way to allay suspicion than to let everyone see you behave

85

as though you thought your victim still alive? Yes, I might well visit his friends, but I would let them see my face, as if I had nothing to hide.'

Rochester slid down in his seat, placing his feet back on the railing. 'Beautiful poet, you worry me.'

Chapter Eight

Aphra walked along the river from the theatre to the timber yard at the foot of her street, clutching a dishevelled collection of loose paper to her chest. Damn that Rochester! Thanks to him, Bevil Cane's play was out of order. It would take her for ever to sort it out; Mr Cane hadn't numbered the pages.

Then, after rehearsal, Rochester had the nerve to say he wouldn't be coming to the funeral after all; he had too many memories of the naval yard at Deptford, all of them dating back to the first war against the Dutch, and all of them bad. Aphra had protested that her own memories of the war were every bit as bad as his, but he would not be moved, even when she reminded him that Matthew Cavell and he had served on the same ship. 'I lost many friends on that ship,' he'd said, telling her again how he watched two of them killed by the same shot. 'I do not wish to be reminded of the war, or the *Revenge*, or anyone who was on it.'

All right, she'd finally told him, she didn't want him there anyway. Then Elizabeth broke in and said that *she* would come.

Aphra stepped around a pile of manure, gritting her teeth. She could think of nothing she would like less than to spend another evening with Elizabeth. What was she supposed to say to her? They had nothing in common except the play, and she didn't dare speak to her about that; she might tell her what she really thought of her performance. She might tell her that she rued the day she had ever agreed to cast her. She might tell her a lot of things.

She'd nearly told Elizabeth there and then that she was giving her three more days; if she didn't improve to a sufficient degree by the end of rehearsal on Saturday, she would be replaced first thing Monday morning, wager or not. But in the end, she didn't say it. Instead, she bit her tongue and left the theatre, saying only that she would make her own way to Deptford.

She felt as if all the anger and frustration of the last few days had formed itself into a huge dark cloud, following her everywhere she went. She forced herself to walk faster, trying to shake the cloud from her shoulders.

Then she came within sight of her house, and broke into a run.

Several raggedly dressed children were gathered around a cart in the street outside her door, chattering to the driver and petting the horses. She recognized the driver and his cart from the previous night. The man smiled and took off his hat at her approach. In the back of the cart, wrapped in a blanket, was Elias's body.

'What are you doing here?' Aphra shouted at the driver. 'You were supposed to take him to Deptford!'

The children fell silent, gaping up at Aphra.

'I did that, missus,' the driver said. 'We had a lovely ride along the water. Pity your friend was in no state to enjoy it.'

Aphra could not believe what she was hearing. 'But you weren't supposed to bring him back!'

A little girl started giggling. Aphra shot her a glance and she darted behind one of the horses.

The driver shrugged. 'I didn't know what else to do with him, did I, missus?'

'You didn't know what else to do with him?' She felt a sudden stabbing pain along one side of her head. She took several deep breaths, telling herself she must remain calm. The pain became a dull throbbing behind her right temple. 'You were supposed to leave him there!'

'And I would have, gladly,' the man assured her. 'But they wouldn't take him, would they?'

'What? Are you sure you took him to the right address? Gospel House, near the naval yard?'

'They wouldn't have him, missus. A woman come out to look at him, said she didn't know him and told me to take him right back where he come from, didn't she?'

Aphra's jaw clenched so hard she heard it click. 'But I wrote to them! I told them to expect another body!'

The driver shrugged to show it was nothing to do with him. The children lost interest and wandered away.

Aphra looked down at her hands and saw they were shaking. All she'd wanted was to help someone who had lost everything in life to regain a little of his former dignity in death, and it was all going horribly wrong. 'You have to return him to Deptford. He is to be buried there tonight.'

The driver told her he would be happy to take the body back to Deptford, for a fee of six shillings.

'Six shillings!' she shrieked. 'The fare on the river is only two!'

'Then you'd best send your friend by river,' the driver said, climbing down from his seat. He walked around to the rear of the cart and lifted up the body. 'I'll leave him on the step for you, missus, shall I?'

'I'll give you three shillings,' Aphra said.

'Five,' said the driver.

'Three and six, and I ride with you.'

Nell stopped off at the print shop to pick up the cards she had ordered the day before. They looked wonderful: similar to Aphra's, but with a lot more skulls. She asked the printer's apprentice to read out the words for her, so she could be certain they'd got it right.

*

Aphra stepped into her hall to find several letters shoved under her door. She carried them into the parlour and opened the shutter to let in some light.

'God's nails,' she said, taking in the scene. The room was exactly the way she'd left it the night before: furniture pushed back against the walls, empty jugs scattered here and there, a trail of muddy footprints across the floor. Someone had placed a chair upside down on her little table to make more room when they'd carried out the body.

Even her bookshelves had been interfered with; several poetry broadsheets lay open across her desk. That would have been Rochester, checking to see that his own verse was included.

She tossed her letters on to the desk top, placed Bevil Cane's disordered manuscript in a drawer and went upstairs to get changed.

She came back a short while later, dressed in mourning. She could see the cart driver through the window, fidgeting impatiently. For three and six let him fidget, she thought, sitting down to read her letters.

It was lucky she did. One of them was from the coffin-maker, writing to inform her he had been unable to deliver the second coffin, as it had been turned away. 'Ye Gods!' she said out loud, crushing the letter in her hand.

Another was from the coroner, requesting her presence at the inquest into Elias's death.

And one was from John Hoyle. She glanced at the signature and tossed it into the grate, unread.

The others were all demands for payment.

The throbbing in her head became worse than ever. Calm, she told herself, stay calm. She took a long, deep breath, then stood up to close the shutter, plunging the room back into darkness.

When she opened her front door she noticed a man standing in a doorway further down the street. By the time she'd closed the door and locked it, he was gone.

'Ready to go now, missus?' the driver asked her wearily.

'We need to stop at the coffin-makers first; it's on the way.'

'Stop? You said nothing 'bout no stop,' he protested. 'Stops is extra.'

Nell's maid greeted her with the news that her mother was in the kitchen again.

Nell raised a hand to silence her. 'Has my mourning attire been delivered?'

'Yes, mistress. I placed it in your chamber.'

'Thank you, Lucy,' Nell said, dismissing her.

As the maid curtsied and left, Bevil Cane appeared at the top of the stairs. 'What did she say, Nelly?'

'Who?'

'Mrs Behn,' he said, hurrying down to meet her. 'What did she say about my play?'

She sighed and shook her head. 'She said nothing, Bevil.'

He paused where he was on the stairs, looking dejected. 'Nothing?'

'You only gave it to her this morning,' Nell reminded him gently. 'She's barely had time to read the title.'

He considered this a moment before resuming his journey downwards, this time at a slower pace. 'I suppose you're right,' he admitted. 'But what about Mrs Decker? What did *she* say? Did you mention me to her?'

Nell sighed. 'I never got the chance. I promise you, I shall speak to her tonight, and I will tell her all about your play and how much you wish her to be in it.'

'Tonight?' Mr Cane repeated, looking puzzled. 'I thought you were attending a funeral tonight.'

'And so is Mrs Decker,' Nell said, heading towards the kitchen. 'I'm taking her in my coach.'

'Oh Nelly, please say I may come with you!' Mr Cane called after her.

*

Nell stood in the kitchen doorway, amazed. Her mother and her cook were in the room together, her mother seated at one end of the table eating something from a plate, the cook standing at the opposite end, chopping vegetables which she tossed into an iron pot.

'Hello, my little duck,' Madam Gwyn said, looking up from her meal. She leaned to one side, straining to see around her daughter, and smiled, exposing several long dark threads stuck between her yellow teeth. 'Hello, Bevil,' she said, waving.

Nell swung around, startled to see Mr Cane standing behind her; she thought she'd left him in the front hallway. Then she turned back to her mother. 'This peaceful scene is unexpected.'

'We have reached an agreement,' her mother announced. 'I will not prevent her presence in the kitchen and she will not prevent me preparing my own victuals whenever I so desire.'

Nell glanced at the cook. The cook nodded, but said nothing, a sly expression on her face. Nell gazed down at the contents of her mother's dish: a pile of shiny black crumbs which she was eating with her fingers. 'Did you prepare that yourself?' she asked her mother.

'I did,' her mother said proudly.

'What is it?' Nell asked.

The cook made a little snorting sound, as if she was trying not to laugh.

Her mother shrugged. 'Some kind of dried vegetable; I don't know what it's called. I found it in a wooden box in the larder. It had a pleasing fragrance, so I boiled it in water.' She pushed the dish forward. 'Try some. The texture is odd, but the flavour is good.'

Nell looked at the cook; her cheeks had gone bright red. She lifted some damp black shreds from the plate and held them to her nose. 'God's death, mother! You've been eating tea!'

'So that's what you call it,' Madam Gwyn said, raising another handful to her mouth.

'Mother – '

'Mistress,' the maid interrupted, hurrying into the kitchen. 'A visitor awaits you in the withdrawing room.'

'Who?'

'It's the Duke of Monmouth, mistress.'

She raised both eyebrows; this was a surprise. 'Bevil,' she said, turning to leave, 'please explain tea to my mother. And *you*,' she said, looking back at the cook, 'I will speak to you later.'

Chapter Nine

Thomas Alcock stood among the rabble on the balcony of the Banqueting House, looking down at the king at his table. Alcock's wig today was brown, his clothing made of wool.

The king, oblivious to the gaping onlookers gathered above him and the two dozen violinists in Indian-style gowns and turbans playing behind him, tore into his food as if he hadn't eaten for a week. But that, Alcock knew, was the way His Majesty approached every meal. The courtiers seated around him were a little more restrained, behaving as if it had only been three or four days since they last encountered food.

The king's younger brother, James, Duke of York, was at the table, as was His Majesty's latest *amour*, the Duchess of Mazarin, wearing a gown of pure white satin, a string of shimmering pearls woven through her waist-length raven hair.

A man standing close to Alcock said he had never seen a more beautiful woman – who was she? One ventured a guess she was the Duchess of Portsmouth. Another snorted in disgust. That was not Madam Carwell, he informed them, mispronouncing the Frenchwoman's name, that was *another* Popish whore, even worse than most because her uncle was a cardinal. 'Did we bring back the monarchy for this?' he went on, 'That we may be ruled by a vicious court, crawling with Papists?'

'Mind your tongue,' someone warned him, adding in a whisper, 'You never know who may be listening.'

Nell leaned back on a thickly padded couch, trying not to yawn as the young Duke of Monmouth paced up and down in front of her, launching into another of his tirades against the Catholics in his father's court. 'Sometimes I think you and I are the only Protestants left at Whitehall,' he said, shaking his head.

'You exaggerate, Jamie.' He was still pacing relentlessly up and down, back and forth across the room. It was making her dizzy to watch him. 'And you are wearing a hole in my carpet. Will you please sit down?'

'I apologize, Mrs Gwyn,' he said, sitting down across from her. 'It is only that I see what is happening around me, and I fear for the future of this country if the king continues to deny me my rightful place.'

'He's denied you nothing, Jamie,' Nell said. 'He acknowledges you as his son, he has given you offices and a title – '

'But he refuses to admit I am his legitimate heir!'

Nell sighed, but remained silent. She didn't want to get into the old argument again. Monmouth always insisted that Charles had married his mother; the king vehemently denied it. Monmouth said he had proof, but was never able to produce it, claiming it had been stolen.

'I fail to understand how His Majesty can persist in his foolish determination to block my rightful claim to the throne in favour of my uncle,' he went on, ignoring the look of warning on Nell's face.

'You must not refer to His Majesty as foolish,' she scolded him. 'There are those who might interpret such a remark as treason.'

'Please, Nelly, I know there is no one more loyal to my father than you.' He leaned forward, looking earnest. 'A loyalty I assure you I share with all my heart; you and I are natural allies. But I must speak freely with you, to make you understand the danger.'

Nell didn't like the turn this conversation was taking; she'd thought this was a social call. 'Danger? What danger?'

'My uncle is a Papist, my uncle's wife the bastard daughter

of the Pope. If my father continues to insist on his brother's succession, it will mean civil war.'

'Civil war?' Nell shook her head. 'No, Jamie, I can't believe that. Dismal Jimmy of York is simply too dull a character to provoke such a confrontation. The only fear you might have of him is that he'll bore you to death.'

Monmouth raised his hands in surrender. 'Nelly, I apologize. It was not my wish to start an argument.'

'Ha!' Nell said, refilling his glass of brandy. 'You mean it was not your wish to lose one.'

The duke raised his glass, taking several careful sips. 'Let us speak of something else,' he said quietly. 'How are the children?'

Nell smiled. 'They're having a nap. You may go see them if you wish, but you must be quiet.'

He shook his head. 'I have no wish to disturb them.' He stood up and walked over to the fireplace, checking his reflection in a silver-framed mirror above the mantel. 'It was a pleasant surprise to see you yesterday, in the fields at Lincoln's Inn. Do you go there often?'

'I used to have a house near there,' she reminded him, 'soon after I left the stage.'

'Oh yes,' he murmured thoughtfully, still examining his reflection. 'So you did. Is that why you were there yesterday? To visit your old haunts?'

'Not really.' She glanced from the duke to a jewel-encrusted clock nearby on the mantel, gasping when she saw the time. She leapt to her feet, hurriedly explaining that she had to get dressed for a funeral.

'A funeral?' The duke put down his drink and swung around from the mirror, raising a leather-gloved hand to his forehead. 'I'm so sorry, Nell,' he said, crossing the room to clasp her hands in his. 'Truly, I had no idea. Pray tell me, who has died? I hope it was no one close.'

'Not close to me. But I have promised to attend, as a favour to a friend of mine: a Mrs Behn.'

His grip on her hands faltered slightly. 'Mrs Behn?'

'I see you know her.'

'Only by reputation,' he said, letting go of her. He crossed back to the fireplace, retrieving his glass of brandy from the mantel. 'She's that widow who writes immodest plays, isn't she?'

Nell could hardly keep from laughing; Jamie was so easily offended. 'That's right.'

'And who has Mrs Behn lost?'

'Two friends from her time in Surinam: a man named Matthew Cavell, and his brother, Elias.'

The duke's glass slipped from his hand on to the floor, spilling brandy over Nell's Persian carpet.

'Her gown was simple and unadorned, her only jewels a few pearls woven through her hair, yet no man in the gallery could take his eyes away from her,' Thomas Alcock enthused. 'I heard one say he had never seen such a beautiful woman, and I had to agree with him.'

A liveried servant removed his master's periwig, revealing a shaven dome caked with powder. His master pulled off his gloves, tossed them on to a table and sat on the bed, scratching his scalp. 'Thomas,' his master chided him, 'you were looking down at her from the gallery. Anyone may appear beautiful when viewed from such a distance. Even you.' He stopped to examine the powder collecting beneath his fingernails. 'I shall not deny the lady Mazarin is well-favoured, but pray tell me something of interest.'

'There was much grumbling of Popery among the common rabble – '

His master waved a dismissive hand. 'Tell me something new.'

97

'I heard some murmurings about the Duchess of Portsmouth. They say she has taken to her bed – '

'Again?' his master interrupted. 'I said I wanted something new!'

' – and is refusing all sustenance, declaring she would starve herself to death for love.'

'That's better.' His master stood in order for the servant to remove his cravat and coat, then sat back down to allow the removal of his shoes and stockings. 'And what was His Majesty's reaction to this news?' he asked, cracking his toes.

'That Mademoiselle de Kéroualle had never known a day's hunger in her life, and he hoped the experience might do her some good.'

His master chuckled evilly. 'Excellent!'

The other servant continued to fuss around the room, eventually crossing to a cupboard, which he opened with a key.

'And what about my Lord Buckingham?' Alcock's master licked his lips in anticipation. 'Any more news of his conquests?'

Alcock shook his head, laughing. 'No, my lord, I did not see him today.'

'Pity.'

The other servant crossed back to the bed and laid out a selection of ragged clothing, suitable only for a beggar.

Alcock looked at his master questioningly.

His master gave him an enigmatic smile. 'A social engagement,' he said.

Chapter Ten

Aphra had a shouting match with the coffin-maker when he insisted on immediate payment, another with the driver when he wanted to stop off at a tavern in Southwark – 'Stops is extra,' she reminded him – and then she had one with Mrs Barrow, the matron of Gospel House who had earlier turned Elias's body, and then his coffin, away. The woman vehemently denied ever receiving Aphra's letter, but Aphra couldn't shake the suspicion she was lying.

For some reason she couldn't fathom, this large, grey-haired woman had taken an instant dislike to her. From the moment she'd charged into the room where Matthew's body had been discovered on Monday, she'd treated Aphra as if she was some kind of particularly repellent insect. And when Aphra had offered to organize and pay for the murdered man's funeral – with music and refreshments for everyone – Mrs Barrow didn't show the least sign of gratitude, storming out of the room while Aphra discussed the arrangements with several inmates of the house.

Two of those same inmates – elderly men with limbs like twigs – were now struggling to unload Elias's coffin from the back of the cart. The driver stood by with his arms crossed, humming to himself. 'They will do themselves an injury! Help them,' Aphra hissed.

The driver stopped humming and raised an eyebrow.

'You've had nearly four shillings from me already!'

The driver resumed his humming.

She gave the driver what she hoped was a look of utter

contempt, told the two men to wait, then went inside to fetch some help. She came back with two more elderly men in gowns. The four old sailors finally managed — with a lot of puffing and wheezing — to carry the coffin into the house.

The driver remained where he was, still humming the same annoying little tune.

'You've been paid,' Aphra reminded him, struggling to keep the edge of exasperation from her voice.

'Yes, missus, I know that. Thank you, missus.'

'Then what are you waiting for?'

'I was just wondering how far it was to the church.'

'Why?' she asked him sarcastically. 'Do you wish to go and pray?'

He chuckled softly to himself. 'No, missus. It's just ... well, I've seen your bearers now, haven't I? And I was thinking if you expect such as them to carry the coffins, by the time you get to church you'll need to bury them as well.'

Aphra realized to her horror that he was right. She looked up at the wording on the sign above the door: '*Gospel House Hospital And Almshouse For Sick And Decayed Seamen*'. Except for the matron, the cook, and four or five children employed as servants, there was no one in that house who wasn't old and ill. Most of them couldn't even walk the half a mile to the church, let alone carry two coffins that distance. The only other people she expected this evening were Nell and Elizabeth. She couldn't imagine the two of them carrying a coffin, either.

She sighed and closed her eyes, feeling utterly defeated. 'How much to use your cart?'

Her next stop was the church. At least they didn't deny receiving her letter, but the sexton told her there was no more room beneath the centre aisle; one of the bodies would have to go outside. 'It's only so wide, you see,' he said, showing her the space he had marked out. 'And I'm having to jostle some of the others about as it is.'

'Is there no other space left inside?' Aphra asked, gazing around the small church. 'Beneath a pew, perhaps?'

He shook his head. 'Under the pews is more full than the aisle.'

Aphra sighed, defeated once again, and told the sexton to put the gold-handled coffin beneath the aisle; the plainer coffin could go into the ground outside.

The sexton nodded. 'Of course you'll have to pay for the extra digging.'

Aphra nearly forgot she was inside a church; she stopped herself from swearing just in time. 'How much?' she asked him, reaching up to rub her temples.

'Oh, half a crown at least,' he said casually. 'There's the cost of the land, and the workmen to be paid . . .'

Aphra stiffened, narrowing her eyes. She had a good idea what was coming next.

'Though I wonder . . .' the man said thoughtfully, pacing carefully around the spot he'd marked for Matthew's grave. He followed this with a great show of measuring it, counting his steps, stretching out his arms, holding up a thumb and squinting. 'I just *might* be able to squeeze them both in after all, though it would take quite a bit of rearranging things below, if you see what I mean – '

Aphra raised a hand to silence him. 'Just tell me how much.'

She arrived back at Gospel House to find Virtue Hawkins keeping watch over the bodies in a tiny storeroom next to Mrs Barrow's office. Aphra paused in the storeroom doorway, taking in the scene. The floor had been swept and spread with green rushes, and the room cleared of everything except a pair of long tables draped with dark cloth, on which the coffins rested side by side, surrounded by burning candles. Matthew's coffin was open. Someone had washed his face and hands and dressed him in a fresh gown. Elias's coffin remained closed.

Virtue stood beside the open coffin, dressed in the high-collared dark clothing that had been fashionable under Cromwell, her grey hair pulled back into a bun beneath a white linen cap. The old woman didn't see Aphra; her eyes were closed. Aphra started to say something, but stopped when she saw the woman's lips moving. It seemed that Virtue was praying.

Aphra hesitated, uncertain whether she should make her presence known or leave. She had just decided to leave when Virtue opened her eyes. 'It's a wonderful kind thing you be doing here,' the old woman said, 'to remember your friend in such a way.'

There was no doubt in Aphra's mind as to who had taken the time and care to ensure Matthew's corpse was presentable enough to be displayed in an open coffin. 'It seems to me that you have done every bit as much. Or more. For which I am truly grateful.'

Virtue shook her head. 'I never seen my husband's body. He went off to fight for Parliament and died at sea, leaving me a widow these thirty-three years, with no children, and nothing to remember him by.' She gestured towards the body in the coffin. 'Helping your friend get ready today – that was my way of saying goodbye to my husband, the way I would have done those many years ago if I'd only had the chance. What I did I did only for myself, so there be no need for gratitude. Not from your kind self, nor any other.'

'I still thank you.' Aphra moved away from the doorway, to stand beside the table where the open coffin lay. 'Did you know Matthew well?' she asked, gazing down at the one-legged corpse.

'I don't talk much to the men. It wouldn't be seemly, me being a widow and all. And he wasn't here but a couple of weeks, anyway.'

Aphra looked up from the coffin, telling herself she couldn't have heard right. 'Weeks?' she repeated. 'Did you say he'd only been here a couple of weeks?'

The old woman nodded.

Aphra tapped her fingers on the table, perplexed. The way Elias had spoken of his brother, she'd assumed he'd been an inmate of the almshouse ever since he'd lost his leg on board the *Revenge*.

She looked down at the body again. He seemed so frail and old beyond his years, she found it difficult to imagine how he could have managed to survive before he came to Gospel House. Of course, she reminded herself, he may have become ill only recently. But he was terribly ill when he was murdered; that much was obvious. Matthew had not been more than forty-six or forty-seven, yet the man lying dead in front of her might easily have been nearer to seventy. How could a man his age come to be in such a deteriorated condition? If he hadn't been murdered, she doubted he would have lived much longer anyway. She wondered what kind of person would murder someone already so close to death.

She thought back to Monday night, and what was said: several inmates had heard Matthew arguing with a man named Josiah Mullen, who had since disappeared. 'Has Mr Mullen been arrested yet?' she asked Virtue.

'No, they've not been able to find him.'

'I thought your parish constable said he would not get far.'

'And so we all believed,' Virtue told her. 'But it seems Mr Mullen got far enough after all, though the parish has offered a reward for his capture.'

It had never occurred to Aphra that the murder of both brothers within such a short period of time was anything more than a horrible coincidence – largely because everyone had been so confident that Matthew's killer would be arrested without delay. But what if the same person had killed both men? 'You're quite certain Josiah Mullen killed Mr Cavell?'

'It could have been no one else.'

Aphra's mind reeled in horror at the idea that she may have helped Matthew's killer track down Elias. She had spoken to so many people in Lincoln's Inn Fields. One of them may well have been Josiah Mullen. 'What does Mr Mullen look like?'

Virtue shrugged. 'An elderly man, like most of them here. The constable wrote up a poster with his description; would you like to see it?'

'Very much.'

Virtue left the room, telling Aphra she would be back in a minute.

It was the first time Aphra had been alone with either corpse. She stared down at Matthew's body, his wounds hidden from view beneath a long blue gown, and considered the possibility that the same man had committed both murders. She crossed over to the door and closed it before turning her attention to Elias, bracing herself for what she was about to see, and smell.

She lifted the coffin lid, holding her breath. Poor Elias. Though the coffin interior had been sprinkled with hyssop, wormwood and rue to signify repentance, and a plate of salt placed upon his chest to delay corruption, there had been no time to do anything else for him. He still wore the same ragged clothing, stiff with dried blood.

The searcher had cleaned some of the blood away from his throat, revealing several deep, gaping wounds. No wonder there had been so much blood; the man's head was nearly severed. There were cuts all over his face and hands, and his coat had been slashed to ribbons in the struggle. It must have been a ferocious attack.

Matthew had struggled, too; the cuts on his hands testified to that. But – mercifully, she supposed – his struggle would not have lasted as long, or been so intense. He was weaker and, unlike his brother, unable to run. He would have known he had no chance of escape.

Elias, on the other hand, probably thought he could elude his killer. Confronted inside the house, he ran out the back way, only to find himself trapped in a tiny garden surrounded by high stone walls.

But who did he meet inside her house? Could it have been Josiah Mullen? She was willing to concede that two men, regardless of age or infirmity, might get into a violent argument, resulting in the death of one of them. But she found it difficult to believe that someone old and ill enough to be a resident of Gospel House would then cross London to commit another murder. Or that Elias would not be able to escape any inmate of this institution, no matter if they were armed. If Josiah Mullen was at all typical of the men she'd seen picking oakum, the instant he came out into the garden, Elias could have simply run past him, back through the house and out the front.

Unless Mr Mullen was not alone.

She shook her head so hard it rattled, curling her hands into fists. This speculation was pointless. The men were dead, and that was that.

She was about to replace the lid when she noticed something metallic protruding from one of Elias's shredded coat pockets. She doubted it was anything of value – the men who'd taken the body away would have helped themselves to anything of worth before delivering him to the searcher – but it might be something that could help her understand what had happened, and why.

She started to reach for the object, then froze, horrified at what she had been about to do. She started to replace the lid, then reminded herself that Elias had entered her house while she was away, without her knowledge or consent. Surely that entitled her to enter his pocket.

She bent across the body, holding her breath. Elias was due to be buried in less than two hours; if she didn't look now, there would never be another chance. She gingerly removed a thin wedge of metal, about six or seven inches long. It looked like a dull knife blade, ground down to make it slimmer.

She'd seen something similar when she was in prison. If this was what she thought it was, it would answer at least one question that had been worrying her. She decided to keep the metal wedge, in order to test her theory later. She took the drawstring purse from her skirt pocket and slid the piece of metal inside it. It only fitted because the day's unexpected expenses had left her purse nearly empty.

There was something else, visible through the ripped cloth of his coat. Bracing herself, she dug her hand all the way into the pocket and removed a handful of shredded paper as slashed and torn as the pocket itself. She held one fragment up to a candle, and was able to make out two smeared letters among the bloodstains: SH. The other fragments appeared to have something written on them as well; she held another to the light and saw the number four.

Virtue's voice came from behind her. 'What be you doing, Mistress Behn?'

Aphra jumped; she'd been so engrossed, she hadn't heard the door open. She stuffed the shreds of paper down her bodice before she turned to face the old woman, her hands in front of her chest in a prayer position. 'May God rest their souls,' she said piously.

'May God rest their souls,' Virtue repeated, briefly raising her own hands into a kind of loose prayer position, necessarily modified by the scroll she clutched in one hand. 'But I think it best you close that lid. The poor man is too badly injured; it would not be seemly to view him in such a state.'

'Forgive me. I only wanted one last look.'

'I know,' Virtue said, walking towards her, 'but we must do what is seemly.' She reached into her pocket for a handkerchief. 'I'm sorry to say this, but your friend has a dreadful strong smell.'

Aphra replaced the lid on Elias's coffin. 'Is that the constable's description of Josiah Mullen?' she asked, eyeing the scroll Virtue was holding.

Virtue nodded and handed it to her. 'I lack reading, so I cannot say how accurate it be.'

'Then I will read it to you,' Aphra said, unrolling the

parchment sheet. '"Thirty shillings reward. Wanted for murder. Josiah Mullen, aged about sixty-two years, five feet seven inches high, long visaged and sallow complexioned with a malicious expression, few teeth, grey hair to the shoulders, a pronounced limp, and eyes of a menacing brown, dark and squinting – "'

'Is that what it says on that poster?' Virtue interrupted.

Aphra continued reading, ignoring the interruption. '"He was last seen wearing the blue gown typical to Gospel House, Deptford, at which he had been resident this past fortnight – "' This time she interrupted herself, staring at the scroll in disbelief. 'This past fortnight? Josiah Mullen had only been here a fortnight?'

'Mr Mullen came to live here the same day as Mr Cavell.'

Aphra raised her eyebrows. She'd thought beds in places such as Gospel House only became available when the bed's previous occupant died. 'Two new residents in a single day? Have there been other deaths recently?'

Virtue shook her head. 'No. Not since early this year, when a bad cough carried one away. Small and crowded as these quarters be, we are well cared for here, with a roof above our heads and food to eat. Then, only the other week, our Mrs Barrow – bless her – somehow managed by God's mercy to find room for yet two more.'

'But how were these two chosen from the many sick and homeless? Was there any indication they might have known each other before?'

'I wouldn't know that, Mistress Behn. I don't like to speak to the men – '

'I know,' Aphra said drily, 'it wouldn't be seemly.'

'That poster,' Virtue said, straining forward to look at the writing. 'Be you quite sure you've read the words correctly?'

It took some effort on Aphra's part to keep the exasperation out of her voice. 'Yes, I am quite sure.' She returned her attention to the scroll. 'There's only a little more. "... He may have since attired himself in the brown frock and white apron in which he was first admitted to the house, and which have since disappeared. Whoever shall apprehend and lodge him in any of His Majesty's gaols shall receive the above reward by applying to the parish treasurer, St Mary's Church, Deptford."'

'Be you sure that's what it says?' Virtue asked again. 'And no mistake?'

Aphra couldn't stop herself rolling her eyes. 'I have been reading for many years now, Mrs Hawkins, and I think I have the knack of it. I promise you, there's no mistake.'

'But it's wrong. Nearly all of it's wrong. Mr Mullen didn't squint, and though I know they say the devil himself may take on a pleasing aspect, his expression never showed any malice I could see.'

'Criminals always squint and have evil expressions,' Aphra explained. 'I've never seen a reward poster where these two elements were omitted.'

'But he never limped and he never wore a frock and apron when he arrived. I saw him walk through the room where we pick oakum, and I tell you he was wearing a long green coat with dark blue breeches.'

This time it was Aphra who asked Virtue if she was sure.

Virtue's eyes flashed with anger. 'I may be old, but I promise you I do not be blind!'

'I meant no offence,' Aphra said soothingly. She walked over to the door, checked that no one was about, then closed it again, crossing back to the old woman. 'It might be best if we are not overheard,' she explained, speaking as quietly as she could and still have the old woman be able to hear her. 'Pray, tell me, is there anything else?'

To Aphra's surprise, Virtue instantly seemed to grasp the seriousness of the situation. She leaned forward, keeping her voice low. 'I only saw Mr Mullen up close on one occasion, but I saw the colour of his eyes quite clearly and they were never brown, but blue.'

Aphra nearly asked Virtue if she was sure, but managed to stop herself in time. 'Is that everything?'

Virtue shook her head. 'There's one way you may recognize Josiah Mullen for certain.' She held up one hand, pointing to the top knuckle of the little finger. 'On Mr Mullen's left hand, the little finger ends just here, the tip sliced clean away.'

Aphra rubbed her temples, thinking. Why would the constable write such an inaccurate description? It almost seemed he didn't wish Josiah Mullen to be apprehended – perhaps they were friends. 'Were Mr Mullen and the parish constable acquainted?'

The old woman shrugged. 'Not that I'm aware of.'

'So how did he compile his description? I assume he questioned the inmates?'

'I don't know who he spoke to,' Virtue said. 'I only know he never questioned me.'

He'd never questioned Aphra, either. Not that she could have helped with a description of Josiah Mullen, but she would have thought he'd want to know who she was and why she was there. Instead, she only saw the briefest glimpse of him on Monday evening. The moment he'd come upstairs, he'd been led away by Mrs Barrow.

Aphra's train of thought was interrupted when the storeroom door flew open, crashing against the wall.

Mrs Barrow stood towering in the doorway, glaring at Aphra with undisguised contempt. 'There's a man in the kitchen with three barrels of oysters,' she bellowed, crossing a pair of massive arms in front of her formidable bosom. 'I suppose that's something to do with you?'

'That's right,' Aphra said, meeting the larger woman's gaze with a look of cool disinterest, despite the fact her legs were trembling. Why did the woman hate her so? 'They're for tonight,' she added, as if it wasn't obvious.

'Oysters!' Mrs Barrow snorted, her contemptuous gaze falling on Matthew's gold-handled coffin. 'Beer and boiled mutton was good enough for him when he was alive.' She took a large step into the room, looming threateningly over Aphra. 'You dare to call the men away from their work so they can carry the stinking corpse of some stranger into the house – some stranger who does not belong here and if it were not for my deep sense of Christian love and charity I would have had thrown into the Thames – and now you would take over my kitchen! Let me remind you, Mrs Behn, you only remain beneath this roof on my sufferance. I am in charge of this institution, and I advise you not to forget it.'

Chapter Eleven

Elizabeth Decker positioned herself in front of the looking glass in her room, practising the transition from love to grief. According to the pamphlet she'd just bought, love was best expressed by a dreamlike expression, combined with a 'gay, soft and charming voice'.

'Judge then what my heart feels, good sir,' she told the mirror, looking dreamlike. 'Yet ...' She raised one hand to her forehead as she moved into grief, abruptly changing her voice to the 'sad, dull and languishing tone' recommended by the pamphlet. 'My father would quench this burning flame ...' She lowered her hand from the forehead to the chest, pointing at her heart. 'Heaping the cold ash of despair upon the passionate fire that burns within my breast.'

She paused to study her grief-stricken attitude in the mirror, feeling especially pleased with the finger pointing to her heart. No one had told her to do that; it was her own innovation.

She was practising hate when the landlady came upstairs to tell her there was a coach waiting outside, adding the pointed observation that it was definitely not the Earl of Rochester's coach.

The presumption of the woman! 'Can you not see I am in mourning?' Elizabeth said, haughtily brushing past her. It suddenly occurred to her that her landlady was a notorious gossip who might start spreading false tales that she was unfaithful — tales that might find their way back to her beloved Lord Rochester. 'If you will insist on knowing my business, I shall be attending a funeral this evening, with Mistress Nell Gwyn.'

The landlady followed Elizabeth downstairs, whistling in appreciation. 'Zooks! To think I knew her when she was an orange-seller. Who would have guessed she'd rise so high, to have such a magnificent coach!'

Elizabeth frowned, puzzled at her landlady's remark. Mrs Gwyn's coach was small and pink; she would hardly describe it as magnificent.

When she reached the front door she was confronted with the sight of a huge red coach trimmed with gold and sparkling rubies. Eight black horses stood waiting at the front, wearing red plumed head-dresses, their bridles studded with jewels.

She was beginning to think there must be some mistake – or perhaps this was another of Lord Rochester's pranks – when Mistress Gwyn stuck her head out of the window. 'Odd's fish,' she said, laughing, 'are we not a fine company to bury a beggar?'

The coach door swung open and a man leapt out. 'Oh, Mistress Decker,' he said, rushing forward to kiss her hand at least a dozen times. 'I have dreamed of this moment! I have long been an admirer – how I wish I might dare say "an imitator" – of your many virtues.'

Elizabeth stopped in her tracks, staring at the man paying such fervent attention to her hand. 'Have we been introduced?'

Nell leaned back in her seat, pondering the strangeness of her situation. She was in a coach full of people, all of them on the way to the funeral of two men none of them had ever met.

To one side of her Bevil Cane was enthusiastically outlining his play to Elizabeth Decker, while to the other the Duke of Monmouth appeared to be deep in conversation with her mother. She shook her head in disbelief – what interest could those two possibly have in common? She leaned slightly to one side and heard her mother tell the duke: 'My Nelly's an Aquarian, she had her horoscope cast by none other than Mr Ashmole himself. Now me, I'm the sign of the virgin.'

Of course, Nell thought. Jamie of Monmouth was obsessed with the stars. She wondered if the stars had predicted he would make an unexpected journey. Why else would he insist on accompanying her to Deptford?

She knew her own reason for going to Deptford: out of friendship for Aphra. She knew why Bevil Cane was there beside her: because of his unrequited passion for Elizabeth Decker.

But why was Elizabeth Decker there? Maybe she felt guilty because Rochester had refused to come. Or maybe she was trying to ingratiate herself with Aphra so she wouldn't drop her from the cast.

Nell suspected it was the latter.

And her mother? Her mother seemed to think she was protecting her. 'These men were murdered, little duck,' her mother had reminded her, shreds of tea still hanging from her teeth. 'You march in their funeral procession, for all you know, the person marching next to you could be the killer of one or both. This business is bad and dangerous, and I'll not let you go without me.'

'It's not dangerous, it's a funeral. There will be plenty of people around, and Bevil will be with me,' she'd protested.

'Bevil is a sweet boy,' her mother had said, 'who knows nothing of the evil in this world. But I've lived with it, my girl.' She tapped her purple-veined nose. 'I can smell it.'

The motives of the others accounted for, Nell returned her attention to the Duke of Monmouth. He wanted something; of that much she was certain.

He had not only provided the coach, but had taken them all to dinner at a tavern near London Bridge. When she told him that none of this was necessary, he protested it was merely his way of honouring their long friendship, showing but a tiny fraction of his gratitude for the many times she had interceded with the king on his behalf.

It was true James Scott had a knack for annoying his father, and it was also true that Nell had risen to his defence on several occasions, alternately pleading and cajoling, reminding His Majesty of the reckless impulsiveness of youth. Which usually worked – despite the fact the king's first-born son was three years older than herself.

She had only been absent from court for a day and a half, but even in so short a time, it was far from impossible that Monmouth had managed to anger his father once again. That would certainly explain his behaviour: his unexpected visit, his railing against the court, this obvious attempt to beguile her with generosity. He was building up to the moment when he would beg her to use her influence on the king.

Oh, Jamie, she thought, what have you done this time?

Chapter Twelve

The inmates of Gospel House and the adjoining widows' residence had gathered in the room where they usually picked oakum. The stronger of them had already cleared the floor of shredded rope and pushed the benches back against the walls. Most were sitting down, conserving their strength for later, while the twelve-year-old maid circled the room, serving everyone present with beer and biscuits. Aphra counted fourteen men – many of them on crutches, at least three of them missing a limb – and nine women. She knew there was another woman in the storeroom, taking her turn keeping watch over the bodies. And Nell and Elizabeth would be arriving soon. Counting herself, that would make a total of twenty-seven mourners. Twenty-eight if Mrs Barrow ever decided to emerge from her office, where she had been skulking since their last confrontation.

She called the maid over and told her not to be so generous with the biscuits.

Everyone had followed Virtue's example, dressing in their best clothes for the occasion. Their best clothes being, in most cases, at least twenty years out of fashion. God save us, Aphra thought, realizing the majority of the men present must have served in the Parliamentary fleet during the Civil War, and that most of the women – like Virtue Hawkins – had been married to Parliamentarians. She told herself it was just as well Rochester had decided not to come. He would never have been comfortable in such a gathering of old Roundheads. She didn't feel all that comfortable herself.

A small boy tugged at her sleeve. 'There's a man at the door asking to see you.'

That would be the cart driver; she'd told him to be back by half past six. 'Tell him to wait outside.'

The boy came back a moment later. 'He said to give you this.'

She looked down at the card in the little boy's hand; it was one of her printed invitations. Other than the occupants of Gospel House, the only man she had invited was Rochester; he must have decided to come after all. 'Well, show him in,' she told the boy. Despite her earlier misgivings about how he would blend in with such a company, she was relieved to learn of his presence, especially since they had not parted on the best of terms that afternoon. This must be his way of making amends.

She took up a position near the entrance to the room, holding out a glass of burnt claret, even though the claret wasn't meant to be consumed until the reception after the service. That would be *her* way of making amends.

The boy reappeared at the end of the corridor, leading a broad-hatted figure, limping with the aid of a crutch. As the limping figure drew closer, Aphra saw he was dressed in a beggar's rags.

'May I help you?' she asked, hiding the glass of claret behind her back.

'Why, Mrs Behn,' the man said heartily. 'Surely you would not forget me so soon, after the long and cordial conversation we had only yesterday, and the most generous charity you offered my humble unworthy self!' The man's hat was pulled low across his forehead, and he wore a patch over his right eye. His hair and beard were red, streaked with white. He spoke with an accent she couldn't quite place; she thought it might be Irish. 'I want you to know,' he went on, 'after you and the other beautiful lady left in that pretty pink coach, I did my best for you. Indeed I did. But though I looked for him high and low, I was never able to pass your card on to Mr Elias Cavell, even though, as I believe I told you yesterday, he and I are among the closest of friends. And having failed you thus, I thought it my solemn duty to come here tonight, if only to return your lovely card – which, I hope you don't mind me saying, must have cost you a fair amount. Lovely workmanship. And while I'm here, I thought it only proper I should pay my respects to the poor deceased brother of my dear friend, Elias.'

Aphra had spoken to so many homeless beggars in Lincoln's Inn Fields that their faces and voices had faded into a blur. But there was something very familiar about this man; she had definitely seen him before, even if she couldn't remember the conversation of which he spoke. And she had handed out a few cards to those who said they knew Elias, but only as proof of her good intentions. She had never expected any of them to turn up for the funeral.

'I hope you will forgive me,' she said, 'but I do not recall your name.'

'O'Bannion,' the man told her. 'Fergus O'Bannion. Did you ever manage to contact Elias then? To tell him about his brother?'

Aphra shook her head sadly. 'Not really.'

'I'm sorry to hear that, Mrs Behn. I thought perhaps I might meet Elias here.'

'There is something that I must tell you,' Aphra said. 'About Elias – '

O'Bannion lowered his voice, winking his one good eye. 'And I must tell *you*, I don't mind admitting the thought has crossed my mind that in places such as this, one man's death equals one empty bed.'

'But this is a house for seamen,' Aphra said.

'Oh, I was a seaman, all right,' O'Bannion said. 'That's how I lost my eye: fighting the Dutch back in 'sixty-seven.'

'You'll have to speak to the matron,' Aphra told him. 'I have nothing to do with the running of this house.' O'Bannion seemed about to speak again, but this time Aphra managed to break in before him. 'Please, Mr O'Bannion, there is something I really must tell you, if you will only allow me to get the words out. Elias is to be buried tonight as well.'

O'Bannion's mouth dropped open. 'I'm sorry?'

'Elias is dead, Mr O'Bannion.'

The man dropped his crutch and sank on to one of the benches, shaking his head in disbelief. 'Oh, what news,' he said. 'What shocking, awful news!' He raised the brim of his hat slightly, looking up at Aphra with a pitiful expression on his face. 'Please, Mrs Behn, I hope it would not be too forward of me if I were to beg you for something to drink?'

She sighed and handed him the glass of claret.

There was a flurry of excitement a moment later, with the arrival of Nell and her companions. Especially when the residents of the almshouse learned they had been honoured by the presence of the Duke of Monmouth. Only Mr O'Bannion seemed unmoved, focusing his attention on the glass of claret in his hand.

Aphra pulled Nell to one side at the first opportunity. 'What is the Duke of Monmouth doing here?'

Nell shrugged. 'He wanted to come.'

'To the burial of two paupers? It doesn't make sense!'

Nell raised a finger to her lips. 'He's behind you.'

Aphra turned and saw the young duke approaching. 'Mrs Behn,' he said, 'I wish to offer my sincerest condolences on your tragic loss.'

Aphra curtsied and muttered her thanks.

'Pray,' the duke said, glancing about the room, 'where are these unfortunate deceased? I should like to pay them my respects.'

Aphra led him down the corridor to the storeroom. The old woman standing watch over the coffins took their arrival as her chance to get a drink and a biscuit, and hurried away from the room.

'What were your friends' names again?' the duke enquired politely.

'Matthew and Elias Cavell.'

The duke nodded towards the open coffin. 'And which is this poor man? Matthew? Or Elias?'

'That is Matthew,' Aphra told him.

'This is Matthew Cavell?' the duke asked, a strange, strained expression on his face. 'Did you know him well?'

'Once. A long time ago.'

The duke raised one eyebrow. 'But not lately?'

'No, your grace,' Aphra said carefully. She hadn't spoken to the duke on either of her visits to Lincoln's Inn Fields, but he had been there each time. And now here he was in Deptford, for no reason she could imagine. What possible interest could the son of a king have in the death of a beggar? 'Not lately.'

'Still, I suppose the loss is no less painful for that,' the duke said sympathetically.

That last statement took Aphra completely by surprise. The Duke of Monmouth understood. For the first time since this whole dreadful business had begun, someone actually understood how she felt.

Rochester certainly didn't. Even Nell, kind and helpful as she'd been, made no secret of the fact she didn't really understand why Aphra felt compelled to do so much for someone she hadn't seen for fourteen years. But this young man, to whom she'd never spoken until this night, understood that sometimes it took more than the passage of time to ease the pain of losing someone you once loved. She *had* loved Matthew all those years ago, and though nothing ever came of it, she often wondered what might have happened if she'd been a little bolder in the expression of her feelings.

Aphra smiled at the duke, sorry to have misjudged him. Of course he understood the pain of loss; they said that when he was eleven years old the king's agents had accosted his mother

119

on the streets of Brussels and dragged the young boy away, leaving her screaming and crying in the middle of the road. She died a few months later.

'You are right,' she said, wiping away a tear. 'The loss is no less painful.'

The duke leaned towards her, his expression earnest. 'Mrs Behn, there is something I would like to do.'

'Yes, your grace?'

'I would like to pray for these poor men's souls.'

The duke had managed to surprise her once again; she had no idea he was so devout. 'That is most charitable of you,' she said, bowing her head.

'If you have no objection, I would prefer to pray alone.'

'Oh.' Aphra turned to leave.

'You may wait for me in the other room. I will keep watch on the bodies,' the duke said, closing the door behind her.

Aphra started down the corridor, hurt and confused by her sudden dismissal; she'd thought they had been getting on so well. She'd only gone a few steps before coming to an abrupt halt. Could it really be possible that the Duke of Monmouth had come all the way to Deptford to pray alone in a room with two corpses? She didn't think so.

She tiptoed back to the storeroom door and placed an ear against it, listening. She told herself she could not be hearing what she heard: the creaking sound of a coffin being opened. She opened the door a crack and peered inside the room, holding her breath. She told herself she could not be seeing what she saw. The eldest son of the King of England appeared to be going through a dead beggar's pockets.

She watched him for nearly a minute, amazed.

'Mrs Behn?' a voice said behind her.

She slammed the door and swung around, her heart pounding, then saw to her relief that it was only Bevil Cane. 'Mr Cane,' she scolded him, gasping for breath, 'you should never come upon a lady so stealthily; you gave me quite a start.'

120

From the other side of the door came the sound of frantic movement, followed by the young duke's voice, 'Oh Lord, have mercy upon their souls...'

'I do apologize,' Mr Cane said, looking first at her, then at the closed storeroom door. 'Why were you standing out here in the corridor? Is something the matter?'

'No,' she said, thinking quickly. She'd only met Mr Cane for the first time that morning, as she and Nell were leaving for their return visit to St Giles. She could hardly confide in someone of so brief an acquaintance that she had been spying on the Duke of Monmouth as he searched a corpse. 'It's just that it's never easy to say goodbye, and I needed to gather my courage for one last farewell before we take them to the church.'

Mr Cane nodded, clucking sympathetically. 'Perhaps you will find it less difficult with someone to stand by your side.' He offered her an arm, the ribbon and lace trim of his shirt cuff falling nearly to his waist. Aphra couldn't help wondering where an impoverished scholar had found the money for such a shirt. The sword hanging from his belt looked expensive as well. Mr Cane was a charming and attractive young man; she hoped he wasn't taking advantage of Nell's well-known generosity.

Of course, she reminded herself guiltily, that was exactly what she herself had been doing the last couple of days – even if she did intend to repay every penny.

'Lean on me, dear lady,' Mr Cane said, his voice mellow and soothing. 'Allow me to be your strength.'

'You're very kind,' Aphra said, having no option but to take the young man's arm.

Mr Cane reached for the doorknob just as the door swung open from the inside. The Duke of Monmouth nodded and walked past them without a word. If Mr Cane noticed the look of annoyance on the duke's face, he gave no sign of it. 'There is a scene in my play where Dorinda believes Aleister to have been killed in a battle against the Turks – have you read that far yet?'

'Not yet,' she said, keeping her eyes on the duke, curious to see what he would do next.

'Well,' Mr Cane went on, enthusiastically ushering her into the storeroom, 'she goes by moonlight on to the blood-soaked field to rend her hair and clothing and bid her lover's spirit *adieu*. So you see, as a fellow poet, I understand your need to say goodbye.' He shut the door behind them, cutting off her view of the corridor.

Aphra had no choice but to go through with it, though if Mr Cane expected her to rend her hair and clothing he was about to be disappointed. She positioned herself in the centre of the storeroom, raising her hands into a prayer position as Mr Cane looked on encouragingly. 'Goodbye,' she said, nodding to the coffins. She turned to hurry back to the other room. 'Thank you, Mr Cane. I feel much better.'

'There you are at last,' Nell said on Aphra's return. 'It's nearly seven; shouldn't we begin the procession?'

'Yes, yes,' Aphra said distractedly, looking about for the duke. 'In a minute.'

Nell started looking about as well. 'Where's Bevil? I sent him to fetch you.'

Aphra shrugged. 'Taking his turn to watch the corpses.' She finally located the duke surrounded by a group of admirers, drinking toasts to the health of the 'Protestant heir'. He seemed quite happy now he was the object of so much fawning praise.

Nell tilted her head towards the group drinking toasts to the duke. 'Who is that red-haired man with the eye patch?'

'One of the mumpers we spoke to yesterday. I think he came here hoping for a meal, and I did not have the heart to send him away.'

'We spoke to him yesterday?' Nell shook her head. 'I don't remember him.'

'I didn't recall him at first, either,' Aphra admitted, 'but he had one of my cards.'

'Did he?' Nell said. 'Maybe I *do* remember him after all; there's something very familiar about him.'

Aphra felt a tug at her sleeve and looked down. The little boy was back again. 'There's a man at the door asking to see Mr Cavell, but he doesn't have a ticket.'

She breathed a sigh of relief; there was only one person that could be. 'So Rochester decided to come after all,' she told Nell. 'I knew he wouldn't stay away.'

Nell looked dubious. 'If Rochester were to arrive without his ticket, I'd expect him to ask for *you*, not the corpse.'

Aphra sighed. 'You have a point.' She looked down at the boy and told him she would go to the door herself.

The tall, thin man waiting at the door peered at Aphra through a pair of thick spectacles, blinking in confusion. 'I've come to visit Mr Cavell,' he said. While the man's blinking, bespectacled eyes reminded Aphra of an owl, his badly-fitting clothes put her more in mind of a scarecrow. He wore a dark cloth coat, much too big for him, with a leather hat, riding boots and a centre-parted brown periwig that hung too close to his hollow cheeks. Between the spectacles and the wig, it was difficult to see much of the man's face, but she guessed he must be in his late forties or early fifties. 'I wasn't made to wait outside last week.'

Aphra remembered the first time she met Mrs Hawkins, the old woman mentioned that Matthew had had several visitors. This odd-looking character must be one of them. 'You're a friend of his?'

'Yes, yes,' he said impatiently. 'May I see him now, please?'

'Please come inside,' Aphra said. 'There is something I must tell you.'

The man stayed where he was; what she could see of his face became creased with concern. 'I pray there is nothing wrong?'

123

'Please come inside,' Aphra repeated. 'I have some distressing news.'

The man followed Aphra into the storeroom, blinking in dismay. 'Oh, this is terrible,' he muttered. 'Truly terrible.'

Bevil Cane was still where she'd left him, watching over the coffins. 'Is it time to begin the procession?' he asked, looking up as the two of them entered.

'In a moment,' Aphra told him. 'Once this gentleman has paid his respects.'

'Shall I tell the others to get ready, then?'

Aphra nodded. 'I would be most grateful if you would.'

'Poor Matthew,' the other man said once Bevil Cane was gone. 'Who would wish to kill him? I can scarce believe it.' His owlish, blinking gaze moved towards the other coffin. 'Is another deceased as well?'

'Mr Cavell's brother.'

'Elias?' the man said, his mouth dropping open. 'Please,' he said, reaching for the coffin lid, 'may I look at him?'

'Before you do, be warned. He was badly injured.'

The man took a deep breath and raised the lid. 'Oh God,' he said, his eyes filling with tears, causing him to blink more furiously than ever. 'Oh, God!' He leaned forward, tentatively touching the gaping wounds on Elias's neck. 'Oh, look at your poor dear throat! What have they done to you?' He moved his hand upward to caress the cuts on the dead man's face. 'What have they done?'

Aphra averted her eyes as the man bent over nearly double, his shoulders heaving. 'Would you prefer to be alone?' she asked him gently.

The man gulped and turned to face her, wiping his cheeks. 'Please,' he said. 'For just a moment.'

She turned and left the room, closing the door behind her.

'Why?' she heard the man wail as she walked away. 'Oh, Elias, Elias! Why?'

She returned to the other room to find Bevil Cane handing out sprigs of rosemary to those well enough to take part in the procession. She saw to her dismay that Mrs Barrow had decided to join them after all.

'Who's that red-haired man with the eye patch?' a voice whispered in her ear. 'Over there, behind Mistress Decker?'

She turned to see Nell's mother standing beside her. 'One of Elias's fellow mumpers. He says his name is Fergus O'Bannion.'

Madam Gwyn tapped her nose. 'He doesn't smell right.'

The mourners picked up their torches, forming a queue behind the Duke of Monmouth.

'Excuse me,' Aphra said.

She hurried back down the hall to make sure the stranger had managed to compose himself; in a moment more than twenty people would be coming to collect the bodies.

To her great relief, the man standing beside the coffins was calmer now. As far as she could tell, the eyes behind his thick glass lenses were red and swollen, but dry.

'Sir, you are welcome to join the procession,' she said, 'and equally welcome to return here for the reception after.'

'I would like that very much.' The man sighed and looked away, embarrassed. 'I must apologize for my earlier display of emotion —'

'There is no need to apologize,' Aphra interrupted him.

The man shook his head. 'It's just that Elias ... and Matthew ... were cursed with much ill fortune in this life. They were once quite different men from ...' He sighed and gestured to occupants of the coffins. 'From the men you see before you now.'

'I know that,' Aphra told him.

The man seemed surprised by her response. 'I see you have a most generous and understanding nature,' he said. 'And now I must apologize again, for neglecting to enquire your name.'

'Mrs Behn.'

'It is my sincere pleasure to make your acquaintance, Mrs Behn,' he said, bowing. 'My name is Frost. Nahum Frost.' He gave her a quizzical look. 'Am I correct in thinking you are the person responsible for arranging the burial of these men?'

Aphra nodded.

'I assume this is part of your employment at this house?'

'Oh, no,' Aphra told him. 'I have nothing to do with Gospel House. I was a friend of Matthew's.'

'You knew Matthew?' the man asked, an odd expression on his face.

'And Elias as well. I shall always remember both men with the greatest affection.'

The man peered at her curiously. 'Affection for them? Why?'

'Why?' Aphra repeated, amazed he would ask such a question. She shook her head. She could hear the others coming; there was no time for an explanation. 'It is a long and complicated story ... Let me just say that Matthew and Elias Cavell once did me a great kindness.'

'I should think,' the man said softly, 'that being kind to you must be the easiest thing in the world.'

Chapter Thirteen

Honoré Courtin rose from his seat, hiding his disappointment as a servant conducted two guests into his withdrawing room; only one of them had been invited. The servant hurried from the room to set another place at the dining table.

Monsieur Courtin tried to tell himself the fact that the Duchess of Mazarin had come at all could be considered a kind of victory. Even if she had brought the young Countess of Sussex with her, which would severely limit the scope of the evening's conversation.

On the other hand, bringing young Anne of Sussex might well be the duchess's way of letting Monsieur Courtin know he had no hope of achieving his aims. Hortense Mancini was not an unintelligent woman; she knew why she'd been asked to dinner. And she must know that her acceptance of the invitation had raised his hopes that she might be persuaded to remember her heritage. So why raise those hopes only to dash them? She knew he could hardly discuss the interests of France in front of the English king's daughter. It was obvious she was toying with him.

Still, he reminded himself, the duchess was an exceptionally beautiful woman, and the young countess could hardly be described as ill-favoured. Even if he could not discuss the business he had planned, the evening would have its consolations.

'Ladies,' he said, bowing to kiss each one's hand, 'I am honoured by your presence.'

*

Aphra supervised the children as they spread the food out on one of the tables in the large downstairs room, and signalled the musicians to start playing. The room took on a party atmosphere, the dead men forgotten as the maid served the mourners with oysters and neat's tongue and ham, everyone present gulping down glass after glass of burnt claret. She poured herself a drink and sat down, glad to be off her feet. A couple of the elderly revellers were already hobbling off to bed; it would all be over soon.

She reached into her skirt pocket and took out her sprig of rosemary. The others had tossed theirs into the grave, but she had kept hers. *Rosemary for remembrance*. She stared at it for a moment then put it back in her pocket, wondering if Matthew had felt the same way after her father's funeral: exhausted, penniless and not sure it had been worth it.

She looked up and saw the tall, bespectacled figure of Nahum Frost staring at her from the other side of the room. The poor man. He was the only person present to show any grief over the deaths of the Cavell brothers. He had obviously been close to them. There must be so much he could tell her about them, yet she hadn't had a chance to speak to him since before the procession. He started to walk towards her. At last she would be able to ask him how he knew Matthew and Elias.

'I do apologize, Mrs Behn,' a voice said. 'I tried to speak to you earlier, but you were always so busy. This is the first time I've found you alone!'

God's life, Aphra thought as Elizabeth Decker sat down beside her. She'd managed to avoid Elizabeth all evening, but now she was trapped; she couldn't just stand up and walk away, as much as she might like to. Mr Frost hesitated, then turned away, apparently not wishing to intrude on the two women's conversation. There is no conversation to intrude upon, she thought furiously, willing Nahum Frost to turn back. I have nothing to say to this woman! To her dismay, Frost joined the admiring crowd drinking toasts to the Duke of Monmouth, temporarily vanishing from view.

'It has been terribly remiss of me, I know,' Elizabeth went on blithely, 'not to compliment you on the arrangements, and thank you for allowing me to come. I pray you are not too angered by my neglect?'

Aphra leaned forward to pat her on the hand. 'Elizabeth, be assured that your neglect is one thing that shall never anger me.'

'Oh, Mrs Behn, you are too kind!' Elizabeth said, blushing.

Aphra sighed and leaned back, resting her head against the wall. She noticed Fergus O'Bannion standing near the food table, urging the children to pile his plate higher. There was something odd about him. She thought back to Madam Gwyn's words about the man: 'He doesn't smell right.'

She frowned. What did the woman mean?

'Have you recommended Mr Cane's play to Mr Davenant yet?' Elizabeth asked her. 'Mr Cane says I am to play the lead; he wrote it especially for me – '

It suddenly occurred to Aphra that Madam Gwyn had meant exactly what she said. 'Excuse me,' she said, rising from her seat.

She walked over to the food table, where Mr O'Bannion was still trying to convince the children to give him a larger portion of meat.

'Only one slice of ham each,' the kitchen maid insisted. 'Those were my instructions.'

'Dear child, I would never dream of asking you to disobey your instructions,' O'Bannion assured her. 'If one slice is all I am allotted, then one slice is what I shall take. My only request is that you make the slice thicker.'

'Give him another slice of ham,' Aphra told the girl. She'd been worried there wouldn't be enough food, but she'd been thinking in terms of the young and healthy appetites of her friends in the theatre, not those of the elderly and infirm residents of an almshouse. All that expensive meat and fish had hardly been touched. She might as well have served them gruel. 'Give him as much as he likes.'

'Why thank you, Mrs Behn,' O'Bannion said, bowing. 'Thank you most kindly. You have a warm and generous soul; I knew it the first moment I saw you.' He turned back to the kitchen maid. 'And another glass of burnt claret, dear, if you please.'

Aphra remembered why she had come over to the table, and took a deep breath. She didn't smell anything unusual. O'Bannion's head was still turned towards the kitchen maid, who was piling his plate with ham and tongue. She stepped closer, positioning herself directly behind him, and leaned forward, sniffing.

O'Bannion swung around. 'Is something wrong with your breathing, madam?'

Aphra stepped back, pulling a handkerchief from her pocket. 'I beg your pardon, Mr O'Bannion,' she said, dabbing the handkerchief at her eyes. She sniffled a little before she went on in a quavering voice, 'I was thinking of the poor deceased.'

'Oh, dear lady,' O'Bannion said sympathetically. 'You have provided me, a poor beggar, with such generous hospitality, I nearly forgot the sad nature of this occasion. Pray, tell me, is there anything I can do for you?'

'No.' Aphra sighed and put away her handkerchief. 'I am all right now.'

'Are you sure?'

'Quite sure.'

'You know best, dear lady,' O'Bannion said, looking at something over her shoulder.

Aphra turned to see what he was looking at, and saw that Bevil Cane had seated himself beside Elizabeth Decker. The two of them appeared to be deep in conversation, Bevil Cane doing most of the talking. Then Mr Cane lifted Elizabeth's hand to his lips.

Aphra turned back to Mr O'Bannion.

'They make a handsome couple,' he said. Leaning on his crutch, he reached forward to take a glass of claret from the kitchen maid, emptied it in one gulp, handed it back to be refilled, then raised it in a toast. 'I drink to you, Mrs Behn, a woman of rare tenderness and mercy, who would greet a penniless stranger such as I as if he were a long lost friend.' He emptied the glass again, and placed it back on the table. 'I only hope that the departed souls of your friends – wherever they are – are able to see, and appreciate, the sacrifices you have made for them. And now, dear lady, I must bid you a fond *adieu*.' He bowed slightly, leaning on his crutch for support, then limped towards the door without a backward glance.

Aphra watched him go, utterly bewildered by the man and his behaviour. She looked down at the plate of food he'd left on the table. After all that fuss he hadn't eaten a bite.

Then it came to her; she knew exactly what the old woman had been talking about. She could never have stood so close to Elias or any of his fellow mumpers without covering her nose, yet this man who claimed to live outdoors at Lincoln's Inn had smelled of nothing until she came within inches of him. And then he had smelled of perfume.

She slapped her forehead, cursing herself. She should have realized the instant she came to stand beside him. But the man had distracted her, misdirecting her attention towards Mr Cane and Elizabeth, talking so much and so rapidly she'd barely had a chance to think.

One thing was certain: he was no beggar.

She followed after him, determined to confront him and demand an explanation. She was halfway down the corridor when she heard the front door slam; by the time she reached the door and opened it, there was no sign of him. She didn't have a torch, or even a candle, but the moon had risen and was bright enough to light the way. She hurried out into the road, looking up and down. O'Bannion had vanished.

Not only was he no beggar, it seemed he had no need of his crutch, either.

'Mrs Behn,' a voice called behind her. She turned to see Nahum Frost blinking at her from the doorway. 'I pray I am not disturbing you.'

She walked back to the door; there was no hope of finding O'Bannion now. 'No, Mr Frost. I only stepped out for some air.'

'Night air?' What she could see of the man's face looked dubious. 'Need I remind you, madam, that we are south of the river?'

'Perhaps it would be best if we went back inside,' she said.

'Perhaps it would,' Mr Frost agreed. 'But – ' He extended an arm to block her way. 'Whatever ill humours the air may carry, I fear it is too late. We have already inhaled them in abundance. So what difference will it make if we remain here a moment or two more? So that I may speak with you in private?'

'That depends on what you wish to say.' She'd been wanting to speak to Mr Frost all night, but outdoors by moonlight was not the way she'd envisaged their conversation. If she didn't know better, she might suspect this odd, blinking scarecrow, with his leather hat and ill-fitting, mismatched clothes, had something more than talk in mind. But she couldn't allow herself to believe that – the prospect was too laughable.

'I merely hoped you might be so kind as to enlighten me as to the origin of your acquaintance with Matthew and Elias Cavell.'

'That is a happy coincidence, sir,' she said, relieved to see the man had lowered his arm and was now keeping a respectful distance between them. 'I was hoping you might enlighten me about precisely the same thing. Pray, tell me, how did you come to know the brothers?'

'I shall gladly tell you anything you wish to know,' Frost said, bowing slightly. 'But I pray you, madam, do me the honour of speaking first.'

*

The Duchess of Mazarin and the Countess of Sussex sat holding hands on an embroidered sofa as a servant poured the wine.

Honoré Courtin sat across from them, raising his glass in a toast. He couldn't help thinking they looked like an exquisite pair of matching book-ends, their hair arranged in identical curls bedecked with identical ribbons. They were even dressed alike, both in gowns of rich dark velvet. The duchess in a deep shade of red, the younger girl in green.

To Monsieur Courtin's great relief, the one in green was being quiet for the moment. She'd spent most of the evening regaling him with one long, pointless anecdote after another. It was part of his duty as a diplomat to appear interested when he was not, but by the fifth or sixth story he had followed the duchess's example and concentrated on his dinner.

The three of them were sipping their wine, he and the duchess making polite conversation, when Anne suddenly leaned forward. 'Monsieur Courtin, do you play basset?'

Aphra was about to knock on the almshouse door when it swung open. Nell and Bevil Cane stood before her, a look of relief on both their faces.

'My life! You've had us nearly frantic!' Nell scolded, ushering her inside. 'My mother said she saw you followed outside by that hobgoblin in the leather hat.'

'So your mother has been watching me.'

Nell rolled her eyes. 'She's been watching everyone. She suspects them all of murder. All except us, of course,' she added. 'And Jamie. Even my mother would not dare to suspect the Protestant heir!'

'Nor would I,' Aphra said drily, remembering how the duke had rummaged through Elias's pockets.

'The moment Mother Gwyn expressed her concern for you, my hand went straight to my sword,' Bevil Cane broke in. 'Didn't it, Nell?'

'It did,' Nell agreed, humouring him.

'On my honour,' Mr Cane said, bowing to kiss Aphra's hand, 'I stand ever ready to defend you.'

Aphra looked at Nell and saw she was trying not to laugh. She remembered Rochester's comment as he'd glanced at the young tutor's play, about Nell and her stray puppies. That was exactly what Bevil Cane reminded her of: a harmless, barking puppy. She tried to imagine herself in danger, with Mr Cane rushing to her rescue. Ye Gods, she thought, she'd probably end up defending *him*. 'Thank you, Mr Cane,' she said, struggling to keep her voice even.

Madam Gwyn was waiting for them at the end of the corridor. 'Oh thank goodness, little duckling,' she said, taking Aphra's hands. 'I saw you leave after that man with the eye-patch, and then that other followed, and when you didn't come back – '

'I wanted to see where that first one went – you were right about him, he was not what he appeared – but he was gone before I even reached the door. And then Mr Frost and I had a brief conversation about how we each came to know the deceased. I was never in any danger,' Aphra assured her. 'Though I thank you for your concern.'

'So you admit I was right about that rogue with the eye-patch!' Madam Gwyn said triumphantly. She turned towards her daughter. 'Did you hear that, Nell?'

'Yes, mother, I heard,' Nell said tiredly.

'And what did you notice about him that finally convinced you?' Madam Gwyn asked Aphra.

'I never before met a beggar who smelled of civet.'

Madam Gwyn laughed, her eyes gleaming. She tilted her head towards Nell. 'I've been trying to tell *her* all night, but would she listen to me? I'm only the woman that bore her, after all.'

Nell made a face as Aphra expressed her sympathy.

'Mother Gwyn,' Bevil said excitedly, 'I only wish you had

voiced your suspicions to *me*! I should have run the man through as an impostor!'

'I'm sure you would have Bevil, darling,' Madam Gwyn said soothingly. 'Now be so kind as to pour me a glass of that lovely burnt claret. And be sure you fill it to the top this time, dear.'

'Yes, Mrs Gwyn.'

'And pour another glass for Mrs Behn, while you're about it.' She took Aphra by the arm and led her over to a bench. 'Now sit down beside me, duckling, and have yourself a rest.'

Aphra found herself sitting between mother and daughter, both of them talking at once.

'Did you see which way O'Bannion went?' Nell asked one ear, while Madam Gwyn loudly tutted in the other that she'd known the man to be a villain all along.

'No,' Aphra said, 'I looked up and down the road, but found no sign of him in either direction.'

'It's just as well,' Madam Gwyn said. 'Who knows what he might have done if he saw you following?'

'Why would he do anything?' Aphra asked her. 'He may have lied about who he was, but he seemed totally lacking in malice. In fact, he seemed a man of rare civility.'

'Go to, Mrs Behn! Go to,' Madam Gwyn chided her. 'Do you believe a murderer incapable of being civil? But once they are threatened – ' She was interrupted by Mr Cane's arrival with the wine. 'You are the sweetest of lads,' she said as he carefully handed her a glass filled nearly to overflowing. 'If I had been blessed with a son, I would have wished him to be just like you.'

'With you as a mother and Nelly as a sister, no man could have been more fortunate,' Mr Cane said.

'Odd's bobs, Bevil, sit down and stop your dissembling!' Nell ordered him. Nell was laughing, but Aphra could see the old woman was touched.

He handed a glass to Aphra, then pulled a bench around so

he could sit facing the three women. 'Now, ladies,' he said, 'I must know what you were discussing.'

'Only that my mother believes Mr O'Bannion to be a murderer,' Nell told him.

Mr Cane raised his eyebrows. 'Do you?' he asked Madam Gwyn.

'The murderer always attends the funeral of his victim,' Madam Gwyn said darkly. 'How else can he be sure of his success, but to see the lifeless corpse lowered into the earth?'

'Mother,' Nell said, rolling her eyes. 'Where do you get these ideas?'

'If you are right,' Mr Cane said, 'then the murderer could be anyone here.'

'Does that include me?' Nell asked him.

'No, Nelly,' Mr Cane assured her. 'Not you.' He turned his attention back to Madam Gwyn. 'Why do you believe it to be O'Bannion?'

'Because he came here lying through his throat, that's why. He was no more a beggar than you or I.'

Mr Cane considered this a moment, rubbing his chin. 'I fear you may be right. Why else would he try to deceive us so? And you,' he said, looking at Aphra. 'My heart quakes at the thought you attempted to follow that man, alone. You must promise me now, you will never do such a thing again!'

'But nothing happened,' she protested, lifting her glass to her lips.

'That is not the point,' Bevil Cane insisted. 'The point is that if something had happened you would have been powerless, with no one there to aid you. You should have asked me to come with you. I would have done so gladly.'

'You were busy,' Aphra said pointedly, lifting her glass again. She took another mouthful of claret, then raised a hand to her forehead, feeling giddy. How much wine *had* she drunk tonight? She couldn't remember.

Mr Cane glanced away, embarrassed, as Nell began to giggle.

'Mistress Decker and I were merely discussing my play,' he said. His cheeks had gone so red that Aphra started laughing as well.

'Bevil, you make a bad liar,' Madam Gwyn told him.

He shrugged, and started to laugh himself. 'That was all the enchanting lady would *allow* me to discuss! Still, you must believe me, I would gladly have come to your assistance, whatever you may have interrupted. Now promise me, Mrs Behn, that the next time you wish to chase a murderer, you will come to me first.' He leaned forward, his expression earnest. 'Though Nelly and Mother Gwyn are dear to me as life itself, I fear they underestimate me. They think my skills confined to the scholarly pursuits of poetry and mathematics, but I assure you I am well practised in the use of a blade – '

Aphra reached forward to pat him on the hand. 'And I assure *you*, Mr Cane, I have no intention of chasing murderers, but if ever I should do so, your assistance will be welcome.'

'I see you do not take my offer seriously, Mrs Behn. But no matter. If you need me, I shall be there.'

'Oh, you've offended him now,' Madam Gwyn said, giggling like a young girl.

'No, Mother Gwyn. It's all right. I am not offended,' he said. But the expression on his face showed he was.

Oh God, Aphra thought. Here was a sweet young man, sincere in his concern for her welfare, and she and the other two women were mocking him without mercy. Of course, she reminded herself, they had all had too much to drink over the course of the evening; but she was still sober enough to feel guilty. 'Forgive me, Mr Cane,' she said, feeling the room begin to spin – that last sip of claret had affected her more than she'd realized. 'I assure you, I take you very seriously, indeed.' She raised a hand to cover her mouth, unable to stop herself from laughing. 'You have no idea how seriously I take you!'

'Are you all right, Aphra?' Nell asked her, going slightly out of focus.

137

'Yes,' Aphra said, feeling her head fall back against the wall. 'I'm fine, I'm fine.'

'You said you had a conversation with the other man,' Mr Cane reminded her. 'The one in the leather hat.'

'Oh yes,' Aphra said, her eyes fluttering closed. 'The owl-crow.'

'Owl-crow?' Nell repeated.

'Face of an owl, body of a scarecrow.'

Madam Gwyn nudged her, laughing. 'Owl-crow; I'll remember that!'

'You said he told you of his acquaintance with the dead men,' Mr Cane said. 'What did he say?'

'He knew them in Surinam,' Aphra mumbled.

'Surinam?' Mr Cane repeated.

'Hmm. He said he'd heard about me, though we never had the good fortune to meet. He said he'd heard my name mentioned many times, and always with the greatest reverence.'

'He'd heard about you?'

'From Matthew; they were neighbours. He said he should have known me by my description as a beauty.' She started to giggle. 'Then he said it did not do me justice! And then he said –'

'Why, Aphra!' Nell interrupted, her voice seeming to echo from every wall. 'You sound as if you are sighing for this owl-crow!'

'God's life, no!' Aphra said. 'Sighing for the likes of him? Surely no woman could be so desperate for hot cockles!'

'Mrs Behn!' Bevil Cane said, shocked.

'Poor Bevil has yet to learn about such things,' Madam Gwyn hooted before her head came crashing down on Aphra's shoulder.

'Oh, but his voice ... his voice,' Aphra said, 'soothing and gentle, warm as a tropical night. I could have listened to that voice for ever ...'

'Mother Gwyn,' Bevil Cane said, sounding far away. 'Mrs

138

Behn? Nelly, help me! Mother Gwyn, speak to me ... Mother Gwyn! Oh God, oh God!'

'Five hundred guineas,' Hortense Mancini said as Mustapha helped her into her coach. 'Anne, you are a wicked child!'

'More thán he would have paid you to be his spy,' Anne said, climbing in after her.

'Who said he wished me to be his spy?' Hortense demanded.

'Come, Hortense, do you take me for an idiot? Why else would the French ambassador pay you such homage?'

'Most men pay me homage, my dear,' Hortense informed her, raising her nose in the air.

'Ooh, you are proud, madam,' Anne said, teasing her.

'No more than I should be. Which does not alter the fact that you must stop cheating at cards!' Hortense pulled Anne's head down to rest on her shoulder. 'Look at the moon,' she said, gazing out of the coach window. 'It's bright as day outside.'

'Would you do it?' Anne said, nestling against her.

'Do what?'

'Spy for Monsieur Courtin.'

'Don't be stupid,' Hortense said, batting playfully at Anne's head. 'The French have spies enough without me. Whitehall is crawling with them.'

'I'd like to be a spy,' Anne said.

'Well, you be one, then,' Hortense told her, turning back to the window as the coach began to move. 'Anne, look.'

'What?' Anne said, raising her head.

Hortense frowned. 'Nothing,' she said. 'It's just ... I thought I saw a man watching us from that doorway. There was something about his face ... he seemed to be staring directly at me.' She sighed and shook her head. 'Never mind, he's gone now.'

'Another of your admirers,' Anne said, nestling back against her shoulder.

Chapter Fourteen

Aphra gradually became aware of a gentle motion, alternately rocking her from side to side, then bouncing her up and down. And there was a sound. A loud, rasping sound that grated against her ears. She moaned and rolled her head, trying to get comfortable, but the irritating sound continued, loud and harsh as ever. Then she heard a man shouting somewhere in the distance, but she couldn't make out the words.

Something heavy was pressing down on her. She tried to push it away, but someone caught hold of her hand and held it, squeezing, as a warm breeze blew across her cheek.

She opened her eyes and saw another pair staring into her own. She couldn't make out the other person's features, they were too close. All she could see were eyes, red-rimmed and bloodshot, as if they had been crying. Then the other moved back, and she saw it was Elizabeth Decker.

'Elizabeth, what are you doing?'

'Oh, Mrs Behn! Praise God you know me!'

'Know you?' Aphra pulled her hand away from Elizabeth's tight grasp, flexing her fingers to restore the flow of blood. 'What are you prattling about? Of course I know you.'

The man shouted again, his words clearer this time: 'Make way! Make way for his grace! Make way!'

Aphra gasped, suddenly aware of her surroundings. She was leaning back on a padded leather seat, wedged between the Duke of Monmouth on one side and Elizabeth Decker on the other. Elizabeth was leaning across her, staring earnestly into her face. Aphra could still feel something heavy pressing against her, but had no idea what it was. She shifted to one side, trying to see around the other woman's head.

Nell's voice came from nearby. 'Elizabeth, please move aside. I would like to see Aphra's face.'

Elizabeth moved out of the way, and at last Aphra could see the source of the weight she felt. There was a basket on her lap.

Beyond the basket she saw Bevil Cane leaning forward, staring every bit as earnestly as Elizabeth. Nell sat beside him, her arm around her mother's shoulders. The horrible grating sound was coming from Madam Gwyn; she was snoring.

'Aphra seems to have rejoined us,' Nell told the others.

'Where am I?'

'You are in the Duke of Monmouth's coach,' Elizabeth told her, as the voice in the distance repeated its admonition to make way.

'What?' She tried to think. 'But how?'

Elizabeth's eyes filled with tears. 'You don't remember?'

Aphra shook her head. The last thing she remembered was sitting on a bench in the almshouse, talking to Bevil Cane. 'No,' she said. 'I remember nothing.' She looked down at the basket in her lap. 'What is this?'

'It's the left-over food,' the duke said, staring straight ahead and keeping all expression out of his voice. 'You refused to leave without it.'

Her eyes widened. 'Did I?'

He turned to face her, his look as blank and unreadable as his voice. 'During a brief period of wakefulness,' he said. 'You also shouted something about "serving them gruel", but none of us could understand you.'

'It was then I tried to speak to you,' Elizabeth said, 'and you did not know me!'

'I didn't?'

Elizabeth wiped a hand across her eyes. 'You turned to me and said, "Who are you, to be present at this function?" And I replied, "Surely you know me; I am Elizabeth Decker, the lead actress in your new play." And you said, "No, mistress, you must be mistaken, for you are certainly no actress!"'

Aphra sank down into her seat.

'It was then Nelly explained you were suffering from some kind of delirium, and did not recognize me,' Elizabeth went on, sniffling.

Aphra and Nell exchanged glances. Aphra's expression was one of relief and gratitude, Nell's an ironic smile.

Elizabeth dabbed at her eyes with a handkerchief. 'Though the fact you did not know me cut me deeply, I cannot begin to express my relief at that time to see you conscious again, no matter how briefly, and no matter the state of your reason. I tell you, Mrs Behn,' she said, choking back a sob, 'when I saw you slide to the floor, with Madam Gwyn tumbling after, my heart nearly froze with fear. I thought you were dead!' She lowered her head into her hands, weeping.

Aphra looked at Madam Gwyn, horror-stricken. It hadn't occurred to her the old woman might be ill. 'Is your mother all right?' she asked Nell.

Nell nodded. 'This is not the first time my mother has fallen to the floor from the effects of wine.'

Aphra turned back to Elizabeth, placing a hand on her heaving shoulder. 'Please don't cry,' she said gently. 'It seems Madam Gwyn and I are both quite well.'

'Forgive me,' Elizabeth sniffled, trembling. 'It's just that I love you so, I couldn't bear the thought of losing you!'

The last thing Aphra wanted was a declaration of love from Elizabeth Decker. 'Please, Elizabeth,' she muttered, embarrassed. Mr Cane and the duke both averted their eyes; Nell was staring at her open-mouthed. 'There's no need – '

'You're so like my own dear mother. She died when I was six, but if I close my eyes I can see her face and hear her voice so clearly ... You are her image, Mrs Behn! Her image!'

'I do not deserve such a tribute.'

'But you do,' Elizabeth protested. 'I assure you, you do.'

Aphra sighed, sinking her face into her hands. She would never be able to drop Elizabeth from the cast now. Hell take the woman! Why did she have to say those things? Why couldn't she have just kept quiet? 'I beg of you, Elizabeth, let us speak of something else.'

Elizabeth nodded, then kissed her on the cheek. Aphra felt like crying herself. The play was doomed, and there was nothing she could do about it.

And she had the most dreadful headache. She tried to recall the scene the others had described: tumbling to the floor, then waking just long enough to insult Elizabeth and collect the left-over food. It was impossible to even imagine it; she felt as if her mind had been wiped clean. She'd never disgraced herself in public like this before. How much wine had she drunk?

Nell's mother mumbled something in her sleep, then resumed snoring louder than ever.

The duke's horses came to a halt in front of Aphra's rented house. A liveried servant rushed around to open the coach door, a lantern in his hand.

'Are you sure you will not return with us to Pall Mall?' Nell asked her for the fifth or sixth time.

'Yes, I am sure,' Aphra said. 'I cannot stay away from my own house for ever.'

'But after what happened,' Nell protested.

'The dead have been buried,' Aphra said. 'It is over.' She murmured her thanks to all present, and began to rise.

'Wait,' Mr Cane said, raising a hand to stop her. 'At least let me enter your house first, to ensure that all is well.'

'That will not be necessary, Mr Cane. I can see for myself the door and shutters are closed and the house is dark.'

'Would an intruder leave the door or windows open for all to see? And how else do you think an intruder would lie in wait, but in the dark?'

'Don't talk such rubbish, Bevil!' Nell said. 'Would you frighten poor Aphra to death? Intruders lurking in the dark! Where do you get such ideas?'

'Only from what *you* have said,' Bevil retorted. 'Was it not you who told me you found a blood-soaked body in her house of office?'

Nell sighed. 'Give him your key, Aphra.'

Aphra handed the basket to Elizabeth, then reached into her pocket for the key, inwardly wincing at the thought of her unmade bed piled high with laundry, and the petticoat she'd left draped over the back of a chair. Still, she reflected, if Mr Cane hadn't volunteered to search the house for intruders, she would have been unable to sleep until she had done exactly the same thing herself, taking the poker from beside the fireplace and thrusting it into every corner. She would probably still do it anyway.

The Duke of Monmouth started to rise. 'Allow me to assist you,' he said to Mr Cane.

'That won't be necessary, your grace,' Bevil said, leaping down from the coach and borrowing the footman's lantern. 'Wait here,' he told Aphra. 'I shall only be a moment.'

They sat in silence for several minutes, listening to Madam Gwyn snoring.

'Did I tell you Mr Cane said he wrote the lead role in his play especially for me?' Elizabeth asked Aphra.

'Yes, you told me,' Aphra said, looking at her front door. What could be taking him so long?

'I nearly forgot,' Nell said, reaching into her pocket. She took out a handful of printed cards, passing one each to Aphra, the duke, and Elizabeth.

Aphra shook her head, laughing. She knew what the cards said; she'd been with Nell when she'd ordered them.

The other two held the cards up to their faces, struggling to read them. The duke called for his footman to bring them more light. The man returned a moment later with another lantern.

Aphra looked down at her card. She didn't realize Nell had ordered so many skulls; the card was covered with them. Elizabeth glanced at the invitation in her hand, then shook her head in sympathy. 'Another funeral? I'm so sorry. I didn't know you had lost someone as well.'

The Duke of Monmouth snorted. 'This is a tasteless jest, Nelly.'

'Jest?' Elizabeth took a closer look at her card. 'So it is.'

'How can you be so unfeeling in the face of death?' Nell protested. 'I promise you it shall be a tasteful and moving ceremony, and I, for one, shall weep as the coffin is lowered into the ground.'

'I must tell you, I do not approve of this mischief,' the duke said. 'But I will be there, if only for the sake of our long friendship.'

'If you limited your engagements to events of which you approve, you would never leave the house,' Nell told him. 'And as for you, Elizabeth, I must warn you: the moment a woman steps on to a stage, she loses the right to disapprove of anything.'

'I will be there,' Elizabeth said. 'Though I fail to understand the point of it all. Pray, what do you mean to accomplish?'

Aphra could take no more of Elizabeth's dim wittering. She rose up, stepping over the Duke of Monmouth's feet, and climbed down from the coach.

'Aphra, where are you going?' Nell called after her.

'Into my house.'

'But Bevil hasn't returned yet.'

'Zoors! Do you think I don't know that?' Aphra shouted. 'What *is* he doing in there?'

'I will go and look,' the Duke of Monmouth said.

'There is no need, your grace,' Aphra said, walking towards the door. The last person she wanted inside her house was Monmouth.

Elizabeth's voice was the last she heard before entering the house. 'Mrs Behn! You forgot your basket!'

*

She entered her dark front hall, listening. She heard a number of sounds coming from the parlour. A rustling and crackling, followed by something heavy being dragged across the floor. 'Mr Cane!' she shouted. 'Mr Cane!'

'Just a minute,' he called from beyond the parlour door.

She pushed the door open and stepped inside.

A fire was burning in the grate – the source of the crackling sounds she'd heard. The lantern borrowed from the footman was sitting on her little cloth-covered table, which had been placed back in its usual position, near the entrance to the kitchen. By its light she saw Bevil Cane, pushing a carved wooden chair across the room. 'What are you doing?'

'Ah, Mrs Behn,' he said, looking up. 'I'm nearly finished.'

'What are you doing?' she repeated.

He nodded towards the grate. 'The house was cold, so I started a fire for you.'

'That was thoughtful of you, but what are you doing with that chair?'

He positioned the chair next to the small table at the rear of the parlour. 'I was only trying to help. The room was in some disorder when I came in: chairs and tables stacked and shoved against the wall, mud on the floor, papers scattered everywhere.'

She looked about the room and saw the floor had been swept and cleared, the carpet rolled out and all her furniture put back into place.

'There were several poetry broadsheets lying open across the desk, and more had fallen to the floor.' Mr Cane pointed up to one of her bookshelves. 'I put them up there, in alphabetical order according to title.' He walked over to the desk and bent over, looking at something wedged between the desk and the wall. He reached around behind the desk, pulling out a large sheet of folded paper. 'Another one,' he said. 'May I?'

Aphra looked away, embarrassed. 'Please.' She thought of the dirty laundry she'd left piled on the bed; she hoped he hadn't decided to organize that as well.

Mr Cane looked at the writing on the front of the broadsheet, then placed it between two others on the shelf. He mentioned that he'd observed that Aphra sometimes edited these collections and he hoped the next time she put one together, she would remember her devoted admirer.

'I have no plans to edit another collection,' she said, 'but if I do, I will let you know.'

'That is all I ask,' he said. He spent another moment examining the contents of her bookshelves. 'I don't see my play.'

Aphra sighed, pulling out the drawer where she'd placed the manuscript. 'I'm afraid I dropped it on the way home from the theatre,' she said, giving him an edited version of the truth, 'and the pages fell out of order.'

He picked up the manuscript. 'It will not take me long to rearrange them,' he said, spreading several pages across her desk top. 'I know every line by heart.'

Aphra extended a hand to stop him. 'Why not take the manuscript home, and have Nell return it to me when it is back in order and the pages have been numbered?'

'But I can do that now. It will take me no time, I promise you.'

'Mr Cane, please. I *will* read your play; you may depend upon it. But it has been a long and eventful day, and I would like to go to bed now.'

'I beg your pardon,' the young man said, neatly stacking his papers before turning to face her. 'Are you sure it is wise to be alone at such a time? If you insist on remaining in this house tonight, please allow me to remain here with you.'

Aphra told herself she couldn't have heard him right.

'I would sleep down here, on the floor,' he added quickly, reaching to take her hand. 'My only wish is to know that you are safe.'

Aphra looked at the young man staring into her eyes with so much earnest intensity. She had thought of him earlier as a harmless puppy, but puppies had their attractions.

She started to giggle. She'd thought the effects of the wine had worn off, but now it seemed they hadn't, after all. She decided the best thing would be for the puppy-man to leave before she made a fool of herself.

'Thank you, Mr Cane, but I will be all right.'

'Are you quite sure?' he asked, raising her hand to his lips.

Aphra was beginning to consider the possibility that if Mr Cane spent the night, she might not require him to remain on the parlour floor. Puppies were supposed to curl up at your feet and keep the bed warm. She was about to tell him that when she was interrupted by the sound of approaching footsteps.

Aphra pulled her hand away from the young tutor as the Duke of Monmouth entered the room, carrying the basket of left-over food.

'My life!' Nell said, walking in behind him. 'What is taking you so long?'

'Mr Cane was helping me move some furniture,' Aphra said, stepping away from the desk.

'Mother is awake at last, which is a great relief. She is asking for you,' Nell told Mr Cane.

'Praise God!' Mr Cane said, clasping his hands into a prayer position. 'I trust she is well?'

'Well enough, though she complains of an aching head,' Nell said. 'Pray, go to her. She wishes to speak with you.'

'At once.' He turned, bowing, to Aphra. 'Your servant, madam.'

Nell turned to Monmouth, still holding Aphra's basket. 'Thank you, Jamie,' she said, reaching up to take the basket from him.

The duke held on, refusing to let go. 'No, Nelly,' he said. 'Allow me to put the basket away.' He turned to Aphra. 'Your kitchen, madam?'

Aphra thought back to the duke's earlier request to be left alone with the dead brothers, and how she had witnessed him searching a corpse. Now he wished to take a basket into her kitchen. She felt like giggling again, but managed to suppress it. 'Please, your grace, just leave the basket on the floor and I will attend to it later.'

'But I insist,' the duke said, clinging to the basket.

What could he possibly want in her kitchen? Having searched a corpse, did he now wish to search her larder? And if he did, she asked herself, what would he be likely to find? Nothing but half a loaf of stale bread and a small bag of oats. Let him search, she thought, nodding towards the kitchen door.

'Your servant,' the duke said, taking the lantern from the small table as he passed.

'Aphra, I need to speak to you,' Nell said. 'I found something –'

Aphra shushed her and tiptoed to the kitchen door. If the Duke of Monmouth was searching her larder, she wanted to see it. She pushed the door open and stepped inside.

He wasn't there.

She walked to the outside door and looked out into the garden. There was a light in her house of office.

Chapter Fifteen

Louise de Kéroualle sat up in her bed, listening to the gentle snoring of her maid. The fire burning in the grate lit the room well enough for her to see the time on a gold clock mounted above the mantel. It was after midnight.

She pushed back the blankets, careful not to make a sound, and stood, slipping her feet into a pair of soft-soled satin shoes. She left the room a moment later, a hooded cloak wrapped around her nightdress.

Louise stepped into the corridor and hurried towards the nearest flight of stairs, the hood pulled close around her face. She made her way down to the ground floor, and outside.

She crossed a torchlit courtyard, careful always to remain in shadow; her apartment had several windows overlooking this side of the palace. She glanced up to assure herself no one was watching, then took a large key from a pocket inside her cloak and entered her own kitchen.

She came out ten minutes later, a sack of food hidden beneath her cloak, a slice of cold mutton in her mouth. Swallowing the last bite of meat, she locked the door behind her and went back the way she had come.

Aphra made her way upstairs, relieved to be alone at last. She was tired of everyone asking her if she was well, telling her she was acting strangely and should not be left alone.

She knew she was acting strangely, and that was all the more reason for her to be alone. She dreaded to think what she might have said to Mr Cane if Monmouth and Nell hadn't entered the room when they did, and even more, she dreaded to think what she might have *done*.

She gasped at the sight of the dishevelled pile of skirts and undergarments she'd left sitting on top of the bed. What madness had overtaken her, that could ever make her think of inviting Mr Cane into this room? She thanked God she had never got the opportunity.

She knocked her laundry to the floor and sat down on the bed, kicking off her shoes. She was about to unlace her bodice when she froze, listening.

She'd heard something downstairs, she was sure of it. Something rattling.

She put her shoes on again and walked on to the landing, holding her breath.

The rattling sound continued, coming from somewhere below. She crept down the stairs, telling herself over and over that it was just the wind.

At the bottom of the stairs she heard a muttered curse, followed by a thump. To her relief, both sounds came from outside the door, which was still securely locked. She tiptoed into the parlour and lifted the poker from its position beside the grate, plunging the end into the flames until it glowed. She walked back to the door, gripping the poker with both hands. The doorknob twisted back and forth, and then there was another thump. 'Who's there?' she demanded. 'Who's there?'

No answer.

'I have a pistol,' she said. 'Speak or I will shoot!'

'A pistol?' said a familiar voice. 'Sweet soul, when did you get a pistol?'

Aphra rolled on to her side and opened her eyes, then raised her hands to cover them.

She slowly spread her fingers. 'Oh God,' she said out loud.

Her black mourning clothes lay strewn across the bedchamber floor. A man's jacket, sword and breeches lay in a heap on top of her dirty laundry, and a brown periwig hung from the back of a chair.

'Oh God, no!'

She leapt out of bed, splashing herself with perfume and dressing quickly. John Hoyle rolled over, mumbling something, but did not wake up.

She bent down to gather up her laundry and found several strips of paper. There was no time to look at them now. She scooped them up along with the laundry, tossing the lot into the bottom of her wardrobe.

'I have to go to the theatre,' she told the sleeping body on the bed.

Hoyle pulled the blanket up over his head.

Nell was on stage with the cast. Aphra sat alone in the Royal Box, flicking through Bevil Cane's play. Apparently he'd been up most of the night putting the pages back in order. Aphra nearly said she wished he hadn't bothered, but unlike the previous night when she had said and done many things she now regretted, this morning she had managed to hold her tongue.

She swore to herself that she would never get so drunk again as long as she lived.

'Mrs Decker is late,' Mr Davenant called to her from the stage.

'I can see that,' Aphra called back.

'Where is she?'

Aphra dropped Mr Cane's play on to the seat beside her. 'I don't know!'

'This is the second time she's been late,' Mr Davenant said. 'I'll have to fine her.'

'Then fine her!' Aphra shouted.

'I will,' Mr Davenant muttered, crossing his arms.

Elizabeth arrived ten minutes later, apologizing profusely. Aphra immediately picked up Mr Cane's play and started reading; she wanted to appear casual and unconcerned when Rochester came to sit beside her in the box.

Aphra read through the entire first scene of *Aleister and Dorinda* without interruption. By the time she was halfway through the second, she began to suspect Rochester wasn't going to join her after all.

It occurred to her he might not be speaking to her after the way she had stormed out after the last rehearsal, but she was the injured party, not him. She had a right to be angry. He didn't.

She peered over the top of the manuscript, pretending she was still reading. She couldn't see Rochester anywhere.

She put down the script and leaned over the railing, expecting to see him stretched out on a bench in the pit. He wasn't there.

She sank back into her seat, biting her lip. Why wasn't he here? She wanted to talk to him, to tell him all the things that had happened and ask him his opinion.

Nell, of course, had asked her how she felt this morning, and Aphra had asked after Nell's mother. But she hadn't dared mention that she'd left John Hoyle asleep in her bed; Nell would only have chided her for being a fool.

But Nell was still young and beautiful. She didn't understand what it was like to look into a glass and see a face looking back that is not the face you *thought* you had. Not the face you remembered.

Of course Rochester wouldn't understand that, either. But he did understand John Hoyle. As he'd told her many times, they had the same faults.

She wished he was there.

On the stage below her, they were running through a scene where the heroine, disguised as a man, accidentally rescues a woman by frightening away an attacker. 'For God's sake, Elizabeth,' Aphra shouted. 'Walk like a man! Men do not take tiny little steps, they stride!'

Her face creased in concentration, Elizabeth dutifully took several large, sweeping steps across the stage.

'God's wounds!' Aphra screamed. 'You're supposed to appear bold and threatening. You're not supposed to be sliding on ice!' She stood up and pointed at one of the actors. 'Walk for me, please. Show her.'

The actor swaggered across the stage like a Covent Garden bully.

'There,' Aphra said. 'Like that.'

Elizabeth tried to swagger.

'Now you look as if your hip is out of joint.'

'It's all right, Aphra,' Nell said, taking Elizabeth by the arm. 'Just say the lines,' she told Elizabeth, 'and copy my movements.'

'A lady in distress? What can I do? But wait! I am a man now, and shall behave as one,' Elizabeth declaimed as Nell dragged her downstage, swaggering.

'First, I will make myself look big, like a cat.'

Nell took a deep breath, throwing back her shoulders and spreading her arms and legs.

'Now I'll fix him with my fiercest eye.'

Nell raised one eyebrow.

'Jut out my chin, slap myself on the thigh, and have myself a good long scratch.'

Nell went through the actions described.

'And then at last I'll reach for my sword, and bid the rogue begone, my voice deep and strong, like the roar of a lion.'

Nell mimed reaching for a sword.

'Why, he's gone, just like that, before I ever said a word! This being a man is even easier than I thought!'

Aphra left her seat in the Royal Box as Mr Davenant got up on stage to remind everyone that from tomorrow morning, and for the next two weeks, they would be using the rehearsal rooms in Leicester Square. The cast started leaving for the local tavern before he'd got halfway through his announcement. 'Be there by ten of the clock precisely,' he continued, calmly addressing the empty theatre, 'or be fined two shillings. Thank you.' He bowed and left the stage.

Aphra shook her head. She would never understand young Mr Davenant.

Nell flopped down on to a bench in the pit, yawning. Aphra sat down beside her, clutching Bevil Cane's manuscript to her chest.

'You're not well, are you, Aphra?'

Aphra shrugged.

'You were much affected by last night's wine,' Nell observed.

'Ha!' Aphra said, wondering if John Hoyle was still snoring in her bed. 'More than you know.'

The king swept through the gates of Whitehall Palace and headed into St James's Park for his daily constitutional, followed as usual by his pack of yapping spaniels. A throng of people surged forward, each with an important request, each desperate to speak to His Majesty 'for just a moment'.

The king passed them by, his long-legged strides leaving everyone far behind. Thomas Alcock followed at a more leisurely pace, blending in with the assorted fops and courtiers whose habit it was to accompany the king on these walks. No one around him was saying much of interest. The main topic of conversation seemed to be the Duchess of Portsmouth, who was still refusing all nourishment in her bid to 'starve herself for love'. But the Duchess of Mazarin was walking nearby, and that was consolation enough. She was wearing a pair of tight men's breeches that showed every curve of her legs.

Alcock walked a little faster, trying to get closer to the duchess. She was walking arm-in-arm with another woman, almost as tall as her, with hair almost as dark and lustrous as hers. That had to be Anne of Sussex, the duchess's inseparable companion.

His master had once made some remarks about the women's

friendship which Alcock had found offensive, referring to things he didn't think were physically possible – though his master assured him they were. No, Alcock told himself, he could never believe such things of his beautiful duchess.

He was close enough now to smell her perfume. She turned her head, and their eyes met.

Alcock moved away, fading into the crowd. That was stupid of him. He was supposed to be faceless and anonymous, moving about unnoticed, and the duchess had not only caught him staring at her, she had stared back.

The duchess craned her neck, searching the company. Alcock lowered his head, shifting sideways in order to walk behind two other men.

He felt unnerved. No one had ever paid him the slightest attention on his wanderings among the court. He tried to tell himself the duchess hadn't really noticed him, but in that moment when their eyes met he'd felt as if she knew everything there was to know about him, as if she could see into his soul.

He shook his head. If he were a man of a more romantic disposition, he might think he had fallen in love. But he wasn't, he told himself. And he hadn't.

He leaned to one side, peering around the two men in front of him, and saw the duchess walking ahead, whispering something to her companion. He remembered his master's comment about anyone appearing beautiful when viewed from a distance, but now Alcock had seen the duchess up close. Close enough to touch her. To kiss her. There was no doubt in his mind: she was the most beautiful woman in the world.

A snatch of murmured conversation interrupted his reverie. One of the men in front of him was speaking of something other than the Duchess of Portsmouth's bid for starvation; he had just spoken a name Alcock recognized.

Matthew Cavell.

Alcock only knew the name because his master had mentioned it the previous day. He had never heard the name before, and didn't expect to hear it again. At least not in this company, in these surroundings.

He bent his head forward, trying to hear what the man said next. But it was too late. Whatever the conversation had been, it was over. The men bade each other farewell and went their separate ways. It was only then Alcock saw that the man who'd been speaking wore a black plaster across the bridge of his nose. Arlington!

Alcock cursed himself for being a such a fool. He'd been so distracted by the Duchess of Mazarin he hadn't even noticed he was less than two feet away from the head of His Majesty's Secret Service. Now Arlington was gone, and he had nothing to show for his morning's work but the mention of a name.

He sighed and kept walking, losing himself in the crowd.

Aphra and Nell were about to leave the theatre when Elizabeth walked on to the stage from the tiring room, carrying her cloak.

'Are you still here?' Nell called up to her. 'I thought you'd left with the others.'

Elizabeth stopped in the middle of the stage, shaking her head.

'Why isn't my Lord Rochester with you today? What have you done with him, you wicked girl?'

'I have done nothing!' Elizabeth wailed, bursting into tears.

'I was joking!' Nell rushed up on to the stage and led Elizabeth to a bench in the pit.

'I haven't seen him,' Elizabeth went on, sobbing. 'I don't know where he is ... He was supposed to collect me this morning, to bring me to rehearsal. I waited and waited, but he never came!'

Chapter Sixteen

'John!' Aphra called as she walked through her front door. 'John, are you here?'

She looked into the parlour. Empty. And the fire was out.

She went up to the bedchamber. Empty as well. Sheets and blankets lay tangled at the foot of the bed.

She remade the bed, going over the previous night's events in her head, trying to remember exactly what had happened.

Hoyle had attempted to break into the house, convinced she was with a man. He said he had seen someone get out of a coach and enter her house with a key: the same key, he assumed, that she had falsely accused him of not returning.

She had shouted that he'd been spying on her, and he shouted that it was not without reason. He had come to speak to her the night before, after 'the misunderstanding' in his chambers, only to find she had not returned home. And then he had waited, shivering in the cold street until dawn.

He demanded to know where she'd been that night, and who was in there with her now. Who was this coward who would not face him man to man, but preferred to hide behind a woman's skirts?

She finally let him in, so he could see for himself that there was no one there. Then he had been so sincere in his repentance, and so profuse in his apologies.

Damn him, she thought. And damn herself, for being such a fool. He was *always* sincere and he was *always* repentant, and he was *always*, *always*, *always* gone the next day. Why should this time be any different?

She sighed and went down to the kitchen. The basket of food she'd brought back from the almshouse sat open in the middle of the table. Hoyle must have helped himself to breakfast.

She looked inside and saw it was empty except for three last slices of tongue. She reached into the basket and ate them.

She didn't know how she came to have the basket in the first place. It wasn't hers; it must belong to Gospel House. She would have to send it back. Yet another thing to worry about. Yet another expense.

Still hungry, she looked into the larder and grimaced. Nothing there but a bag of oats.

She emptied the contents of her purse on to the kitchen table. One and six. She had no intention of living on bread and water until the play opened. She would have to get more money somehow.

There was something else on the table: the blade she'd found in Elias's pocket. Another thing she'd forgotten about. This seemed as good a time as any to test it.

It was early afternoon, and there were children playing in the middle of the road. She walked out of her front door, inserted the blade into the crack between the shutters and quickly slid it upwards, undoing the latch and opening her parlour window. If not for her tightly laced bodice and long skirts, she could have climbed inside easily. If she were as tall and thin as Elias – and dressed in something unrestricting – she would be inside the house within seconds.

She looked at the children, still playing. They hadn't even noticed her.

She went back inside and sank down on to the settle, shocked at how easy it was to get into her house in broad daylight. She was going to have to do something about that.

But first she needed money.

She went back upstairs and opened the door to her wardrobe, looking for something to sell. She took out two silk petticoats,

159

trimmed with lace, and laid them across the bed. She should be able to get something for those.

She spent a long time staring at the red satin gown she'd had made after the success of her first play. There were so many memories attached to that gown.

She took it out and tossed it on to the bed. It was just a dress, after all.

Buried beneath the laundry at the bottom of the wardrobe she found a pair of high-heeled brocade shoes she'd never worn. She placed them next to the dress and the petticoats.

The inquest into Elias's death was scheduled to start at three. She looked at the clock beside her bed. Only one-thirty. She'd stop at the pawnbrokers, then get something to eat on the way. There was plenty of time.

She reached under the bed for the chamber pot and carried it downstairs, to empty it in the outhouse.

The garden was a mess. Most of her shrubs and herbs had been trodden on the other night. Wherever she looked, stems had been broken and flowers crushed. She walked down the path to the outhouse, and opened the door.

There was dried blood everywhere: the floor, the walls, even the ceiling. She imagined Elias in his death throes, blood spurting from his throat. Then she looked at the inside of the door and saw the clear imprint of a hand, outlined in blood. Had the hand belonged to Elias, clutching at the door as he cowered in terror? Or was this the blood-soaked hand of his murderer, shoving the door aside as he made his escape? There was no way of knowing.

She dropped the chamber pot and ran back inside the house, tears streaming down her cheeks.

She came back a few minutes later, carrying a bucket of water and some rags. If she didn't clean up the mess, no one else would.

*

The Duchess of Portsmouth lay back in her bed, listening to her maid begging her to eat. 'Please, my lady. You will make yourself ill.'

'I don't care if I make myself ill,' Louise told her. 'I don't care if I die.'

'My lady –'

Louise waved a hand to dismiss her. 'Leave me. I wish to be alone.'

'But –' the maid protested, her eyes filling with tears.

Louise gestured towards the door. 'Go.'

'Yes, my lady.'

'And don't come back unless I call you.'

'As you wish, my lady.'

'And close the door behind you.'

The maid gone, Louise sat up and pulled out the sack she'd hidden beneath her pillow. She ate three oranges, then crossed over to the window to toss out the peelings, along with some quail bones left over from breakfast and a mutton bone from the night before.

'Ow! By the mass!' a voice shouted from below.

She hid behind the curtain.

Nell sat at a table in a back room at Whitehall Palace, facing a middle-aged man with thin, bloodless lips and narrow, deep-set eyes. She took a small glass phial from her pocket and placed it on the table in front of her.

The man picked up the phial. 'What is this?'

'I was hoping you could tell me.'

The man regarded her for a moment, his lips curled upwards as if he was smiling while his eyes remained blank and cold. 'Dear Nelly, what *are* you suggesting?'

She gritted her teeth. This was going to be difficult. 'I am suggesting nothing, Will,' she said carefully. 'I came here because I thought you could help me.'

He tilted his head to one side. 'Help you? How?'

161

She took a deep breath, gathering her courage. 'I have heard that there are certain drops used by spies and informers, and that some of these drops are manufactured here in Whitehall, in His Majesty's own laboratory. I have also heard that you have much experience of these potions and are well-versed in their effects.'

'I don't know what you're talking about.'

She stood up, taking the phial. 'I'm sorry I bothered you,' she said, turning to go.

'Wait, Nelly!' the man called after her. 'I meant no offence.'

She stopped and turned to face him.

'You understand I must be cautious,' he said.

'Cautious? I came here because I thought you were my friend!'

He stood, holding out his hand. 'Let me see what you have brought me.'

She handed him the phial.

He took it over to the window, holding it up to the light. 'Where did you get this?'

She hesitated, wondering how much to tell him. She had come here to find out what the phial had contained and whether it had been meant to harm her mother. Not to give an informer – even His Majesty's informer – a step-by-step account of her activities.

'Come, Nelly,' he urged her. 'Think of it as a trade. You wish information, and I *may* be persuaded to give it. Provided you are willing to give information in return.'

'Very well, I agree.' She sat down, resting her elbows on the table. 'You go first.'

It was William Chiffinch's turn to hesitate; Nell could see him deliberating. He put the phial down on the table, then walked over to a cupboard and took out a bottle of wine and two glasses. 'No one but you could twist me so,' he said, pouring them each a glass before sitting down across from her. 'I myself have experience of two different types of drops: one to elicit secrets from the lips of others, the other to prevent those same secrets being elicited from me.'

'What if someone has no secrets?'

'Everyone has secrets, Nelly. Everyone. And it is my job to discover them.' He took a sip of wine before continuing. 'It only takes one or two drops of a certain tincture to loosen a man's tongue to such an extent he will be unable to hold back, but must speak his every thought. No matter how deep, or shallow and fleeting, it must be expressed.' He smiled, looking towards the window. 'His Majesty finds it comforting to know what those around him are thinking.'

'And the other tincture of which you have experience?'

He raised his glass. 'Doctor Goddard's drops. A small amount is sufficient to make a man impervious to the dulling effects of wine, or any other drink.'

Nell started to reach for her own glass, then thought better of it. 'Would either of these drops put a person to sleep?'

'The second one: no. Quite the opposite, in fact. The first one?' He shrugged. 'A person might become drowsy.'

'But would they collapse on to the floor? Would it be impossible to wake them?' Nell persisted. 'And if they did wake briefly, would they fall into unconsciousness again, almost immediately?'

He picked up the phial. 'Is that what happened?'

Nell nodded.

'If this tincture is what I believe it to be, then I would say that whoever administered it did not know what they were doing.' He handed the little bottle to Nell. 'It's not quite empty. See?'

Nell saw a tiny amount of liquid at the bottom. 'Yes.'

He took the phial back and opened it, holding it over Nell's glass. 'One, two,' he counted, carefully shaking two drops into her glass. 'If I wished you to bare your soul to me, that would be more than sufficient for my needs. The effects have been known to last for hours.'

Nell stared at the glass in front of her, giggling nervously.

'My guess,' William Chiffinch continued, 'is that some fool did it like this.' He held the phial upside down as if he was pouring out the contents. 'If this was full, it must have contained enough for twenty doses. Maybe more.'

'Oh my God,' Nell said, 'this was given to my mother! Could it harm her, Will?'

He shook his head. 'I don't think so. Put her to sleep, as you said. Maybe give her a headache for a day or two. Don't worry.'

Nell gathered her strength for her final, most difficult question. 'Did you have something to do with this, Will?'

He looked shocked at the suggestion. 'Lord, no! What interest would I have in your mother? Besides which, you may be assured that if I had been involved the tincture would have been administered properly.'

'Who else has access to such a tincture?'

He made a steeple with his hands. 'The French know of the king's drops; they may have something similar. The Italians, definitely. The Spanish, the Dutch ... they all have their agents, Nelly, wandering freely through the palace. When you have heard as many whispered plots, bribes and threats as I have, you will learn, as I have learned, that no one is to be trusted.'

'No one, Will? But surely you trust me?'

He shrugged. 'As much as I trust anyone. But your mother ...' He leaned back in his chair, crossing him arms. 'So far, this trade of ours has been rather one-sided. It's your turn, Nell. And I think you'd better start from the beginning.'

Aphra closed the shutters, tying a length of rope around the catch, then went upstairs to get the clothes she intended to sell.

She was halfway up the stairs when there was a knock at the door. She sighed and went back down. 'Who's there?' she shouted through the door.

'It is I.'

Aphra groaned at the sound of Elizabeth Decker's voice. 'I was just about to leave,' she said, opening the door.

'Oh,' Elizabeth said, clutching a crumpled handkerchief. Her eyes were red and swollen from crying. 'I'm sorry; I didn't mean to disturb you. It's just...' She gasped for breath, her voice cracking as she began to sob. 'I didn't know where else to go!'

'For God's sake, come inside,' Aphra said, placing an arm around Elizabeth's heaving shoulders. She led her into the parlour and sat beside her on the settle, feeling awkward. How was she supposed to comfort this woman Rochester had inflicted upon her against her will? This woman she could hardly stand? 'There, there,' she said, patting her on the arm.

'It's dark in here,' Elizabeth observed between sobs.

'I know it's dark,' Aphra said, exasperated. 'I closed the shutters because I am going out.'

'Of course, you said you were. I remember now.' Elizabeth blew her nose. 'You're going to the inquest, aren't you? I received a notice asking me to attend, but my Lord Rochester said I shouldn't go, they would just ask a lot of questions.'

The constable had told Aphra that the inquest was only a formality and would be over within minutes, but she didn't want to argue with the stupid woman. She'd only start crying again. 'Elizabeth,' she said, keeping her voice as soft and gentle as possible, 'why are you here?'

It was obviously the wrong thing to ask; Elizabeth started sobbing louder than ever.

'There, there,' she said helplessly as Elizabeth bent double, sinking her head into Aphra's lap.

'It's my Lord Rochester,' Elizabeth wailed, throwing her arms around Aphra's waist. 'I went back to my lodgings to wait for him, as you and Mrs Gwyn suggested, but I've yet to hear one word from him! Not one word!'

'Men are like that,' Aphra said, running her fingers through the other's hair. 'One minute they're there, and the next they're gone.'

'You don't understand,' Elizabeth protested. 'I have seen my Lord Rochester every day for the last five months!'

Ever since he'd made his wager with Buckingham, Aphra thought. But Elizabeth didn't know about that.

'Except for one or two occasions,' Elizabeth added, 'when he had to visit his wife at Adderbury.'

'Maybe that's where he is now.'

'No,' Elizabeth said, 'he would have told me.'

'He may have received an urgent message.'

'He still would have told me. He would have sent a note at least.'

'There is another possibility,' Aphra told her, 'and knowing Rochester as I do I think it the most likely explanation. While we were at the funeral he went out and got very drunk. My guess is that he is either asleep, or nursing a painful head.'

'You may be right,' Elizabeth conceded. She straightened up, wiping her nose with the back of her hand.

'I know I am,' Aphra said. 'Now go back to your lodgings, and you will hear from him soon.'

Elizabeth shook her head. 'I cannot go back there, Mrs Behn. Not yet.'

'Why not?'

'The house where I live is full of actresses, and it is only since I became...' She hesitated, searching for the right word, '...*friendly* with Lord Rochester that they have treated me with any courtesy. And if it should seem that my lord has abandoned me ... Oh, I cannot bear to think of it, Mrs Behn! They all saw how upset I was; they all saw that I was expecting him and he never arrived.'

Aphra reached up to rub her temples. Her short acquaintance with Elizabeth Decker seemed to consist of one headache after another. Or maybe it was the same headache, dragging on day after day, ever since rehearsals began. Either way, it seemed her head was always throbbing. 'Why should you worry what they think?' she said. 'There is no opinion less important than that of an actress.'

'But *I* am an actress,' Elizabeth said, puzzled.

'Sorry. I forgot.'

Elizabeth looked worried, as if she thought Aphra had failed to recognize her once again.

'That was meant to be a jest,' Aphra said tiredly. She stood up, smoothing down her outer skirt. It was damp, thanks to Elizabeth sobbing into the material. 'I'm sorry, but I have to leave; I am expected at the inquest.'

Elizabeth grabbed hold of one of her hands, looking up at her with a pitiful expression. 'May I stay here while you are gone?'

'Whatever for?'

'Please,' Elizabeth pleaded, her mouth quivering. 'I can't go back to my lodgings. I can't.'

'But what if Rochester comes looking for you?'

'I left a note to say I would be here.'

'I don't have time to argue with you,' Aphra said, pulling herself away from the other's tenacious grip. 'Stay here if you wish.' She raised a hand to stop Elizabeth's effusive thanks, and went upstairs to collect the clothing she'd left on the bed. When she came down again, Elizabeth had opened the shutters and was bent over a copy of the play, mouthing her lines.

'Don't let anyone in while I'm gone,' Aphra told her.

'Don't worry, Mrs Behn,' Elizabeth said, looking up from the script. 'If any dare intrude upon this house, I shall make myself look big, like a cat.'

Chapter Seventeen

Aphra walked into the back room of a tavern, where several rows of chairs had been set up facing a table. Mr Gue, the constable, sat alone in the front row, his baker's apron neatly folded on the seat beside him. Nell sat in a corner at the back, next to Bevil Cane. The rest of the seats were empty.

Mr Gue stood as Aphra entered, brushing a bit a flour from his breeches as he wished her a good afternoon.

She went to sit at the back with Nell.

'Where have you been?' Nell whispered. 'I was starting to think you weren't coming.'

Aphra didn't feel like telling her she'd been arguing with a pawnbroker over the price of a petticoat. 'I had a couple of errands to perform,' she said.

'I am glad to see you looking so well,' Bevil Cane said.

'And I am surprised to see you,' Aphra told him. 'Surely there is no reason for you to be here.'

'He only came in the hope of seeing Elizabeth again,' Nell said.

'That is not true,' Mr Cane protested, the sudden redness of his cheeks indicating otherwise. 'Though I admit I would not be averse to meeting the lady again, should the opportunity arise, I am here today in my capacity as a scholar.'

Nell made a face.

'Besides,' he added, looking disappointed, 'with each moment that passes, it seems less likely the divine lady will honour us with an appearance.'

Aphra winced at the thought of how close she had come to

disgracing herself with the young tutor, when everyone knew he was in love with Elizabeth Decker. She must have been mad.

He leaned towards Aphra. 'By the way –'

'I've read the first two scenes,' Aphra interrupted, anticipating his question. 'I hope to read the rest tonight.'

He straightened back up, looking pleased with himself.

The watchman arrived with his dog, followed by a hunchbacked woman who walked with the aid of a stick. They both sat next to Mr Gue in the front row. The coroner entered a moment later. He sat at the table and called the proceedings to order.

As Mr Gue had promised, the inquest was over within minutes.

The watchman testified first, followed by the constable. Both said more or less the same thing: that they had been called to Aphra's house upon the discovery of a corpse, then taken the body to be examined by the searcher.

At this point, the hunchbacked woman rose to give her findings: the man had been stabbed and slashed many times, both front and rear, with a sharp blade, but the cause of death was a slit throat. She went on to say that she couldn't be certain, but she thought the length and depth of the cuts looked more like those of a sword than a knife.

The coroner asked the searcher if she had been able to determine an approximate time of death.

She said he'd obviously been dead some hours when he was brought to her 'stiff and cold'.

Nell was asked what time she found the body. Aphra was asked what time she left the house that day and what time she had returned. She made no mention of John Hoyle, or the bag of sweets. It didn't seem important now Hoyle had proved that not only did he not have a copy of her key, he had no idea how to get inside her house without one. The feebleness of his attempt at breaking in had at last convinced her beyond any doubt that Hoyle could never have been inside her house the day Elias was murdered.

The constable was asked if there were any witnesses. He replied that he had questioned two other persons present in the house, one of them a peer of the realm, and neither had seen anything. He later spoke to several neighbours; not one of them saw or heard anything. He also added that he thought the searcher was right, the man must have been killed with a long sword rather than a knife, or else the murderer's clothes would have been splashed with the dead man's blood, and surely a man in blood-soaked clothing could not escape unnoticed in broad daylight, 'even in these infamous times'.

The coroner declared the cause of death as: 'Murder by person or persons unknown', adjourned the inquest, and left.

Aphra rubbed her neck, sighing with relief. The nightmare was over at last. There was nothing more for her to do. The dead had been buried, the inquest had been adjourned. 'Bring the curtain down,' she said. 'It's over. It's finally over.'

'That would seem to be the end of it,' Bevil Cane agreed, rising from his seat. 'There are no witnesses, so no more action will be taken. The dead man was only a beggar, after all.' He took a watch from his pocket, checked the time and kissed both women on the hand. 'Pray excuse me, but I have another engagement.'

Nell waited until he was gone, then leaned forward, reaching into her pocket for something which she held out for Aphra's inspection. 'I didn't want Bevil to see this; it would only worry him.'

Aphra looked at the object in Nell's hand: a small glass phial.

'I found it in the road outside Gospel House,' Nell whispered. 'I saw it just in time; I nearly stepped on it.'

'When was this?' Aphra took the phial from her, holding it up to have a better look.

'While Jamie and Bevil were helping you into the coach.'

'Why didn't you mention this last night? Why didn't you show it to anyone?'

Nell rolled her eyes. 'Can you imagine how Elizabeth might have reacted? Or Bevil? I tried to tell you, but you were in no state to listen.'

Aphra opened the phial, sniffing its contents.

'It was empty when I found it,' Nell said. 'I've since had it refilled.'

Chapter Eighteen

Aphra approached her front door, struggling with a loaf of bread, a jug of beer, a sack of flour and a calf's head.

She saw to her relief that the shutters over her front window had been closed. Closed shutters meant Elizabeth must have gone.

She went inside and found the house dark and silent, the fire in the parlour nearly out. She put down the food, flung open the shutters and tossed some wood on to the fire. The script Elizabeth had been studying lay open on the settle. Several letters had come while Aphra was out; Elizabeth had stacked them on the desk.

Aphra decided to ignore the letters for the moment; she'd deal with them later. She picked up the calf's head and carried it into the kitchen.

The basket she'd brought from Gospel House was still on the table where she'd left it. She told herself she must arrange to send it back before that awful Barrow woman had her arrested for stealing it; it seemed just the sort of thing the old harridan would do.

Someone was knocking at her front door. She put down the calf's head and went into the parlour. She looked out the window and saw two men in the red cloth coats of His Majesty's Palace Guard. 'Oh God, no,' she said.

She could think of only one reason they would be at her door: to arrest her. Not for stealing the basket – she knew Mrs Barrow wouldn't really go that far – but for debt. She still owed fifty pounds to a moneylender, and though she had promised to pay him as soon as the new play opened there was nothing to stop him from putting her into prison until then.

Her first thought was to escape. But how? She could never climb over that high wall at the back. She was as trapped as Elias had been.

How many times had she vowed she would die before she would ever let herself be taken to prison again? For that matter, she asked herself, how many times had she sworn she would have nothing more to do with John Hoyle? How many times had she vowed to replace Elizabeth Decker? She might swear her various determinations from morning to night, but in the end, it seemed all her vows had been nothing more than empty words.

She would offer no resistance. She walked towards the door, cursing herself and her fate, and opened it.

'Mrs Aphra Behn?' one of the men said.

She nodded.

'Will you be so kind as to come with us, please?'

She started to step outside, then hesitated, thinking back to her previous incarceration. Nothing was free in prison; she'd need money for food, as well as an assortment of fees. Fees for the turning of keys. Fees for putting on irons and fees for taking them off again. Fees for the chamberlain, the gaoler, the porter, the book-keeper. Fees for a bit of straw to lie on.

She'd be damned if she'd leave her calf's head to rot; fresh meat ought to be worth something towards her garnish. It might make the difference between being housed on an upper floor with a window or left to languish in a cellar. 'There's something I'd like to bring with me,' she said. 'It's in the kitchen.'

The two men exchanged puzzled glances. 'If you wish,' said the first one.

Hortense Mancini stood by her bedchamber window, staring out across the river.

'And then the groom pulled the horse's reins so hard, the horse reared up and kicked him. We all laughed, and then the stable-master said that I could ... Are you listening, Hortense?'

'Hmm?' Hortense turned to look at Anne, who was lying on her stomach across the bed, wearing nothing but a silk chemise, her head propped up on one arm. 'A horse kicked a groom and you laughed. I heard you.'

'And then the stable-master said – ' Anne continued as Hortense turned back to the window.

'He said you could give the horse an apple,' Hortense interrupted. 'You've told me this before.'

'Have I?'

'Yes,' Hortense said, watching two men moving about on the opposite bank of the river.

'Oh.' Anne paused for a moment. 'Did I tell you about the time I performed in a masque at Hampton Court?'

Hortense saw that the men were carrying fishing rods. She watched as they sat down a few feet apart, casting their lines into the water. She thought it seemed late in the day to go fishing. 'I have a bad feeling,' she said.

'About what?'

Hortense shook her head, still watching the men. 'Nothing,' she said. 'It's probably something I ate.' She turned away from the window, forcing herself to smile. 'Get dressed. Let's go downstairs.'

A group of people had gathered into a circle at one end of a corridor leading towards His Majesty's apartments, listening intently to someone speaking. Nell walked towards them, dressed in the black mourning she had worn the night before.

She noticed a young man standing alone to one side of the circle a few feet away from the others; she approached him, holding out one of her cards. She didn't know him, but that didn't matter. She had hundreds of cards; enough for everyone.

By the time she reached the spot where he'd been standing, he was gone.

. She looked about, puzzled. She thought she saw the top of his blond periwig looming behind a woman's head on the opposite side of the circle, but she couldn't be certain it was him.

Then she realized who was speaking. She forgot about the young man and moved in to listen.

'You need to consult a physician without delay,' the Earl of Rochester said, staring down at the outstretched hand of an overweight man who looked at least sixty. 'You are a stout-hearted fellow, not prone to complain, but you have for some time suffered from a painful swelling of the joints in . . .' He paused, tracing a line across the man's palm. 'I believe it's on the left side,' he said, raising the man's hand slightly in order to get a better look. 'Possibly the leg or the foot; I'm not quite sure.'

The man gawped at Rochester, amazed.

'And you have been troubled with visions and dreams these past nights. This has a simple cause, easily remedied. You have been eating too much rich food too soon before retiring. It is this that gives you strange dreams, and this that gives you the gout. You need to cease this bad practice at once, and perhaps lose a little blood.' Rochester prodded the man's palm with his finger, shaking his head. 'Oh, good sir, you are full of blood — too much so. You need to lose . . .' He pursed his lips, thinking. 'About five ounces, I'd say.'

'Lord save me, everything you say is true! I have been troubled with the gout for some time, and have only this morning spoken to a doctor.'

'I am glad to hear it, friend,' Rochester said. 'I feared I would have to insist you seek medical attention. It is a great relief to hear you have already done so.'

'But that is not all,' the man said excitedly. 'What you have just told me: it's almost word for word what he said! He told me that I must not eat late at night, and that I needed to be bled! How did you know? How *could* you know?'

'Whatever small gift of prophecy I may have been born with, I have managed to develop through years of hard work and study.'

The crowd pushed forward, hands outstretched, each pleading to be next.

'Please, please,' Rochester said. 'One at a time, I beg you.' He nodded towards a man in a dark periwig. 'You, sir.'

The man stepped forward, removing his gloves.

Within a few minutes, he too was proclaiming that everything the earl told him was absolutely correct.

'He must be in league with the devil!' someone muttered.

'Devil or not,' said another, 'please my lord, read my hand next.'

'No more, good people, I beg you,' Rochester said, dramatically raising a hand to his forehead. 'My gift cannot tolerate prolonged use; I find it too draining. Another time, perhaps, but now I need to rest.'

There was much muttering of discontent and disappointment until the earl suggested they seek out the lovely Duchess of Mazarin, who he understood to be an equally avid practitioner of the art of chiromancy, though perhaps lacking some of his skill.

'I'm sure the practice would do her good,' he added as the crowd around him dispersed to look for the duchess.

'Does Hortense really read palms?' Nell asked when the others were gone.

Rochester shrugged. 'She does now.'

'You're wicked, John.'

He sighed. 'Not wicked, enough, Nell. Not wicked enough.' He didn't look at all well; his eyes were bloodshot, his face pale and haggard. He looked down at her black dress. 'You're in mourning.'

Nell rolled her eyes. 'Not only a prophet, but observant as

well.' She immediately went into her act, sniffling and dabbing at her eyes as she handed him a card. 'I know you will agree this is a great loss to us all.'

'And you call me wicked!' he exclaimed a moment later.

'You will come?'

'I would not miss it,' he said.

'Yet you missed this morning's rehearsal,' Nell reminded him. 'Have you ceased to care about your wager?'

'It is not the wager I have ceased to care about,' he said, turning to walk away.

This wasn't like him. 'John! Wait,' Nell called, picking up her skirts to run after him. 'What is it? What's wrong?'

He stopped and turned to face her. 'Would you like me to read your palm? I can tell you things, Nell! Things that will astound you!'

Chapter Nineteen

Aphra felt like kicking herself when she saw where they had brought her.

'Your head, madam,' one of the guards reminded her.

'Perhaps I could leave it in the coach?'

The man regretted he could not allow it; the coach was needed elsewhere.

She nodded, her face red with embarrassment as she followed him towards the palace. To her relief, he led her around the back way, where they were less likely to be seen. They entered through a door at the bottom of a narrow, twisting stairway, and climbed all the way to the top.

He led her along a maze of dimly lit corridors lined with doors. He finally stopped and knocked on one of them.

'Yes?' a shrill voice called from the room beyond.

'You may go in,' the guard said, opening the door.

She entered a large room overlooking the river. The door behind her closed. Another door led into a room to her left. She noticed it was ajar.

A man in a black wig sat behind a desk, quill pen poised above a stack of papers. The only light came from the candles on the man's desk, bathing him in a pool of light while the rest of the room remained wreathed in shadows. She stood in the darkness, watching him. The way he was lit, she couldn't help wondering if she'd been brought there to view a particularly impressive tableau: *Important Man At Work*.

It must have been ten years since their last meeting, but she recognized him at once. His dress was as eccentric as ever: an embroidered shirt with an old-fashioned ruff collar topped with a short Spanish-style cape, bright red in colour. And he still wore that plaster across his nose to commemorate a minor injury received decades ago. The pompous ass. No wonder the court wits found him such a figure of fun.

It was at least a minute before he looked up. That was one of the many things she remembered about him: he liked to keep people waiting. It reminded them who was in charge. 'Ah, Mrs Behn,' he said as he finally deigned to acknowledge her presence, 'pray have a seat.'

She thought back to the way he had left her stranded, penniless, behind enemy lines. She owed him nothing – least of all civility. 'I trust this will not take long,' she said, remaining in the shadows.

Henry Bennet, Earl of Arlington, head of His Majesty's Secret Service, smiled and spread his hands, palms up, as if to show he had nothing to hide. 'Not long.'

'Then I prefer to stand, my lord.'

Arlington lowered his hands, no longer smiling. 'And I prefer you to be where I can see you.' He gestured towards a chair facing the desk. 'Sit down, Mrs Behn.'

It was all she could do not to cringe at the sound of his high-pitched voice carefully enunciating every syllable. She walked over to the chair and sat, cradling the calf's head in her lap.

Arlington's eyes widened. 'It has been much too long,' he said, staring at the head. 'I trust you have been keeping well?'

'So you have brought me here after all these years in order to enquire about my health. Thank you for your interest, my lord.'

Arlington leaned back in his chair, tapping his fingers on the desk top. He was still staring at the calf's head. 'Time has changed you, Mrs Behn.'

She put the head on the floor. 'It changes us all. Why am I here, my lord?'

Arlington finally pulled his gaze up to her face. 'Pray, what can you tell me about a man named Matthew Cavell?'

Her mouth dropped open. Why would the head of His Majesty's Secret Service wish to question her about a dead pauper?

Arlington nodded, noting her reaction. 'I see you know him.'

'I once knew a man by that name,' she said carefully. 'But only briefly, and a long time ago.'

'Oh?' Arlington said, his eyes darting towards the door to Aphra's left. 'That's not what I heard.'

'Then you heard incorrectly.' Aphra turned her head to see what he was looking at. She leaned forward, squinting, but it was impossible to see anything; the door was open by less than an inch, and the room beyond was dark.

Arlington abruptly shifted his gaze forward. 'You knew of his death, and you distributed these.' He held up one of her printed cards.

'I did,' she said, wondering where he'd got it. Someone must have given it to him, but who? Whoever was standing behind that door, she decided. She would have loved to know who it was.

'Yet you knew him only briefly, and a long time ago.' He crossed his arms.

She threw up her hands. 'I hadn't seen the man for fourteen years!'

'Then how did you know he was dead?'

'I didn't!'

Arlington narrowed his eyes, his shrill voice scathing. 'You had funeral invitations printed.'

'I mean I didn't know he was dead until after I arrived at Gospel House. I happened by chance to meet his brother — whom I had also not seen for fourteen years — and he told me where Matthew was. I had no idea I would find him murdered.'

'How *close* were you to Matthew Cavell?'

'I knew him only slightly, my lord.'

Arlington looked dubious. 'Were you close to his brother, then?'

'Certainly not. I hardly knew him. I told you, I had not seen either man for fourteen years.'

Arlington shook his head. 'A man you hardly know is found murdered in your house of office, then you bury this man you hardly knew alongside his brother, whom you knew only slightly.' He leaned back in his chair, drumming his fingers on the desk top. 'To me, this seems ... unusual.'

'I had good reason, my lord.' She told him the story of her father's funeral in Surinam.

'Why would he go to such expense for you?' Arlington persisted. 'Were you his mistress?'

'No, I was not!' Aphra protested angrily. 'There was never the least hint of intrigue between us!'

'You could not be expected to say otherwise,' Arlington observed drily.

Aphra gritted her teeth, seething. 'My lord, I resent – '

'Yes, yes,' he said, waving a dismissive hand. 'Surinam, your father, a near stranger and his brother acting as the only pallbearers, then no further attempt at contact for fourteen years.' He leaned across the desk, his dark eyes gleaming in the candlelight. 'Who else, besides yourself, was acquainted with both Matthew Cavell and his brother?'

She had a horrible feeling she was falling into some kind of trap. 'My lord, I assure you I have no information about the death of either man.'

He looked down at his notes and sighed. 'Thank you, Mrs Behn. You may go.'

She picked up her calf's head and left.

Nell looked at her hand, then at Rochester's face. He'd told her a young man had recently surprised her. He had to be talking about Jamie; his insistence on attending the funeral last night had been a surprise to everyone. Then he said she had encountered someone who was not what he seemed – he had to be talking about Fergus O'Bannion. 'How do you do that, John? How can you tell all that from a few lines on my palm?'

'Years of study and practice,' he said, pretending to look at something over her shoulder.

When did Rochester find the time for years of study and practice? She knew he was lying by the way he refused to meet her gaze, but she also knew a way to make him tell the truth. Of course she'd promised Aphra she would put the drops away and never use them, but just this once couldn't hurt.

She widened her eyes, looking impressed. 'Someone so dedicated to study deserves a glass of wine,' she said, fingering the small glass phial in her pocket. 'Wait there, and allow me to get you one.'

Aphra expected to find the guard who'd brought her waiting outside the door to take her home again. He wasn't there. It seemed she was expected to make her own way home. How typical.

She started down the corridor towards the stairs, then stopped.

Someone had given one of her invitations to Arlington, and someone had been in the adjoining room, listening. They had to be one and the same person. She decided to find out who.

She checked no one was nearby. The corridor was deserted. She walked back to the door and pressed her ear against it. She could hear the murmur of voices, but it was impossible to make out any words. No wonder the internal door had been left ajar for the benefit of Arlington's eavesdropper.

She knelt down to look through the keyhole – not easy in her tight bodice and voluminous skirts. All she could see was a keyhole-shaped chunk of flickering shadows. She turned her head so that her ear was next to the keyhole, just in time to hear the sound of a chair being pushed across the floor. She leapt up and hurried away.

She hid around a corner further down the hall, waiting to

see who came out of the office. The door opened a moment later. A grey-haired man in filthy clothes stepped out into the corridor. Aphra gasped, unable to believe her eyes. She'd met this man only two days earlier, in St Giles.

He walked away in the other direction, disappearing around another corner. She picked up her skirts to run after him. She didn't like people informing on her to Arlington, and she certainly didn't like people spying on her conversations. She was going to have a talk with this man.

By the time she reached the other corner, he was gone.

She looked up and down, but he was nowhere to be seen. It was almost as if he'd vanished through the wall.

Louise de Kéroualle was sitting up in bed eating an apple when her maid burst into the room without knocking.

'How dare you?' Louise demanded, shoving the half-eaten apple under the blanket. 'I told you I was not to be disturbed!'

The maid crossed to the bed, holding out a card. 'I am sorry, my lady, but I thought you would wish to see this at once.'

Louise snatched the card from her and examined it, frowning. It was a printed invitation, bordered with skulls. '*Mon dieu*!' she shrieked as she read the words printed across the centre of the card. '*Mon dieu*! I will kill her! I will murder her with my bare hands!' She leapt out of bed, tearing the card in two. 'Tell Monsieur Courtin I wish to speak to him immediately.'

Rochester leaned against the wall, staring at the ceiling. The glass in his hand was full.

Nell could hardly contain herself; he hadn't touched his wine. 'Let's drink a toast, John,' she urged him, raising her own glass to her lips. 'To Elizabeth's triumphant performance.'

He groaned and shook his head. 'I will not drink a toast to her, Nell. Not ever again.'

'Why not?'

'I don't want to talk about it.'

So that was why he hadn't come to rehearsal. He was angry with Elizabeth. But why? Yet another reason to get him to drink his wine. 'What will you drink a toast to, then?'

'Nothing,' he muttered. 'Nothing at all.'

'To nothing at all, then,' Nell said, holding up her glass.

Rochester sighed and took a drink.

Nell watched him, waiting. Nothing happened. He was still being unnaturally quiet – not at all like the Rochester she knew. 'Where were you last night?' she asked him.

'At home,' he said, still staring at the ceiling.

She was starting to wonder if she'd stolen the wrong drops. Maybe she'd taken the ones that made a man impervious to wine rather than the ones that compelled him to speak his every thought. Or maybe Rochester was immune to the drops' effects. In either case, she decided, it couldn't do him any harm to have a tiny bit more.

Aphra knocked on the door of 79 Pall Mall. The maid opened it. 'Mrs Behn! I fear my mistress has gone out –'

'It is Madam Gwyn I wish to speak to,' Aphra interrupted, adding, 'If she is well enough, of course.'

The maid glanced at the head Aphra was holding, then led her into the parlour to wait.

Aphra had been sitting for less than a minute when she heard rapid footsteps approaching. The door swung open. To her dismay she saw it was not Nell's mother but Bevil Cane who rushed into the room, his face flushed with excitement. 'Mrs Behn! Lucy told me you were here. Does this mean you've finished my play?'

She shook her head. 'Not yet. I am here to enquire after the health of Madam Gwyn.'

'Oh,' he said, disappointed.

'Is she feeling better?'

'I believe so, though she has spent the day in bed.' His gaze moved to her lap. 'You are holding a calf's head.'

'It's a prop for my new play.'

She was relieved to see the maid standing in the parlour doorway. 'Mrs Gwyn says she will be happy to see you, but bids you come upstairs to her chamber as she is somewhat indisposed.'

Aphra stood to follow the maid.

'I'll take her, Lucy,' Bevil Cane said.

The maid curtsied and left.

'This way,' Bevil said, leading Aphra towards the stairs. He knocked on Madam Gwyn's door a moment later. 'Mother Gwyn. Mrs Behn is here to see you. She wishes to enquire after your health.'

'For God's sake, Bevil,' the old woman called from the room beyond. 'Don't keep her standing out in the hall!'

He opened the door, ushering Aphra through.

Madam Gwyn sat in a large bed with sterling silver posts and velvet curtains, her back propped up against a stack of pink satin pillows. She wore a white shawl over her nightdress with a matching cap over her hair, and was clutching a half-empty bottle of brandy. 'Sit down, little duck,' she said, patting the bed beside her.

Aphra placed the calf's head on the floor and sat on the edge of the bed.

Madam Gwyn leaned her head to one side, looking over Aphra's shoulder. 'Are you still there, Bevil? Mrs Behn and I both speak English; we don't need you to interpret.'

'You'll call me if you need anything?'

'Yes, yes.' Madam Gwyn waved a hand to dismiss him. 'Now go along, dear. We'll be fine.'

'As you wish.' He bowed and left the room.

Madam Gwyn sighed and took a long drink of brandy from the bottle. 'He says I frightened him to death last night,' she explained, wiping her mouth with the back of her hand. 'Now he won't leave me alone, for wishing to help me with everything. At least I had a few hours' peace this afternoon when he went off to his meeting.'

'Meeting?'

'At Gresham College,' Madam Gwyn said. 'He goes every Thursday afternoon, though he nearly didn't today. I had to insist I would be all right, with only the maid and the cook and God knows how many other damned servants to look after me. All my life I've had to take care of others and now they think I can't take care of myself.' She drank from the bottle again. 'I'm forgetting my manners,' she said, thrusting the bottle towards Aphra. 'Would you like a sip?'

'No, thank you.'

Madam Gwyn nodded towards the floor. 'That's an impressive head.'

'I'm going to make a pie.'

The old woman closed her eyes, letting her head drop back against the pillows. 'I used to make a wonderful calf's head pie. People used to clamour for my pies, for anything I cooked, but in this house they do their best to keep me away from the kitchen.' She opened her eyes and took another drink of brandy. 'My daughter's servants don't like me touching things, you see.'

'Madam Gwyn, I need your help with something.'

The old woman straightened up, placing the bottle on her bedside table. 'What is it, little duck?'

'The other day when Nell and I went to St Giles, we met a man who said he used to know you. I think his name is Toby.'

'Toby Rainbeard. Nell told me you saw him.'

'What do you know about him?'

'I know enough to curse him as a thief and a scoundrel,' Madam Gwyn said. 'After my husband died in prison, leaving me a penniless widow with two small children to feed, I was fortunate enough to obtain a position managing a tavern.'

Aphra had heard it was more a brothel than a tavern, but she said nothing, keeping her face impassive.

'It was there I first encountered Toby Rainbeard,' Madam Gwyn went on. 'He would come in now and again, bringing treats for my little ones. I'd known him some years when one evening I was called into the kitchen for some reason I no longer remember and asked him to keep watch on the bar should any require a drink while I was gone. That night, when I counted up the takings, nearly five pounds was missing. I never saw him after that.'

'Did you summon the watch?'

Madam Gwyn shook her head. 'This was St Giles. There was no watch to summon. And even if there had been, I would not dare call for him.' She winked. 'I didn't have a licence.'

'But when we met Toby Rainbeard the other day Nell believed him to be your friend.'

'She was no longer with me by then. She was seven when she obtained her employment as servant to Madam Ross.'

Another notorious brothel-keeper, Aphra thought. 'I hope you will pardon me for saying you should hardly have been surprised at what happened, managing an establishment as you did in a thieves' sanctuary such as St Giles.'

'I knew Toby to be a footpad, but I never knew a padder so low as to steal from his friends.'

'So you knew he was a thief,' Aphra said. 'Did you ever suspect him to be an informer?'

The old woman reached for her bottle. 'No, child. Never. But now I think of it, I heard of several arrests of people I knew . . .' She took a large gulp of brandy.

'Mrs Gwyn, do you have any idea where I might find him now?'

'Why? What possible reason could you have for wanting to find a rogue like him?'

'I just want to talk to him,' Aphra said.

Madam Gwyn leaned against her pillows, clutching her bottle. 'The last time I saw Toby Rainbeard, Cromwell was still

Lord Protector. And I never knew where the rogue lived even then. I'm sorry I cannot be more help to you, duckling.'

'You've been more help than you know,' Aphra said.

'Take my advice, and keep well away from that old villain. I promise you, he's not to be trusted.'

Aphra walked homewards along the Strand. There had to be someone else she could talk to. Someone who had known Toby more recently than under the Protectorate.

She raised a hand to hail a passing hackney carriage.

The driver pulled back on the reins, bringing the coach to a stop. 'Where to, my lady?'

Chapter Twenty

Nell stood in the doorway of a massive ballroom, swaying to the music as she watched the others dance. They were doing one of those lively country dances where everyone moved in a large circle, changing partners every few steps. 'Come, Nelly,' a voice said beside her.

She turned to see the Duke of Buckingham, face flushed, periwig askew, offering her his arm.

'I mustn't dance, George. Can't you see I'm in mourning?'

'Oh, a pox on your mourning,' he said, leading her on to the floor to join a group of dancers. 'I hear you are plotting against me,' he said as they promenaded behind the others, touching hands.

Everyone in the circle swung around to walk the other way. 'I don't know what you mean,' she said.

'You have been aiding Rochester in his wager.'

'Oh, that.'

'It's hopeless, you know. You'll never win.'

The men began to circle in one direction, while the women went the other.

'Hello, Charles,' Nell said, coming face to face with the king.

'Nelly, I've seen those cards of yours,' the king said, taking her hand. 'And I must tell you, I think you're being wicked.'

'I thought that's what you liked about me, sire.'

The king raised an eyebrow, but said nothing.

'I have missed your company,' Nell said, lowering her voice suggestively. 'Will you visit me tonight?'

'But you're in mourning,' the king reminded her.

'A black dress may be as easily removed as any other.'

The king laughed, his gaze moving along her body. 'Await me at midnight.'

Once again, the men and women moved in opposite directions. 'I shall expect you,' she called after the king, loud enough for all to hear.

The next time the circle stopped, she was face to face with the Earl of Arlington. They finished the dance in silence.

Aphra raised a handkerchief to her nose as the coach crossed the bridge at Ludgate Hill, then turned north along the eastern bank of the foul-smelling Fleet River, taking her to the prison.

A porter directed her to 'Bartholomew Fair', which turned out to be a dank cellar crowded with bodies. People lay huddled, shivering and coughing, on straw that stank of sickness and excrement. A few had threadbare blankets; most did not.

She found the woman she was looking for sitting with her back against a damp wall, cradling her sleeping children in her lap. Her legs were in irons.

Aphra knelt down beside her. 'Mrs Adams?'

The woman didn't respond.

'It's Aphra Behn. I came to your house with Nell Gwyn.'

'Nell Gwyn?' The woman turned her head, her grey hair hanging lankly across her narrow face, her eyes red from crying. 'You're not Nell Gwyn.'

'No, Mrs Adams. I was with Nell Gwyn. I'm Aphra Behn. Don't you remember? We met two days ago.'

She shook her head. 'Two days? Is it only two days?'

'Meldrick Bridger told me what happened. I'm truly sorry.'

'Meldrick's granddaughter,' Mrs Adams said, 'how is she?'

Aphra thought of the child she'd seen lying ill in a cot. For all she knew the girl was dead by now. 'I understand she's getting better.'

'Praise God for that,' she said, closing her eyes.

'Mrs Adams,' Aphra said, thinking the woman had gone to sleep. 'Mrs Adams?'

'I fear for my own children,' Mrs Adams said, opening her eyes again. 'How long can they survive in this dungeon? The boy already has a fever. Look how he sweats despite the cold.' Her eyes filled with tears. 'Twelve pounds. They would kill my children for a debt of twelve pounds!'

Aphra sighed. It seemed her calf's head was destined to be used as garnish after all. She handed it to Mrs Adams. 'Offer this to the keeper in exchange for better quarters. It should be worth a few days on an upper floor, at least.' She reached into her purse, taking out a coin. 'And this should be enough to have your irons removed.'

'God bless you,' Mrs Adams said, choking back a sob. 'I only wish there was some way I could repay you.'

'There is.' Aphra leaned forward. 'Tell me everything you know about Toby Rainbeard.'

Mrs Adams wiped the tears from her cheeks, her filthy hands leaving streaks across her face. 'Toby Rainbeard? There's little I can tell you. He came to my house in search of lodging, perhaps an hour before you arrived with Mrs Gwyn.'

'An hour?' Aphra repeated. 'I thought he lived with you.'

Mrs Adams shook her head. 'He said he'd met someone who used to lodge with me at a tavern in Alsatia.'

It seemed Mr Rainbeard spent his time moving back and forth between thieves' sanctuaries, Aphra thought grimly. 'Did he mention the name of the tavern?'

'I believe it was the Blacksmith's Arms.'

'Is there anything more you can tell me? Anything at all?'

'About Toby Rainbeard? No, nothing.'

'Mr Bridger said a man came to see him shortly after Mrs Gwyn and I left — '

'Yes, I remember. I'd never seen him before either.'

'Do you know what he wanted with Mr Rainbeard? Where they went?'

Mrs Adams shook her head again. 'I have no idea. I'm sorry.'

'What did the man look like?'

'Tall,' Mrs Adams said. 'Dark hair, turning grey. I would guess him to be about fifty. He seemed upset about something.'

Aphra was about to get up when another question occurred to her. 'Have you ever met or heard of a man named Fergus O'Bannion?'

'No, never.'

'What can you tell me about a man named Matthew Cavell?'

'Nothing,' she said, looking away.

'What about Elias Cavell? What can you tell me about him?'

The woman lowered her eyes, not wishing to answer.

'I know he used to lodge with you whenever he had the money,' Aphra prompted her.

Mrs Adams remained silent.

She thought back to her first visit to St Giles, and how no one in the house would speak about Elias. 'Nothing you say will harm Elias now. He is dead, Mrs Adams.'

The woman gasped. 'Elias? Dead?'

'I saw him buried.'

'So his protector failed him,' Mrs Adams said.

'Protector? What do you mean?'

Mrs Adams's son whimpered softly in his sleep. 'Hush,' she said, stroking the boy's sweating forehead. She raised her head to look at Aphra. 'I had not seen Elias for some weeks, perhaps a month. Then he knocked on my door late on Monday night. He asked to speak to me outside, so the others would not hear. He then told me that if any strangers came to my door I was to deny I ever knew him. I asked him why, and he said that some-one might come looking for him because of something he had stolen – '

'Did he say what it was?' Aphra interrupted. 'Or who he stole it from?'

'I asked him those very same questions, but he refused to tell me. He said it was best I didn't ask, as even the knowledge of what he possessed could be dangerous. I said if the knowledge of something was dangerous, surely the possession of it was more so. He said it might be, had he not found himself a powerful protector. I asked who would take an interest in such as him, and he said I would be amazed, though he dared not say more until his current business was completed, when he would become a wealthy man.' Mrs Adams wiped a tear from the corner of her eye. 'I thought he was drunk. I didn't believe a word of it. Until just as he said, a stranger came to my door asking if I knew him.'

'Are you referring to Toby Rainbeard?'

'No,' Mrs Adams said, 'I was referring to *you*.'

'I saw you dancing with Arlington,' a voice said as Nell left the dance floor.

She turned to face the Duke of Monmouth. 'It wasn't by choice, I assure you.'

Monmouth looked about, then lowered his voice. 'What did he say to you?'

Nell laughed. 'Not a word. Lord Arlington never speaks to me for fear I might speak back.'

He took her by the arm and led her to a quiet corner. 'Look at them,' he said, nodding towards the doorway where the French ambassador appeared to be deep in conversation with the Duchess of Mazarin. 'She had dinner at his house last night,' Monmouth whispered. 'Do you understand what this means?'

'She was hungry?' Nell whispered back.

'Courtin is recruiting agents to promote the interests of France at court. They say he has offered Mazarin a similar arrangement to the one he has with Portsmouth.'

'Really?' Nell said. 'And what exactly is his arrangement with Squintabella?'

'She receives gifts of money and jewels from the government of France in exchange for using her influence on my father. It's been going on for years, Nell; I would have thought you knew about it.'

'They pay Squintabella? S'teeth, they should spend their money more wisely.'

Several people approached the Duchess of Mazarin, holding out their hands. Hortense sighed, then nodded, reaching for the hand of the nearest one. It seemed Rochester had told the truth about one thing after all: the Duchess of Mazarin did read palms.

Monsieur Courtin moved to one side; it seemed his conversation with the duchess was over.

Nell ran her fingers through her hair. 'Excuse me, Jamie.'

She crossed over to Monsieur Courtin, putting on her sweetest smile.

'Ah, Mistress Nelly,' Courtin said, bending down to kiss her hand. 'Seeing you is always a pleasure.' He tilted his head towards Hortense and her crowd of admirers. 'You should ask the duchess to read your palm. She's very good.'

'Perhaps another time,' Nell said. She took one of her cards from her pocket and handed it to him. 'I find this evening too fraught with emotion for me to indulge in such frivolous entertainments.'

'I have seen one of these cards already,' the French ambassador said, shaking his head. 'Though the one I saw had been ripped in two.'

Nell laughed out loud. So her cards had found their way to Squintabella. She'd hoped they would. 'Tell me, Monsieur Courtin, are you really wasting the French treasury on that weeping willow? Everyone knows she has no influence left at court whatsoever. And as for Hortense,' she added confidentially, 'she's not really the sort you want for an agent. She hasn't been in England long; she doesn't understand our ways. You want someone with knowledge and experience. Someone with real influence, not only with His Majesty but with his entire court. In other words,' she said, batting her eyelashes, 'you want me.'

The French ambassador was about to say something when he was interrupted by Rochester, lurching towards them.

'Nell!' Rochester said, grabbing hold of her arm. 'There is something I wish to ask you.' He was slurring his words so badly she could hardly understand him.

'Not now, John.'

He shook his head. 'Now. I have to ask you now.'

Monsieur Courtin bowed and excused himself, murmuring that he would speak to her another time.

'God's flesh, John,' Nell said, pulling her arm away. 'Could you not see I was speaking to the ambassador?'

Rochester leaned forward, squinting. 'Was he trying to recruit you as a spy?'

'No, I was trying to recruit myself, you blockhead! All these years the French have been paying Squintabella to do absolutely nothing. Why shouldn't they pay me for doing nothing as well?'

'Wicked, Nell, you are wicked!' Rochester slapped his thigh, laughing so hard he bent over double. Several heads turned to look at him.

'Maybe we should sit down, John,' Nell said quietly.

He stopped laughing as suddenly as he'd started. 'Nelly, why do you remain faithful to someone who has never been, and never will be, faithful to you?'

'Come with me,' she said, leading him out into the hallway.

'He's unfaithful, Nell,' Rochester taunted her in a sing-song voice. 'Unfaithful. Unfaithful.'

She looked up and down to make sure no one was about. 'Are you referring to His Majesty?' she hissed.

'God's death, who else _could_ I be referring to? Who else is there?'

'No one, of course,' she said, mentally counting the number of drops she'd given him. It hadn't seemed much at the time.

'Of course,' he repeated bitterly. 'Of course.' He walked over to a padded bench along the wall and sat down, wringing his hands. 'He plays you and Portsmouth against each other like pawns in a game of chess, and now he dangles his new prize, Mazarin, in front of you both, goading you. Baiting you. And that's not all, Nelly. You know there have been others. There have been dozens – maybe even hundreds – of others. Why do you put up with it? Why? Tell me.'

She thought the whole point of the drops was that she could *ask* questions, not have to answer them. 'He's the king,' she said. 'And even if he wasn't . . . I love him, John.'

'You love the cully of Britain,' he muttered. 'There is no man more flagrant in his intrigues, and yet you say you love him. I, on the other hand, have always treated women with the greatest gentleness and civility – '

Nell snorted, trying not to laugh.

' – and what do I get for it? Betrayal. Lies and betrayal. I often wonder how different my life might be if I had a woman who'd be true to me, no matter what I did, a woman I could trust – '

'Crimine!' Nell said, wishing she'd never given him a single drop. 'I can usually tolerate you when you're drunk, John, but tonight you are more than a soul can bear.'

'Am I drunk?' he said, swaying slightly. 'I suppose I might be. Does it matter?'

'I'll talk to you when you're sober,' Nell said, walking away.

Buckingham approached her the moment she returned to the ballroom. 'What did that young popinjay Monmouth want? I saw you talking to him earlier.'

'Jamie?' She shrugged. 'He sees Papist spies everywhere he looks.'

'He may be right, Nelly. Be careful what you say, and who you are seen with. I could not help noticing you spoke to Courtin as well.'

'God's teeth! Are you spying on me, George?'

'Just be careful, Nelly,' Buckingham told her. 'That's all I'm saying.'

'Do I need to be careful of you as well?'

'Oh yes,' he said, winking. 'You must always be careful of me.'

Rochester staggered into the room. 'Ge-e-oo-orge! George, I've been looking for you,' he said, slapping the Duke of Buckingham on the back. He bowed to Nell, chuckling evilly. 'I lied to you earlier. Would you like to know what I was lying about?'

Buckingham gave him an appraising look. 'Perhaps you should sit down, John.'

'No, no, I don't wish to sit,' Rochester protested. 'I am here to read your palm.'

'Thank you, but it isn't necessary, John. I've already had my palm read once this evening, by the Duchess of Mazarin.'

'No matter.' Rochester leaned forward to whisper in Buckingham's ear, 'I will tell you things, George, the lovely duchess could never tell you. She does not have my gift.' He lost his balance and almost fell into Buckingham's arms. 'Perhaps we should sit down,' he said.

Nell and Buckingham led him back to the bench in the corridor.

'Give me your hand,' he ordered Buckingham once the three of them were seated.

Buckingham sighed and dutifully removed his glove. 'Very well, John. What do you see?'

Rochester raised Buckingham's hand to within a few inches of his face.

'This is ridiculous,' Buckingham muttered. 'The duchess did not have to twist my arm into such an uncomfortable position.' He started to pull his hand away, but Rochester refused to let go.

'I see a name,' Rochester said.

Buckingham stopped struggling. 'A name?'

'Written in your hand,' Rochester intoned as if he had gone into a trance. 'I see you with a pale-haired woman, young. Her dress is green.'

Buckingham's mouth dropped open. 'You see this is in my hand? Where?'

'There,' Rochester said, pointing to a line on Buckingham's palm. 'See how this line moves across to intersect with another and then another, to form the letter "W". This is the woman's initial.' He threw back his head. 'The name is coming to me ... it's coming to me. It's ... it's ... Winnifred!'

Buckingham's eyes widened in amazement.

Rochester returned his attention to Buckingham's palm. 'See how the flesh in this part of your hand is redder than elsewhere?'

'Yes,' Buckingham said excitedly, 'I see!'

Rochester dropped Buckingham's hand, howling with laughter. 'That's the colour your face was when Winnifred slapped you!'

Aphra stood at the top of a narrow street between the Savoy Prison and the river. At the bottom of the road she saw the glow of a blacksmith's forge. A sign hung from a building to her right: the Blacksmith's Arms. As she approached it, she heard the sounds of voices and raucous laughter. She took a deep breath and walked inside.

The room fell silent, every head turning to look at her. Several men stood together, each with an identical white mark in his hatband, probably to signify membership in some thieves' guild. She had to walk past them to get to the bar.

The woman behind the bar looked as old as Madam Gwyn, with frizzled grey hair and large red veins across her cheeks and nose. 'I wonder if you might help me,' Aphra said. 'I am looking for my uncle.'

She left a few minutes later, cursing herself for making a

wasted journey. No one there had ever heard of a man called Toby Rainbeard.

She returned home to find the bread, flour and beer she'd bought earlier exactly where she'd left them, in the middle of the parlour floor. She carried the bread and beer over to her desk and sat down to read her mail.

The first letter was a demand for payment. She tossed that on the fire.

The second was from the Earl of Arlington, saying he wished to speak to her and would send someone to collect her at five of the clock. She threw back her head, groaning.

She glanced at the others: a printed notice of a new tobacco shop opening in the Strand ('The Best Tobacco By Farr', Louis J. Farr, Proprietor), another extolling the virtues of 'Apricot Paste, imported from Paris', and a list of new pamphlets available from a bookseller near St Paul's. She threw them on to the fire as well.

What now? she thought, stuffing a chunk of bread into her mouth. Bevil Cane's play. She promised him she'd read it tonight.

She took a gulp of beer, then picked up the manuscript, flicking past the first two scenes she had already read. She found the first page of Scene Three and settled back into her chair to read.

She'd read about four or five pages when she realized she hadn't taken in a single word. She flicked back to where she'd started and tried again. None of it made any sense; it was all meaningless blots of ink.

She sighed and rubbed her eyes. The problem was she couldn't concentrate. Though she was going through the motions of reading, her mind was elsewhere.

She couldn't stop thinking about what Mrs Adams had said: Elias had stolen something dangerous. Dangerous how? Was that why he was killed?

But what bothered her even more was Mrs Adams's

statement that Elias had claimed to have found a powerful protector. Why was Arlington so interested in the deaths of Matthew and Elias? She wondered if he might have been the protector Mrs Adams had referred to.

Imagine having Arlington as a protector. No wonder Elias was dead.

She put the manuscript away. She couldn't read it now; she could barely keep her eyes open. It had been another long and tiring day, and all she wanted to do was sleep.

She carried a candle up to her bedchamber, opened the door and screamed. There was someone in her bed.

The person woke with a start. 'Wha'? Where am I?'

Oh God, no, Aphra thought. It was Elizabeth.

Chapter Twenty-one

Aphra woke up freezing; Elizabeth had stolen all the blankets. She rolled over and saw the other woman lying curled up on her side, her thumb in her mouth. 'Ye Gods,' Aphra muttered, getting out of bed.

Elizabeth had never left the house. She'd said studying her lines had made her tired, and she'd gone upstairs to have a nap. By the time Aphra woke her last night, it had been too late to expect her to return to her lodgings alone in the dark.

Aphra went down to the kitchen. There was no bread left; Elizabeth had finished the last of it the night before. There was still the sack of flour, but Aphra didn't feel like baking her own loaf. Besides, it would take too long.

And the basket from Gospel House was still sitting in the middle of the table. She told herself she really must return it.

She tossed it in the larder, out of sight.

Inside the larder was a small bag of oats she'd forgotten about. She opened it and checked the contents: just enough to make two bowls of caudle.

She was still in the kitchen making breakfast when she heard someone pounding on the door. Oh no, she thought, not again. She took a deep breath and walked to the front of the house, tying her dressing gown closed. 'Who is it?' she called.

'It's me, Aphra! Let me in!'

She opened the door to see Nell standing on her doorstep, face flushed and hair dishevelled.

'You'll never believe what happened, Aphra! You'll never believe it!'

'What is it?' Aphra asked. 'Are you all right?'

Nell walked past her into the house. 'Of course I'm all right! It's Rochester.'

'Rochester? What about him?'

'He's been banished from court.'

'What?'

'He's been banished,' Nell repeated, louder this time. 'Rochester's been banished!'

'For God's sake, keep your voice down,' Aphra whispered, glancing towards the stairs. 'You'll wake Elizabeth.'

Nell's eyes widened with amazement. 'Elizabeth? What's she doing here?'

'It's a long story,' Aphra said, leading her through to the kitchen. She told Nell to sit down, then closed the door and poured them each a mug of beer. 'First tell me about Rochester.'

'He got drunk and started insulting people. You would not believe what he said to poor George!'

'George?' Aphra said, sitting across from her at the table.

'The Duke of Buckingham. Anyway, George was so upset he would have challenged him if I had not been there to calm him down. And George was not the only person he upset; within half an hour he'd managed to offend most of the court. Then he went out into His Majesty's Privy Garden and started screaming obscenities at a sundial adorned with a portrait of the king.'

Aphra started to laugh. 'I'm sorry,' she said, 'but surely Rochester wasn't banished for shouting at a dial!'

Nell shook her head. 'No, Aphra, it wasn't the shouting that got him banned.' She sighed and took a drink of beer. 'He attacked the sundial with his sword, and when the sword would not slice through it he threw himself upon it as if he was trying to strangle it, finally knocking it to the ground and smashing it to pieces. Charles was furious.'

'Why would he attack a sundial?'

Nell lowered her eyes, embarrassed. 'He called it a prick, standing there to fuck time.'

'I don't understand why he would behave that way,' Aphra said. 'I've seen Rochester drunk, but never – ' She had a sudden horrible recollection of what she'd been told about her behaviour at the funeral. 'Oh, no. Please tell me you didn't do what I think you did.'

Nell blinked, putting on her most innocent expression. 'I don't know what you mean.'

'Oh, my God,' Aphra said. 'You did. Why, Nell? I thought he was your friend.'

'I didn't mean any harm,' Nell protested. 'He seemed unhappy about something, but he wouldn't talk about it and I thought that if I knew what was wrong I might be able to help him.'

'You thought you were helping him?'

Nell nodded. 'Yes, of course I did.'

'I can't believe you did such a stupid thing, Nell. You saw what the drops did to me.'

'But I didn't give him that much.'

'Those drops are dangerous, Nell. I don't know why Will Chiffinch ever agreed to refill that bottle for you. I'm going to have a talk with that man.'

'That would not be a good idea.'

'Why not?'

Nell squirmed in her chair. 'He didn't exactly refill the bottle for me.'

Aphra crossed her arms. 'Didn't he?'

'No. The phial I showed you yesterday isn't the one I found outside Gospel House. Will Chiffinch kept that one. So, on my way home, I stopped off at the king's laboratory. They know me there; I've often visited Charles while he was working on his experiments. Then, when no one was looking, I – '

'Are you mad?' Aphra said, throwing up her hands. 'God's

nails, you don't just take things from the king's laboratory. They could hang you for something like that!'

'Don't be ridiculous,' Nell said. 'I am in His Majesty's favour. I can take what I like from his laboratory, or anywhere else in the palace, with no fear of reprisal.'

'As long you don't get caught,' Aphra added drily.

'No, Aphra, you're wrong. I know the king, and I know what he likes.' She giggled. 'He likes me to be wicked, the wickeder the better.' She stood and lifted up her skirts to show a white silk petticoat trimmed with ribbons and lace. 'Look what Charles himself gave me, not one hour ago, precisely for being wicked. And I have half a dozen more just like it.' She lowered her dress and sat back down. 'Why do you think my hair is in such disarray? I haven't had time to comb it since he left my bed.'

Aphra rolled her eyes. Nell could never sleep with the king without boasting about it afterwards. 'But what do you intend to do about Rochester? What happened to him is your fault.'

'I know that. I know. I tried to speak to Charles, but His Majesty wasn't in the mood for' – she raised a hand to her mouth, giggling – 'talk. He had other activities in mind. I will try again, of course, at the first opportunity, and will keep on trying until I get John recalled to court. And in the meantime...' She shrugged. 'I suppose I shall have to do everything I can to ensure he wins his wager. It seems the least I can do. Which reminds me, why is Elizabeth here?'

Aphra sank her head into her hands, moaning. 'I wish I knew!'

Aphra and Nell agreed between them that it would be better to say nothing about Rochester's disgrace to Elizabeth; she'd only spend the rehearsal in hysterics. Nell told her instead that Rochester had to go away on urgent business, which Elizabeth accepted without too much fuss, complaining only that he hadn't told her. Nell assured her he would have, but the business was very urgent indeed, so urgent he had no time to notify anyone. Elizabeth seemed satisfied with this, it never occurring to her to ask how, if he had notified no one of his urgent departure, did Nell know all about it?

By the time the three of them climbed into the back of Nell's coach to ride to the rehearsal rooms at Leicester Square, Elizabeth was her usual chirpy, annoying self, full of confidence in her performance. A confidence Aphra had no hope of sharing.

Aphra was leaning back with her eyes half-closed, doing her best to ignore Elizabeth's inane prattle as the coach turned north off the Strand. A moment later, she heard the sound of hoofbeats coming up fast behind them. 'Nell,' she said, 'I think someone is pursuing us.'

Nell stuck her head out the window, looking back, and laughed. 'Slow down,' she told her driver as another coach came up alongside them.

'Nelly,' shouted a woman's voice, 'where are you bound this fine morning?'

Aphra leaned forward, peering around Elizabeth and Nell to see a dark-haired woman leaning out of the other coach's window.

'Leicester Square,' Nell shouted back. 'Barely fifty yards away!'

The other woman laughed. 'So are we. We'll race you!'

Aphra was thrown back in her seat as the horses broke into a gallop, Nell and the other woman both shouting to their drivers, urging them to go faster.

Sitting in the middle, Elizabeth was buffeted from side to side, first crashing into Nell, then throwing her arms around Aphra. The two of them toppled forward as the coach came to a stop.

Nell leapt down from the coach, whooping with delight. 'Victory!' she shouted, applauding her driver. 'Victory!'

The other coach, black trimmed with gold, pulled up beside

her. 'You are fiercer competition than I guessed,' the dark-haired woman said.

Aphra walked over to where Nell was talking to two almost identical women, both tall with long dark hair, both dressed in men's clothing, each with a sword hanging at her side.

'Hortense, Anne,' Nell said, 'this is my dear friend, Aphra Behn.'

'I have heard of you, Mrs Behn,' the one Nell had addressed as Hortense said. 'They say you are immodest and immoral.' She took off her hat, bowing like a court gallant. 'In which case, it is a pleasure to make your acquaintance.'

Aphra suddenly realized who the woman was. She had to be the infamous Duchess of Mazarin, the woman who had replaced Louise de Kéroualle as Nell's chief rival for the king's attention. And Anne was of course the sixteen-year-old daughter of Barbara Castlemaine.

She hadn't realized the duchess and the king's daughter looked so much alike. It was only up close that she could see the differences between them, the chief one being that Hortense was nearly twice the other's age. And their eyes were different. Anne's were blue, while the duchess's were a strange mixture of green, grey and hazel.

'And this is Elizabeth Decker,' Nell said, as Elizabeth came to stand by Aphra's side.

Aphra could hardly keep herself from cringing at the sound of Elizabeth's voice, gibbering about what an honour this was.

'You're wearing swords,' Elizabeth went on to observe.

'We are on our way to a lesson with our fencing master,' the duchess explained, 'at the academy, just over there.' She nodded to a building on the other side of the square.

Elizabeth gasped, obviously impressed.

It suddenly occurred to Aphra that if Elizabeth had been dressed in men's clothing, or the duchess and countess in gowns, the three of them would be almost indistinguishable at a distance. Though once more, up close, it would be impossible to mistake Elizabeth's vacuous expression for the duchess's air of confident intelligence.

There was less to distinguish Elizabeth from Anne, though, even up close. They were only a few years apart in age, and Anne, at the moment at least, looked every bit as vacuous as Elizabeth. She kept glancing down at her feet, a silly little half-smile on her face, before briefly raising her eyes only to lower them again.

She heard Elizabeth giggling at her side. She turned and saw she was looking down at her feet with precisely the same stupid smile. Aphra rubbed her temples, not certain what was going on.

'Are you and Anne coming to Pall Mall this afternoon?' Nell asked the duchess.

'I don't think so, Nell. Though I find your invitation amusing, it would not be tactful for me to take part in such an event.'

'I'm going to be there,' Elizabeth blurted out.

The Duchess of Mazarin gave her a knowing smile. 'We may come after all. We'll have to see.'

Thomas Alcock had seen his master drunk before – in fact he saw him drunk nearly every day – but never like last night. He approached his master's bedchamber cautiously, expecting to find him in bed with a headache and – following the previous night's disgrace – in the foulest of tempers.

He knocked on the door and went in. To his surprise the earl was up and dressed, supervising a team of servants in the packing of his luggage. 'Ah, Thomas,' his master said brightly. 'There you are at last.'

'Are you going away, my lord?' Alcock asked him.

'Observant as ever, Thomas,' the Earl of Rochester said, his eyes sparkling with amusement. 'Now go and pack your things; you're coming with me.'

Chapter Twenty-two

Elizabeth wittered all the way home from rehearsal, babbling on and on about how incredible it was that two women should be taking lessons from a fencing master. 'Do you think I should take fencing lessons, Mrs Behn? So I may be more convincing in the scene where disguised as a gallant, I find myself challenged to a duel?'

'Elizabeth,' Aphra told her, 'in my opinion, lessons of any kind would be wasted on you. I doubt there is anything in the world that could make your performance more convincing.'

'Why, thank you, Mrs Behn! Thank you.'

Aphra buried her head in her hands, groaning. The woman was impossible to insult.

Hortense sat in front of a mirror in her bedchamber, a servant combing her hair. Anne lay sprawled on her stomach across the bed, scowling at a stack of letters. 'They're from my husband, every one of them. He wishes to know why I have not replied to his earlier missives, and insists upon my immediate return to Sussex, or else he shall "take action", whatever that means.'

'Persistent, isn't he?' Hortense said, yawning. She glanced towards the window. Someone was moving about on the opposite bank of the river. She waved the servant away from her hair, and stood up to get a better look.

The fishermen she had seen the previous day were back.

Aphra was handed a glass of sherry the instant she stepped into Nell's parlour. The room was crowded with a chattering collection of court wits, fops and ladies of dubious reputation. About half of them were dressed in mourning, as Nell requested. She also noticed a group of four rather sour-faced gentlemen standing together in one corner, looking on the gathering in silent disapproval. Aphra wondered who they were and what they were doing here; they seemed so out of place.

In the centre of the room a miniature coffin sat on a table surrounded by burning candles, a plate of salt balanced on the lid. Elizabeth stood beside the coffin, staring down at it with her usual bemused expression. She looked up as Aphra approached her.

'I see you have been paying your respects to the deceased,' Aphra said.

'There isn't any deceased, Mrs Behn,' Elizabeth informed her earnestly. 'The funeral is meant to be a jest.'

'Is it?' Aphra said, widening her eyes in mock surprise. 'I hadn't realized.'

The parlour doors swung open to reveal Nell descending the stairs, draped from head to foot in black. Bevil Cane followed behind her, carrying a basket of rosemary.

'Oh, woe!' Nell declaimed, wringing her hands. 'Oh, woe! This is a tragic day!'

She paused at the bottom of the stairs to produce a black handkerchief from her pocket. 'Thank you for coming,' she sniffled, first dabbing at her eyes, then loudly blowing her nose.

She entered the parlour to rapturous applause from all but the four sour-faced gentlemen in the corner, knocked the plate of salt to one side and threw herself over the miniature coffin, weeping.

'It's all right, Mrs Behn,' Elizabeth whispered, 'she's only acting.'

Nell raised a hand for silence, then straightened up to speak, obviously struggling to compose herself. 'My dear friends. My dear, dear friends. As you know, we are gathered here today to pay our last respects to the late hopes and ambitions of Louise de Kéroualle, Duchess of Portsmouth. I'm sorry the coffin has had to remain closed, but the sight of the duchess's ambition was never a pleasant one.' She nodded to Bevil Cane, who had positioned himself beside the door ready to distribute the rosemary. 'Let us begin the procession.'

A young fop acted as pallbearer, lifting the little coffin and carrying it out of the door. The others followed, each taking a sprig of rosemary as they filed past Bevil Cane.

'Mrs Behn,' he said as she went by him, 'you haven't said that you liked my play.'

She hastily explained that she hadn't had the opportunity to finish it as Elizabeth had been visiting her last night.

He seemed disappointed, but agreed it would be impossible to think of anything else while the divine Mrs Decker was present.

She heard giggling, and turned to see Elizabeth standing behind her. She hurried outside and came face to face with the Duke of Monmouth.

'Ah, Mrs Behn. It seems once again we are destined to meet at a funeral.' He raised an eyebrow, looking at her quizzically. 'I pray you are recovered from the last one?'

She curtsied politely, inwardly seething at the duke's sarcastic tone of voice. 'Quite recovered,' she told him frostily.

'Good,' he said, going into the house to collect his sprig of rosemary.

Aphra made her way to the front to walk alongside Nell. She indicated the four men she'd noticed earlier, now walking respectfully behind the young Duke of Monmouth. 'Who are those men that look as if they've each swallowed a lemon?'

'Members of the Country Party, a faction within the House of Commons,' Nell informed her. 'They believe they represent the interests of the people, as opposed to the Court Party, which they see as representing a vice-ridden den of Papists.'

Aphra knew about the newly formed parties. As far as she understood it, the Country Party had stated its opposition to the

Duke of York's succession on the grounds of his rumoured Catholicism. 'What are they doing here?'

'It could be they enjoy my company,' Nell said, shrugging. 'Though I suspect it's Jamie they're here to see.'

Of course, Aphra thought, the Country Party would support Monmouth's claim to be Charles's rightful heir to the throne.

As the procession of mourners turned the corner into the inner courtyard of Whitehall Palace, Aphra got a nagging feeling that she was looking directly at something but failing to see it. She glanced back at Monmouth, remembering how she had watched him search Elias's pockets.

The mourners came to a stop around the small hole that was to serve as the coffin's final resting place and tossed in their sprigs of rosemary. And then there was the sound of someone sobbing.

She looked across to see Elizabeth bent over nearly double, weeping into her hands as the coffin was slowly lowered into the ground. The Duke of Buckingham stood beside her, muttering, 'There, there,' and patting her on the shoulder. He moved aside, looking relieved, as Bevil Cane rushed over to comfort her.

'What's she crying about?' Aphra demanded, crossing over to the duke.

The Duke of Buckingham made a little clucking sound of sympathy. 'It seems the poor girl had no idea that Lord Rochester has left for France.'

'What?'

'I called at his house this morning, and was told he had left for France.' The Duke of Buckingham shook his head in disapproval. 'To think he didn't even leave the poor girl a note. I ask you, is that not the most shocking behaviour?'

Aphra gritted her teeth. Buckingham was obviously trying to upset Elizabeth in order to undermine her performance. She couldn't believe he would sink so low just to win a bet. She was about to tell him so when she heard somebody screaming.

She looked up to find the source of the noise and saw a woman leaning out of an upstairs window, shaking her fist and shouting threats. 'I will kill you! I will strangle every one of you with my bare hands!'

The duchess's outburst was greeted with a round of applause. Her face turned bright red. She slammed the window closed and drew the curtains.

'Ah, the lovely Lady Portsmouth,' the Duke of Buckingham said appreciatively. 'Is it not wonderful to see so much energy in one who is meant to be starving herself to death?'

Elizabeth left immediately after the burial, accepting Bevil Cane's offer to escort her home. The rest returned to Pall Mall for a lavish reception, with more guests arriving as the evening progressed. The Duchess of Mazarin and her young friend the Countess of Sussex were among these late arrivals, though Aphra hardly saw them; they'd vanished into a room with several others, apparently to gamble at cards.

It must have been after ten when a fair-haired man of about thirty walked over to Aphra, introducing himself as one of her greatest admirers. 'I see your glass is empty,' he said, speaking with a slight foreign accent. 'Allow me to get you another.'

'I don't know your name,' she said when he returned a moment later.

'Grootvader,' he said, bending down to kiss her hand. 'Jan Grootvader.'

'Is that a Dutch name?' she asked him, taking a sip from her glass.

The next thing she remembered, she was dancing around the garden with the Duke of Buckingham, not certain how she'd come to be there.

Chapter Twenty-three

Aphra woke with a start, raising an arm to shield her eyes from a blinding light. She sat up, squinting at her surroundings, then fell back against the pillow, suddenly aware she had a blistering headache.

A girl stood beside a large window tying back a pair of curtains. 'My mistress said I should wake you so you wouldn't be late for rehearsal.'

'I am awake,' Aphra mumbled, still shielding her eyes, 'now please close the curtains.'

'Don't you want the light, Mrs Behn?'

'No, I do not.'

The girl drew the curtains and left.

Aphra rolled on to her side, groaning. There was a terrible taste in her mouth; she needed something to drink. She thrust out a hand, feeling for the jug on the bedside table.

She got up, then stumbled around in the dark, trying to find her clothes. She crossed over to the window, opening the curtains just enough so she could see what she was doing.

Nell was standing on a terrace at the top of the garden wall, apparently talking to someone in the adjoining garden. All Aphra could see of the other person was the top of a man's hat. Nell was giggling and gesturing expansively, occasionally throwing back her head to shake her curls.

Then she blew the man a kiss.

By the time Aphra went downstairs, Nell was back inside the house, eating a huge ling and herring pie for breakfast. 'Good

213

morning, Aphra,' she said, her voice seeming to bounce off the walls. She pushed her plate across the table, offering a slice of pie.

Aphra averted her eyes; she couldn't bear the sight of it. 'I'm not hungry.'

Nell chuckled knowingly and ordered a servant to pour Aphra a mug of ale with sugar. 'That should improve your head,' she said.

'How can you be so well when I am dying?' Aphra moaned.

'It might be something to do with the amount of wine you drank.'

Aphra sank her head into her hands. 'It's that Dutchman's fault. He wouldn't stop refilling my glass.'

'Dutchman?' Nell repeated. 'What Dutchman?'

'Grootvader, I think his name was. Jan Grootvader.'

'I never heard of him,' Nell said, shrugging. 'But then I handed out so many cards, I have no idea how many people I invited, or who half of them were. Which reminds me . . .' She curled her lips into a sneer of disgust. 'His Majesty has just congratulated me for getting the Duchess of Portsmouth out of bed. It seems Squintabella ordered a hearty breakfast this morning, and is already dressed and plaguing the Stone Gallery with her presence. And Charles says it's all thanks to me.'

So that was who Nell had been speaking to in the garden. But where was Bevil Cane this morning?

Nell smiled slyly, explaining that Bevil had not come home until after dawn and was still asleep.

'You don't think — ?' Aphra said.

'I don't know. He is too much of a gentleman to say. But I intend to find out from Elizabeth.'

Monsieur Honoré Courtin sat at his desk, composing another letter to his king.

Your Majesty, he began, writing in a cipher that substituted numbers for letters.

It is my pleasure to inform you that Mistress Nelly Gwyn has graciously offered her services towards the promotion of our cause at the English court. Though I must admit I did not take her offer seriously, it seems she has already begun work on our behalf. Thanks to the actions of Mistress Nelly, Mademoiselle de Kéroualle may yet regain her influence over your cousin. I saw the Lady Portsmouth this morning, and can report that I have never seen her so determined. (Though I fear this was never the delightful Mistress Nelly's intention!)

He stopped to look out of the window, chuckling to himself. Poor Mistress Nelly! How could someone so worldly be so naive?

You may also be interested to know that the volatile young Earl of Rochester has lost Charles's favour and is rumoured to have left the country, most likely bound for our fair shore.

As to the other matter, I have been informed of the apparent involvement of a widow named Aphra Behn, who by an interesting coincidence is also a close associate of our new unwitting ally, Mistress Nelly.

Aphra Behn is a woman of no social importance, subject to much disapproval for her lack of modesty, indulging as she does in the unfeminine occupation of writing for money. However, she was not only acquainted with both the deceased men; I have also learned that the second murder occurred in the grounds of this infamous woman's house, and that she then organized and paid for a funeral which was attended by none other than the bastard Duke of Monmouth, of whose ambitions we are well aware.

I am currently attempting to trace two other people who attended the funeral — a Mr O'Bannion and a Mr Frost — in order to determine the significance, if any, of their presence.

I also understand that Aphra Behn has been asking questions about an elderly criminal named Toby Rainbeard. I do not yet know what involvement he has in this matter, but rest assured I shall find out.

Elizabeth was already at the rehearsal room when Aphra and Nell arrived. She was sitting on a bench along the wall, looking pale and tired. 'She doesn't look like she's had much sleep,' Nell whispered gleefully.

Aphra slumped into a chair, only half-listening to Nell's playful interrogation of the actress. Elizabeth seemed shocked at the suggestion that anything improper had occurred between herself and Mr Cane, protesting he had behaved like a gentleman.

'And we all know how gentlemen behave,' Nell said, winking and nudging her with her elbow.

But Elizabeth would not admit to anything. She continued to insist that Mr Cane had left early, despite Nell's repeated assurances that it would remain their little secret.

Aphra was staring into space, more asleep than awake, when she was startled by a woman's voice. 'I saw your friend John Hoyle last night, in a tavern in Holborn, having dinner with a woman.'

She looked up to see one of the other actresses standing over her, looking smug. The woman was a notorious gossip who loved to stir up trouble. She obviously expected Aphra to get angry, or run from the room in tears.

Aphra decided to laugh instead. 'If you see him again you may tell him that while he was having dinner in a tavern, I was dancing with a duke.' She neglected to mention that the duke in question had brown teeth and a purple nose, and was so overweight that when he bent down to kiss her hand he'd burst his waistcoat; that might ruin the effect.

The actress walked away, disappointed.

Aphra returned home with a loaf of bread, fresh from the oven at Mr Gue's shop, and a handful of fruit bought from a street vendor. She walked through the parlour into the kitchen, opened the larder, and was once again confronted with the sight of the basket she'd brought back from Gospel House.

She was beginning to hate that basket. It represented all the things nagging at the back of her mind, all the things she kept meaning to do but never got around to. Like reading Bevil Cane's play.

She was about to pick up the basket when she heard a knock at the door.

She reached the front hall to find a piece of crumpled paper shoved underneath her door. She opened the door and looked out; there was no one there.

She bent to pick up the paper, and saw three words, written in a barely legible scrawl: the Blacksmith's Arms.

Chapter Twenty-four

Toby Rainbeard was sitting at a table, waiting for her. She sat down across from him. 'You wanted to see me?'

The old man raised an eyebrow. 'I was under the impression it was you who wished to see me. Niece.'

'I notice you had no difficulty in determining who your niece was,' Aphra said.

'And I notice my niece had no difficulty in locating me, which I must say I find surprising. I'd hoped I was more elusive than that.' He called to a little boy serving behind the bar, telling him to bring two mugs of beer, then turned back to Aphra. 'Now pray tell me, how may I assist you, Mrs Behn?'

'I should like to know why you have been spying on me, Mr Rainbeard.'

The old man opened his mouth to speak.

She interrupted him before he could get a word out. 'I can see the denial forming on your lips, but I shouldn't bother if I were you. I know you gave my funeral invitation to Arlington, then hid in the adjoining room while he questioned me about Matthew and Elias. I saw you, Mr Rainbeard.'

He shrugged, resigned. 'I assure you I had no choice in the matter.'

'What do you mean, you had no choice?'

Toby signalled silence, indicating the boy approaching the table with two mugs. 'I mean,' he said once the boy was gone, 'I was brought to Arlington's office just as you were, Mrs Behn. Except that this was some weeks ago, and I was not treated so courteously. My Lord Arlington told me he wanted me to trace a man named Matthew Cavell. He did not say why. I thought I was close to finding him when I learned he had a brother named Elias who sometimes stayed with a woman in St Giles. Then you came to this woman's house, and I learned the man I was seeking was dead.'

He bent forward across the table, looking earnest. 'I promise you, when I gave your card to Arlington, it was merely to show him there was nothing more to be done. I honestly thought that would be the end of the matter.' He paused to heave a dramatic sigh. 'It is only now I see how wrong I was,' he added, sighing again.

Aphra regarded him silently for a moment. Then she applauded. He'd been very convincing until he ruined it by sighing once too often. 'If only I'd known you were such a good actor, I would have cast you in my new play,' she said.

Toby drank the contents of his mug in one gulp. 'I must say you impress me, Mrs Behn,' he said, wiping his mouth on the sleeve of his coat. He smiled, exposing a set of broken teeth. 'Just how well did you know your so-called friend, Matthew Cavell? Did you know he was a traitor?'

'What?'

Toby raised his empty mug, signalling for the boy to refill it. 'He went over to the Dutch in 'sixty-seven and lived in Holland for some years after, not daring to return to England for fear of being hanged. Didn't you know that, Mrs Behn? Ah, I see by your face that you did not.'

'But that is not possible,' she protested. 'He lost his leg while serving on the *Revenge*!'

'Where did you hear that, Mrs Behn?'

'From Elias,' she said.

The boy came to the table to refill Toby's mug. Again he waited for him to go before he spoke. 'So you did speak to Elias after all.'

'Of course I did!' She took a sip of her beer, telling herself to remain calm. The man seemed to be playing some kind of elaborate game with her, purposely trying to provoke her for some reason she couldn't fathom. She told herself that whatever the game was she would refuse to play along. 'I spoke to Elias on Monday. That was my reason for seeking him on Tuesday: so I might speak to him again.'

'Elias was as much a traitor as his brother,' Toby said, lifting his mug to take another drink. 'Maybe even more so.'

'I don't know what you're talking about,' Aphra said.

'Don't you?' Toby put down his mug and wiped his mouth, looking at her curiously. 'I think you may be telling the truth.'

'I wish *you* would,' Aphra muttered.

'But I have been, Mrs Behn. I assure you, everything I've said is true.'

Nell opened the nursery door and saw her sons were having their afternoon nap. She hadn't been to bed herself since early the previous morning, and then she hadn't got much sleep, thanks to the attentions of His Majesty.

She went downstairs to the kitchen. 'Is Bevil not up yet?' she asked her maid, Lucy.

'Not only up, but gone out again, mistress. He said it was something to do with his scholarly pursuits.'

Nell nodded, laughing. Scholarly pursuits, indeed. More likely pursuit of Elizabeth Decker. Now Rochester had gone to France, there was nothing to stop him declaring his passion for the actress.

She left the kitchen, yawning. It was only the middle of the afternoon, but she could stay awake no longer.

She was about to get into bed when Lucy knocked on her bedchamber door with the news she had a visitor.

'S'teeth,' Nell muttered. 'Who is it?'

'It's Mistress Decker.'

The sky clouded over, the temperature dropped and it began to rain. Aphra huddled shivering in a narrow space between two buildings a little further up the street, waiting to see where Toby Rainbeard would go when he left the tavern.

Madam Gwyn had been so right about him. She'd never met such a lying rogue. How dare he slander Matthew's memory like that?

The only thing he'd told her that sounded true was the reason he gave for his employment with Arlington. He said that some years earlier he'd been in Newgate for theft, and given a choice between the gallows and informing on certain confederates, he chose the latter. She had no trouble believing a villain like him would betray his friends to save his own neck.

She'd been waiting for about half an hour when she saw him leave the tavern. He turned and walked a few doors down, towards the blacksmith's. And then he vanished from sight.

Aphra came out of her hiding place and hurried after him. She looked into the blacksmith's shop and saw a man hammering on something beside the forge. There was no sign of Toby.

Then she noticed a narrow path running alongside the building. She followed it around to a door at the back. It wasn't locked. She opened it and peered through into a large, high-ceilinged space full of tools and bits of metal. She could see the blacksmith working at the front. He was too intent on his hammering to notice her.

A few feet away from the back wall, a tall wooden ladder led up to a hole in the ceiling. She stepped back outside and looked up towards the roof. There was a tiny window just below the eaves.

Aphra returned home to find her books and papers scattered across the parlour floor, her bed tipped over, and the bench removed from her house of office.

She was still trying to clean up when Elizabeth Decker came to visit the next day.

'I just wanted to let you know,' Elizabeth said, standing

221

outside on the doorstep, 'that my Lord Rochester's absence has only increased my determination to work harder than ever on my performance.'

'Thank you for telling me that,' Aphra said, making no move to let her in. 'Now if you'll excuse me, I am busy.'

'But I have brought you something,' Elizabeth said, holding out a cloth-covered parcel, tied with string.

'You might as well come in then,' Aphra sighed.

Elizabeth paused in the parlour doorway. 'Your books are on the floor.'

'I noticed that,' Aphra said drily. 'Just be careful where you step.'

Elizabeth spent a long, careful moment taking in the scene before she came to the conclusion: 'You've had burglars, haven't you?'

Aphra walked past her into the room, kneeling down to gather up some papers. 'It does appear so.'

'Have you informed the constable?'

'There is nothing missing and no one dead in my house of office, so why bother poor Mr Gue? All he would do is ask the neighbours if they saw anything, then write a report to say they hadn't. I spent a large part of last evening and this morning questioning the neighbours myself, which is why I haven't finished clearing up yet.'

'And did your neighbours see anything?'

'Of course not.'

Elizabeth entered on tiptoe, gingerly stepping around a number of scattered pages. 'I don't understand it,' she said, gesturing to the various paintings and tapestries on the walls. 'Why did they leave those? Surely they have some value.' She held up a corner of the cloth draped across the table next to the kitchen entrance. 'Why would they leave this?' She dropped the tablecloth and pointed to Aphra's fire screen. 'And that? Embroidered cloth is very dear.'

Aphra looked up, surprised. Elizabeth Decker had actually

demonstrated a capacity for logical thought. 'Something must have frightened them away,' she said. 'Maybe they thought someone was coming.'

Elizabeth put her parcel down on the table, apparently happy with Aphra's explanation, and knelt to help collect the papers scattered across the floor. 'Here's a letter that looks as if it hasn't been opened,' she said.

'That will be from John Hoyle,' Aphra said, enjoying Elizabeth's shocked expression as she tossed it on the fire.

Elizabeth stacked her books and pamphlets on the shelves in a rather haphazard manner, but at least she got them off the floor.

Aphra refolded the last of her broadsheets and sank down on to the settle, exhausted, while Elizabeth went into the kitchen to pour some beer. Her gaze drifted over to the parcel Elizabeth had brought her; she still didn't know what was in it. She got up and crossed to the table, cutting the string with the little knife she used to open letters.

Elizabeth came back into the room as she was removing the cloth wrapping. 'I hope you like it,' she said. 'Mrs Gwyn said you'd told her mother you had a fondness for calf's head pie.'

Chapter Twenty-five

Louise de Kéroualle sat in front of her mirror, shouting at the maid who was combing her hair. The girl was new, and was an idiot; she didn't have the least idea what she was doing. 'Ow!' Louise screamed, snatching the comb away. 'You are supposed to be curling my hair, not ripping it from my scalp!'

'I'm sorry, my lady.'

'Leave me,' she ordered the girl, 'while I still have some hair left.'

'Yes, my lady. I'm sorry, my lady.'

'Send in Marie. At least she will not pluck me bald!' She pointed at the door. 'Go!' She stood and crossed to the window, gazing down at the river with tears welling in her eyes.

She'd watched Charles again this morning, frolicking in the water with Mazarin. Now they were gone. Back to Mazarin's apartments, she supposed. Back to Mazarin's bed.

She rested her head against the glass windowpane, angrily choking back a sob. Something moved on the opposite bank, catching her eye. She looked up, wiping her cheek, and saw two men, carrying fishing rods.

Them again.

It seemed they were there every day now, most hours of the day and night, though they never seemed to catch anything.

She picked up her telescope, curious. After quite a lot of pushing and pulling and sliding, she managed to get their faces into focus. They were a pair of rough-looking, heavy-set men, with cruel expressions she found frightening. She recognized one of them as the man she had seen looking up at the palace through a spyglass.

They didn't seem to be paying the slightest attention to their fishing. Instead, it seemed they were staring up at the palace. Not at her, she was relieved to see, but at another set of windows further along.

She put down her telescope, wondering if she should speak to someone about this.

Aphra lifted her head, horrified to see bright sunlight pouring in through the crack between the shutters. She must have fallen asleep at her desk.

She glanced down at the manuscript she'd been using as a pillow, cursing Bevil Cane for writing the damned thing, and herself for still not reading it.

She walked into the kitchen and ate a slice of pie for breakfast, cursing Elizabeth for going to all that trouble, spending her Saturday night and Sunday morning cooking something especially for her. She didn't want Elizabeth to be pleasant and helpful, she wanted to detest her. Damn the woman, she thought. Damn her to hell.

Damn Rochester, too, for running off to France, abandoning her and the play in the middle of rehearsals.

Damn John Hoyle, just for being John Hoyle.

And damn whoever had broken into her house.

It was that, she realized, that was making her angry. The idea that someone had come in while she was gone, and torn everything apart, leaving the house in a shambles. Damn them!

She groaned, rubbing her aching neck and shoulders, and went upstairs to get dressed. She screamed when she saw the time.

She was more than an hour late for rehearsal. And to her dismay Bevil Cane was there.

'Mrs Behn,' he whispered, hurrying over to meet her, 'we've all been so worried. Mistress Decker says you had burglars!'

'I'm sorry, but I still haven't read your play,' she whispered before he could ask her. 'I shall read it tonight, I promise.'

'Oh, I quite understand,' Mr Cane murmured sympathetically. 'Was anything taken?'

'Not that I know of.'

'Nothing?' he said. 'Are you quite certain? You found nothing missing at all? Not even the smallest item?'

'Nothing!' she shouted, exasperated. 'I told you, there was nothing!'

Everyone turned to look at her, bringing the rehearsal to a halt.

'I think we should sit down,' Mr Cane whispered, looking embarrassed.

She walked over to a bench, fuming. It wasn't her fault she'd started shouting. It was Mr Cane asking the same annoying question over and over that had disrupted the rehearsal, not her.

Bevil Cane sat beside her, watching the action intently. The actors were running through the scene where the heroine tests her lover by pretending to be a Turkish dancer. To Aphra's relief, Mr Cane only laughed at the right places.

Elizabeth knew all her lines, and while she was far from brilliant she was better than she'd ever been. It seemed she meant it when she said she was going to work on her performance.

Maybe there was hope for the play after all.

Once again, Aphra found herself waiting in a coach while Bevil Cane went in first to ensure the house was safe for her to enter.

'There's no one in there,' she told Nell. 'There's no reason for him to do this.'

'But he wants to,' Nell sighed. 'It makes him feel better to think he's helping.' She nudged Aphra with her elbow.

226

'Elizabeth was much better today, wasn't she? We spent most of Saturday afternoon going over her part, line by line. And you know why she was so keen to go over it again and again, don't you?'

Aphra shrugged.

'It's her revenge against Rochester for abandoning her. She intends to show him she can do perfectly well without any help from him.' She lowered her voice, a mischievous expression on her face. 'I hate to say it, Aphra, but giving Rochester those drops may be the best thing I ever did. For the play, I mean. Speaking of dear Rochester, have you heard from him?'

Aphra shook her head. 'Not a word. I've no idea what he's doing in France.' She shifted uncomfortably in her seat. Once again, Bevil Cane was taking an age. 'Zoors! What is he doing in there?'

'Bevil likes to be thorough,' Nell said. 'I wouldn't be surprised if he checks the pot beneath your bed.'

Aphra leapt down from the coach, tired of waiting.

'I was joking,' Nell called after her.

She found him in the parlour, taking the books down from one of her shelves and neatly stacking them on the settle.

'I'll have this finished in no time,' he assured her, rearranging the various books and pamphlets into alphabetical order.

'There's no need for this, Mr Cane.'

'But I insist,' he said. 'I want to help you, Mrs Behn, in any way I can. And please call me Bevil.'

She waved goodbye to Bevil Cane, her shelves once again in perfect order. She told herself she should be grateful the young man was so willing to be of assistance. Then she remembered his play, and her feelings of gratitude vanished.

She couldn't help thinking there was one reason, and one reason only, for his always appearing so pleasant and helpful: he wanted her to recommend his play to Mr Davenant.

She sat down at her desk, opening the drawer where she'd placed the manuscript. She was going to have to read it some time.

But not now, she thought, closing the drawer again.

She couldn't stop thinking it seemed an interesting coincidence that her house was broken in to on the same afternoon she'd been called away to meet Toby Rainbeard.

Chapter Twenty-six

Aphra stood at the rear of the blacksmith's shop, looking at the hole in the ceiling. It was a long way up, and the ladder didn't appear very stable.

She placed a foot on the bottom rung and began a slow and careful ascent, the ladder swaying beneath her. She didn't dare look down.

She paused near the top, carefully sticking her head through the opening. The ladder led to a small furnished attic.

The middle of the tiny room was almost completely taken up by a table and two chairs. To one side of the table there was a cot. The tiny window she'd seen from outside was set high in the wall, with no glass or shutters. A blacksmith's apron hung from a nail above the frame, serving as a makeshift curtain. Below the apron a fragment of mirror had been mounted on the wall. Beside the mirror was a tall wooden wardrobe.

Toby Rainbeard was sitting at the table, his back to her.

'Hello, Mr Rainbeard.'

He swung around, startled. 'Mrs Behn! What are you doing here?'

'It would seem you are not used to callers,' she observed, enjoying the expression on the old man's face. She imagined she must make an odd sight, her head and shoulders protruding through the floor.

He got up, and stretched out a gloved hand to help her up the last couple of steps into the room. 'How did you find me?'

'It wasn't difficult,' she said, taking a closer look at her surroundings. Everything in the room seemed to be covered in a layer of soot. Though the air was cool outside, the room was unbearably hot. And then there was the noise: a constant sound of hammering from the blacksmith's shop below.

'Once again, I am impressed.' The old man gestured to one of the chairs. 'What can I do for you, Mrs Behn?'

She sat down across the table from him, looking him straight in the eye. 'My house was broken into on Saturday.'

'I pray nothing of value was taken?'

'Nothing at all.'

'Nothing missing?' The old man raised an eyebrow. 'Then what makes you think anyone broke in?'

'I came home to find my books and papers scattered across the floor, and the bench from my house of office lying in pieces among the rose bushes.'

The old man grimaced, sucking air between his teeth. 'I may know something of your burglary after all.' He stood and walked over to the wardrobe.

'What do you mean?' Aphra demanded. 'What do you know?'

'I told you before, Matthew Cavell was a traitor,' the old man said impatiently. He opened the wardrobe, rummaging for something in a drawer. 'We suspect he was trying to sell something to the Dutch. Something important.'

'But what's that got to do with my house being broken into?'

'What Matthew had he passed on to his brother for safekeeping. And his brother died in your house.' The old man turned around, slipping a knife into his waistband.

'So they think whatever he had might be in my house?'

'Exactly.'

'But what is it? What did he have?'

'My Lord Arlington does not confide such things in me,' the old man said. 'He instructs me to find something, but will not say what it is. I only know the Dutch must not have it.' He walked past her to the ladder.

'Where are you going?'

'Go home,' he said. 'And leave your burglar to me.'

Toby Rainbeard was in good condition for his age, but not so good that Aphra couldn't easily keep up with him, staying out of sight a short distance behind.

He came to a stop in front of a small house near Covent Garden. He walked around to the back. She followed a minute later, finding a ground floor window forced open.

She took a deep breath to gather her courage, then climbed in after him.

The house was a shambles. And there was a terrible smell.

She found Toby standing over a body on the upstairs landing. The walls around him were splashed with blood. 'What are you doing here?' he demanded furiously.

She bent down to look at the corpse of a man lying sprawled on his back, his bloodstained clothing cut to ribbons, his throat slashed from side to side. She reached for her handkerchief, trying not to breathe. The man had been dead a day or two at least. 'I know him,' she gasped, recognizing the face of the young Dutchman she'd met at Nell's.

'There is much going on here you do not understand. I beg you, leave now and involve yourself no further.'

Aphra walked the short distance from Grootvader's house to the Theatre Royal in Drury Lane, determined to expose Toby Rainbeard as a liar. She arrived at the theatre in time for the third act.

She found the man she was looking for sitting in the bottom row of the middle gallery peeling an orange. 'Mr Pepys,' she said, 'may I have a word?'

He looked up, regarding her appreciatively. 'I am always happy to have words with a beautiful woman. I only pray they may be kind ones.'

'We have met before,' she said, 'at the Duke's Theatre in Dorset Garden.'

He gave her a blank smile that made it obvious he had no idea who she was.

'I'm a friend of Nell Gwyn's,' she reminded him. 'Aphra Behn.'

'The playwright!' he exclaimed. 'Of course, I recognized you at once. Pray sit beside me, Mrs Behn.'

She sat, keeping an empty seat between them. Samuel Pepys's wandering hands were well known among women who worked in the theatre.

He moved down a seat, closing the gap between them. 'This is a poor play,' he said, offering her a segment of his orange, 'though some of the actresses are very pretty.'

Everyone around them was talking, no one paying the slightest attention to the action on the stage. 'I wonder if you might help me,' Aphra said. 'I am interested in the naval records of someone who served on the *Revenge* during the Dutch war of 'sixty-four to 'sixty-seven.'

'It may take some time; many of our records were destroyed by fire a few years ago. But tell me his name,' Mr Pepys said, placing a hand on her knee, 'and I will see what I can do.'

Aphra had been home less than five minutes when a printed announcement was shoved underneath her front door. She picked it up and read the words:

To All Gentlemen, Ladies and Others, whether of City, Town, or Country: Alexander Bendo wishes you Health and Prosperity.

Good people, do not waste your money on fakes and charlatans, but come to one awarded his Doctor's Degree at Montpellier, with knowledge of medicines physical, chemical, and Galenic, and genuine abilities in the various arts of astrology, physiognomy, palmistry, alchemy, and mathematics.

Do you have a question for which you earnestly desire an

answer? Come to Alexander Bendo. He will tell you what you wish to know.

If only it was that easy, she thought, tossing it on to the fire along with the other announcements and the latest letter from John Hoyle.

Chapter Twenty-seven

Virtue Hawkins looked up as Aphra entered the room where the inmates of Gospel House picked oakum. 'Mrs Behn,' she called, patting the bench beside her, 'we have all been so worried about you.' She went on to scold her that she'd frightened everyone half to death the night of the funeral. 'We thought you were dying.'

Aphra shook her head, embarrassed; everyone in the room was looking at her. 'It was merely the effects of too much wine,' she said, preferring not to go into Nell's theory about drops.

'Wine?' Virtue snorted. 'You hardly touched a drop all evening; I was watching you. It was exhaustion made you collapse, Mrs Behn. Exhaustion.'

'Then how do you explain the collapse of the other woman?'

'*That*,' Virtue said, wagging a rough, gnarled finger, 'be too much wine.' She sighed and shook her head, returning her hands to the bundle of rope she was working on. Dressed once more in her blue gown, sitting hunched over a coil of rope, she looked older than Aphra remembered. As Aphra gazed about the room, it seemed to her that everyone there was older than she remembered.

'Your poor friend had someone asking for him the morning after the funeral,' Virtue said, looking down at her rope. 'Very upset he was when the boy told him Mr Cavell was dead and buried, begging could he see the room where Mr Cavell had passed away so he might say a private farewell. The boy told him if he wished to say farewell, the man was only buried down the road. But he said he wished to visit the place Mr

Cavell had last been alive, so the boy let him go upstairs. He was foreign,' she added, shrugging.

'Foreign?' Aphra repeated. 'What did he look like?'

Virtue put down the rope she was working on and raised a hand to her forehead, looking tired. 'He was a fair-haired man, not much older than thirty.'

Aphra shivered, suddenly feeling very cold. 'Did he tell you his name?'

'It was the boy who spoke to him, not I.'

Aphra found the boy in the kitchen. She asked him if a foreign gentleman had come asking for Mr Cavell the morning after the funeral, and he said yes. She asked how he knew the man was foreign. He said it was because he had an accent. Then she asked if he remembered the man's name. He shook his head, saying all he remembered was that it didn't sound English. 'It wasn't Grootvader, was it?' she said.

His face lit up. 'That's it exactly. However did you know?'

Aphra grabbed hold of a table to steady herself. 'Had he been here before?' she asked the boy.

'Oh yes,' the boy told her. 'He'd been here three or four times at least, including the day Mr Cavell died.'

She went back to sit beside Virtue Hawkins. 'You didn't mention the foreign man had been here before.'

'Did I not?' The old woman shrugged her thin shoulders. 'Your friend had so many visitors in the short time he was here.'

'But the boy told me this man came to visit Matthew on the day he died.'

'That's right,' Virtue nodded.

'And were there any other visitors that day?'

Virtue wrinkled her forehead, thinking. 'A tall, thin man, the foreign gentleman, and then your good self.'

'So the foreign man was the last to see Matthew alive.'

'No, Mrs Behn,' Virtue said, exasperated. 'I told you before, your friend was killed by Josiah Mullen! The men heard them arguing after the other man had gone.'

Aphra had forgotten about Mullen. 'Have they found him yet?'

'No, not yet.'

Aphra felt as if her head was spinning. The person she should be concerned about was Josiah Mullen. He was a murderer, and he was still at large. Maybe he was the one who murdered Grootvader, which — judging by the identical slashes across the throat — meant he'd also killed Elias.

Which meant he'd been inside her house at least once.

'Who heard Matthew and Mr Mullen arguing?' she asked Virtue.

The old woman tilted her head towards two men sitting on a bench near the entrance to the kitchen.

'I'll go and speak to them,' Aphra said.

'What?' Virtue asked her, horrified.

'I just want to ask them what they heard.'

'But ... but you can't just walk over and speak to them,' the old woman told her. 'It would not be seemly.'

'But I spoke to them the other night at the funeral.'

'Funerals be different,' Virtue said.

Aphra stood up. 'This will only take a moment.'

The old woman put down her rope and stood to follow her. 'It will be less unseemly if I am with you.'

'Mrs Behn wishes to speak to you,' Virtue announced, giving the men her sternest look.

Ye Gods, Aphra thought. She remembered the men's names from the other evening as Mr Smith and Mr Wilson. Neither was a day under seventy, one had a pair of crutches and the other had no teeth. What did Virtue think she was protecting her from?

She sat on a bench opposite the men, Virtue standing guard

behind her. 'I understand you heard Mr Cavell arguing with someone the day he was murdered.'

'That's right,' Mr Wilson, the man with the crutches, said. 'He was arguing with Josiah Mullen.'

'Do you know what they were arguing about?'

Both men shook their heads.

'Did you hear what they were saying?'

'Not really. Though I heard one word quite clearly, and that word was "traitor",' Mr Wilson told her.

'Traitor?' she repeated, feeling sick at the thought that Toby Rainbeard may have been telling the truth after all. 'When was this? Did you notice the time?'

Both agreed it was between four and five in the afternoon. They said they went upstairs to get something, but stopped outside the door when they heard shouting. Neither thinking it right to listen in on another's conversation, they immediately returned downstairs.

'If only we had intervened,' Mr Wilson said, 'your friend might still be alive. But neither of us could guess their disagreement would end in such a way.'

'The two of them argued all the time,' added Mr Smith.

'Did they know each other before coming here?'

'It seemed so,' said Mr Wilson. 'Neither came down to pick oakum, but always remained upstairs together, never speaking to anyone in the house unless it was necessary. Then it was usually Mr Mullen who did the talking for both of them.'

Aphra was more confused than ever. Hiding away, never speaking? This didn't sound like the Matthew Cavell she had known. 'So he and Mullen were friends?'

'Not friends,' Mr Smith said darkly. 'It was my impression that Mr Cavell was frightened of Mr Mullen, as I told them at the inquest.'

'You only say that now Mullen's killed him,' Wilson chided him. 'You never knew that when he was alive.' He turned to Aphra. 'They seemed bound together in some way. They were always whispering between themselves, so no one else could hear.'

'What were the findings of the inquest?'

'That he was killed with a knife,' Virtue said from behind her.

Aphra twisted to look up at her, surprised.

'I attended the inquest also, Mrs Behn.'

'He wasn't murdered with a sword?' Aphra said, thinking of what her parish searcher had said at the inquest into Elias's murder.

'The searcher said he was stabbed four times with a small knife. She said there was little blood on his clothes because he did all his bleeding inside, and it was the blood collecting in his chest that killed him.'

It seemed odd that Matthew and Elias should each be murdered in such a different manner, with different weapons, when Elias and Mr Grootvader had both been murdered in such similar fashion. She asked if Mullen owned a sword and was told the inmates were not allowed to keep weapons; Mullen must have kept his knife hidden. She told herself that explained it. Mullen didn't obtain a sword until after his escape. 'You say he rarely came downstairs. What about the times Matthew received visitors?'

'Mullen always remained by Mr Cavell's side,' Wilson said. 'Visitors or no.'

'What kind of man was Josiah Mullen?'

'Lazy,' Mr Smith told her, going on to say Mullen claimed to be too weak to work, though no one believed that now.

'Because he was strong enough to kill Matthew?' she asked.

'I hate to say this, Mrs Behn,' Virtue's voice came from behind her. 'But I was strong enough to kill your friend. The searcher said if the poor man hadn't been murdered she doubted he would have lived another month, he was so frail and ill from a growth in his stomach.'

238

'Oh God,' Aphra said. 'Poor Matthew.'

'The only way Mullen could have escaped with no one seeing him was through the upstairs window,' Mr Smith said. 'And how could someone too weak to pick oakum leap from a window?'

'He did have a fingertip missing, just here,' Mr Wilson added, holding up his gloved left hand and pointing to the little finger. 'But it was an old injury, and nothing to stop him from working.'

Aphra remembered that Virtue had mentioned Josiah Mullen's missing fingertip, and that it hadn't been included in the description on the constable's poster.

The men said it was Mrs Barrow who spoke to the constable, not them.

'Did you mention it at the inquest?' she asked them.

They admitted it hadn't occurred to them.

The men could tell her nothing more about Matthew or Mr Mullen, but suggested Mrs Barrow might have something in her records.

She thanked Virtue and the men, then stood up, bracing herself for another meeting with Mrs Barrow.

She'd only gone a few steps when another thought occurred to her. 'I don't see anyone new here,' she said. 'Have you still not filled the empty beds?'

The men told her they had not.

Aphra headed towards Mrs Barrow's office, passing the stairs to the men's quarters on the way. She stopped and placed a hand on the railing, thinking how Grootvader had pleaded with the boy to allow him up there.

What had he been looking for?

She was halfway up the stairs when she heard Virtue's voice calling from below. 'Where be you going, Mrs Behn?'

'Upstairs,' Aphra called back over her shoulder.

'But the men sleeps up there,' Virtue sputtered.

Aphra swung around to face her. 'They're not sleeping now.'

'But — '

'I've been up there before,' Aphra reminded her. 'And so have you.'

'But that was when we found your friend. That was different.'

Aphra decided to change her tactics. 'You allowed some foreign stranger to have a last look at the place where Matthew died,' she said, looking hurt. 'Would you deny me the same chance to say one final farewell?'

The old woman hesitated for a moment. 'It will look very bad if you go alone. I best come with you.'

Aphra did her best to hide her exasperation as she waited for the old woman to catch up, telling herself she hadn't expected to find anything anyway.

Virtue stood in the doorway, looking worried, while Aphra examined the room. It was obvious which cots had belonged to Matthew and Mr Mullen; they'd been stripped of sheets and blankets.

Aphra touched the mattress on which Matthew had died, feeling for any unusual lumps, then lifted it.

'What be you doing, Mrs Behn?' Virtue asked her, wringing her hands.

If Aphra was honest with the old woman, she would have to tell her she did not have the slightest idea what she was doing, or why she was doing it. She told her instead that she thought Matthew might have left a will.

Virtue bit her lip, unconvinced.

Aphra moved on to examine Mr Mullen's bed. It wasn't far from the window, which was easily big enough for a man to get through, and set fairly low in the wall, so it wasn't too great a distance to the ground. Aphra imagined the men were right that this had been Mullen's escape route.

She moved away from the wall, bending down to examine the floor.

Virtue walked over to see what she was looking at. 'What be you doing *now*, Mrs Behn?'

'Checking for loose floorboards.'

'But why?'

'Sometimes people hide things under floorboards.'

'Hide what?' Virtue asked her.

Aphra threw up her hands. 'I don't know!'

'What is going on here?' a woman's voice thundered from the doorway.

Aphra looked up to see Mrs Barrow glaring at her with undisguised hatred. The woman was quivering with rage.

'Ah, Mrs Barrow,' she said, keeping her voice light. 'I brought back your basket. I gave it to the maid.'

'Get out of here!' Mrs Barrow shouted, a vein in her forehead bulging. 'Get out of here, now!'

'I think it best you go now, Mrs Behn,' Virtue said quietly. The old woman took her by the arm, quickly leading her past the seething matron.

'But I wanted to ask her a few questions,' Aphra protested.

'If I were you,' Virtue whispered, pulling her down the stairs, 'I would leave Gospel House this minute, and I would not come back.'

'Why not?'

'Please, Mrs Behn,' Virtue said as they reached the front door. 'Just go.'

Aphra could see the door to Mrs Barrow's office standing open beyond the storeroom, her desk piled high with papers. If only she could get a look at the woman's files. 'All I want is to find out what happened to Matthew,' she said.

There was the sound of heavy footsteps on the stairs; Mrs Barrow was coming.

'Please,' Virtue said, her eyes wide with fear. 'Please go.'

'He was my friend and he was murdered in this house,' Aphra reminded her.

Mrs Barrow's heavy tread reached the bottom stair.

Virtue pushed Aphra out of the matron's line of sight, into the street. 'Sunday morning,' she whispered, 'from seven to nine of the clock Mrs Barrow be at church.'

Aphra returned home to find Elizabeth Decker waiting on her doorstep with a trunk, wailing that she'd been evicted from her lodgings.

Chapter Twenty-eight

Aphra woke early Sunday morning to find one of Elizabeth's arms draped across her chest. She disentangled herself and crept from the room, careful not to wake the snoring actress.

She arrived at Deptford shortly after sunrise, carrying the thin blade she'd found in Elias's pocket.

She knelt down behind a bush, watching the front of Gospel House.

Mrs Barrow left a little before seven, accompanied by the children and several of the fitter inmates. Virtue Hawkins was not among them.

She waited until Mrs Barrow and the others were out of sight, then crossed the road to approach the almshouse. The door swung open. Virtue beckoned to her from the hallway, urging her to hurry.

Aphra headed straight for Mrs Barrow's office. Virtue followed, nervously wringing her hands.

Aphra tried the office door; it was locked.

Virtue rocked from side to side, moaning that she'd told Mrs Barrow she was too ill to go to church; she'd lied, and all for nothing.

'It's all right,' Aphra told her, slipping Elias's blade into the door frame.

'I've never done such a thing before,' Virtue groaned as the office door swung open.

Mrs Barrow's bed stood in one corner behind a curtain. Next to the bed was a small dressing table and a wardrobe containing a handful of dark-coloured dresses and several aprons.

On the opposite side of the room was a large cabinet.

In the centre was Mrs Barrow's desk. Aphra checked the papers on the desk top first. Kitchen accounts. ·

The desk drawer was locked, but a moment's work with the blade got it open. Inside, Aphra found a set of keys tied together with string. She crossed over to the large cabinet. It was locked. She fumbled with the keys, trying them one by one.

'You're not thinking to steal anything?' Virtue whispered, trembling.

Aphra rolled her eyes. 'No, of course not!' She sighed with relief as she finally found the right key.

Inside the cabinet was a collection of ledgers, standing upright on shelves. She took down the first one and opened it. It was a day-to-day journal of expenses and activities for the year 1604. She put it back. She took down another, flicked through it and put it back.

She opened another volume, stopping as she came across the entry: '*17 November 1645. Admitted today one Virtue Hawkins, a childless widow of good character, age twenty-eight years. Recently evicted from Oakdale Farm, Essex. Husband lost at sea two years ago, serving under the Earl of Warwick, Lord High Admiral of the Parliamentary Fleet.*'

God's death, Aphra thought, looking at the old woman keeping a nervous eye on the door. She'd been here more than thirty years. She tried to imagine Virtue at the age of twenty-eight, and was horrified to find she couldn't do it.

She flicked through several more volumes, briefly scanning such entries as: '*Delivered today, seven sacks of flour*', '*Augustus Lennon, dead overnight of the griping guts*', and '*Praise be to God, this day we are still spared the plague*'.

But she couldn't find the ledger for the current year.

She put the last of the volumes back on its shelf and began a desperate search of the room, Virtue wringing her hands and moaning that the others would be back at any moment.

Aphra could have kicked herself when she found the book

for the current year had been in plain view the whole time, on the dressing table beside the bed.

She opened it, ignoring Virtue's frantic pleas to hurry as she carefully examined every entry for the month of September. Then she went back and checked August. There were deliveries of meat and beer, a broken banister that needed repair, a man who injured himself in a fall, but no mention anywhere of Matthew Cavell or Josiah Mullen.

She looked at the entry for the date of Matthew's death. Nothing.

The date of the funeral. Nothing.

She looked everywhere she could think of. There was nothing about Matthew, and there was nothing about Josiah Mullen.

She'd hoped to find some background details, perhaps a previous address, for either or both of the men. Instead she seemed to be finding that — as far as the records of Gospel House were concerned — neither man had ever existed.

Nell sat in the second to last row of seats in a large room at Whitehall, the Duke of Buckingham on her left, Sir Charles Sedley on her right, the three of them ignoring the preacher who'd been invited to deliver this week's address.

Buckingham leaned across Nell to whisper to Sedley. 'I see young Monmouth's here in his role of Protestant icon, sitting at the front, looking if he is actually paying attention to the sermon.'

Sedley yawned loudly. 'I find the boy unspeakably tiresome.'

Nell felt a tap on her shoulder. She turned to see two Maids of Honour leaning forward. 'Have you been to see Alexander Bendo yet?' one of them asked her.

Nell shook her head.

'We went yesterday, and he was amazing,' the other one enthused. 'It was as if he already knew us, and knew everything about us.'

'I found it terrifying,' said the first. 'The very moment I entered the room, I could feel disembodied spirits, swirling around my head.'

'It was a *little* frightening,' the other admitted. 'But the doctor said I had a natural psychic ability that only needs to be developed, and he was willing to give me lessons in occult lore.'

Nell turned towards the front of the room just in time to see Anne of Sussex take a seat beside her father.

Charles Sedley leaned across in front of Nell, nudging Buckingham's arm. 'Now there,' he said, nodding towards the young countess, 'is someone I find most intriguing.'

'Do you think she and her lovely friend might let us watch?' Buckingham asked, sniggering like a little boy.

'Watch what?' Nell asked.

Her question sent Buckingham and Sedley into whoops of hysterical laughter. Everyone in the room turned to look at them, except the king, who was asleep.

Still dressed in her nightgown, Hortense Mancini was brandishing a sabre in front of her mirror, striking various poses, when Mustapha knocked on the door and announced a visit from the Duchess of Portsmouth.

She hid the sword under the bed and put on a dressing gown.

Louise de Kéroualle entered a moment later, curtsying.

Hortense bowed. 'A visit from you is a rare pleasure,' she said. 'And on the Sabbath, too. Though I hope you haven't come to invite me to mass. Anne has gone downstairs to attend the Protestant service, which is more than enough religion for one day, and I'm hardly dressed for church, don't you think?'

'I am not here to ask you to mass.'

'In that case, have a seat,' Hortense said, gesturing towards a chair. 'And a drink,' she added, clapping her hands to summon a servant.

Louise crossed to the window, looking nervous. 'Do you mind if I close the curtains?'

Hortense shrugged. 'If you wish.'

Louise pulled the curtains across. 'This is not easy for me,' she said. 'I am afraid you will think me foolish. But on the other hand I thought you should know.'

'Know what?'

'It is probably nothing,' Louise said. 'But they're out there again. Two men, on the opposite bank. They've been sitting there every day for the past two weeks.'

'You mean the fishermen?'

'They're not fishermen,' Louise said. 'I've watched them through a spyglass, and half the time they don't even bait their hooks.' She took a deep breath. 'I think they are watching someone in the palace, and I think it is you.'

Aphra stood in her bedchamber doorway, watching Elizabeth kneel on the floor in front of the wardrobe, muttering at a pile of Aphra's dirty laundry.

'What are you doing?'

Elizabeth looked up, startled. 'Mrs Behn! You're home.'

'What are you doing with my clothes?'

'I'm so sorry, Mrs Behn,' Elizabeth said. 'I opened the wardrobe and they all tumbled out on to the floor! I keep trying to push them back, but they just fall out again.'

'Please, Elizabeth,' Aphra said, picking up an armful of laundry and tossing it back into the wardrobe, 'just leave my things alone.'

Elizabeth frowned, holding up a piece of bloodstained paper. 'What's this?'

'Oh, my God,' Aphra said. It was one of the strips of paper she'd found in Elias's pocket. With everything that had happened since, she'd managed to forget all about them. She dumped the laundry back on the floor and knelt beside it, searching for the rest of the paper.

*

Elizabeth followed her downstairs, watching her spread the torn paper across her desk, then lift the sections up to the window one by one, straining to see what was written beneath the blood.

Despite a constant stream of interruptions – 'What are you doing? Why is that paper so dirty? What does it say? May I look? May I? Please? ... Please? ... By the law, it smells!' – Aphra eventually managed to make out the words: 'Gresham College, 4 of the clock, Thursday.'

Nell returned home from Whitehall to find the Duke of Monmouth waiting in her parlour. 'Keep coming round to see me like this, and people will talk,' she teased him.

'This is not a time for joking,' he said gravely. 'Many things are happening of which you are not aware.'

She sat down, sipping a glass of sherry. 'What things?' she said, hoping he wasn't there to launch into one of his diatribes.

He was. She could tell by the way he refused to sit, preferring to pace up and down on her carpet.

'Plots and conspiracies,' he told her.

'Let me guess,' she said, yawning. 'Papists.'

'This is a serious matter, Nelly. Feelings in the country are running high –'

'You mean feelings in the Country *Party*,' she interrupted.

'This is a time for caution. A time you must know who you can trust, who your friends are and where their loyalties lie.'

'Jamie, if you wish to have a drink you may trust me to be your friend. If you wish to attend a play or dance at a ball, I shall be forever loyal. But if you continue to shout at me about conspiracies you may find our relations become strained.'

'I was not aware that I was shouting.'

'I wish my neighbours could say the same. Please, Jamie, I pray you sit down and be quiet!'

He sat down on a padded chair, sulking.

'All right,' Nell said finally. 'I give up. You wish to tell me about conspiracies, tell me about conspiracies. I am listening.'

He stared down at the floor, thinking. 'I do not wish to upset you,' he said eventually. 'Or to worry you. But the Papists are plotting to take over the nation, and we must stop them.'

Nell rolled her eyes. He'd be talking about civil war again in a minute.

'How much do you know about your friend, Mrs Behn?'

That question took her by surprise. 'Aphra? What do you wish to know about Aphra?'

'How well does she know Samuel Pepys?'

That question surprised her even more. 'The Samuel Pepys who's always trying to grope the orange girls?' She threw up her hands. 'Hardly at all.'

'She was seen talking to him the other day during the afternoon performance at the Theatre Royal.'

'So?'

'There are those who suspect Pepys may be a secret Papist.'

'God's death! You're talking about the Secretary of the Admiralty, Jamie.'

'Exactly.' Monmouth nodded, looking triumphant. 'And how has he risen so high? Through his long association with my Papist uncle.'

'But what has this to do with Aphra?'

'Maybe nothing,' he said. 'Though I find her choice of company interesting, don't you?'

His Majesty's evening visit over, Hortense put on a dressing gown and made her way down the hall to Anne's room.

Anne was sitting up in bed, reading. She put her book away as Hortense got into bed beside her.

'I've been thinking,' Hortense said, placing an arm around Anne's shoulders, 'that it might be better for you to return to Sussex.'

Anne stared at her in disbelief. 'What? You can't mean that!'

'But I do,' Hortense said.

Anne's eyes filled with tears. 'Have I done something to anger you? Or are you just tired of my company?'

'It's nothing like that,' Hortense assured her. 'I am concerned for your safety.'

'My safety? Why?'

'Louise de Kéroualle was here today. She told me there is much anti-Catholic feeling in this country, being whipped up by certain parties, and that she herself has been the victim of many threats. It is her belief that I may be an even greater target for their hatred, simply because I had a cardinal for an uncle.'

'And you believed her?' Anne asked, incredulous. 'She's just trying to frighten you, to make you leave Whitehall.'

'But what about those men on the riverbank? We've both seen them. She says they are watching us through a spyglass.'

'I wouldn't be surprised if she'd hired them herself. She'd do anything to be rid of you, just as my mother would once do anything to be rid of Nelly Gwyn or Frances Stewart. I'm not going anywhere,' Anne said, snuggling up to her. 'And neither are you.'

Honoré Courtin sat up late, writing an encoded message informing his king of the interest shown by the Duke of Monmouth in a conversation between Aphra Behn and the Secretary of the Admiralty, Samuel Pepys, reported to have taken place during a performance at the Theatre Royal.

Chapter Twenty-nine

A phra came downstairs the next morning to find another printed announcement shoved beneath her door, this time for a poulterers offering: *'Fresh fat chickens delivered to your door.'*

She tossed it on the fire just as Nell's coach pulled up in front of the house. She looked out the window to see Bevil Cane approaching the front step to escort her and Elizabeth to rehearsal, as he had insisted on doing every morning since Elizabeth came to stay with her.

'I understand from Madam Gwyn that you attend a weekly meeting at Gresham College,' Aphra said once they were in the coach.

'I attend the college every Thursday afternoon from four to six. I have recently been made a fellow of the Royal Society.'

Aphra wondered who a Lincoln's Inn mumper could possibly have arranged to meet at the Royal Society. 'Have you noticed anything unusual at the meetings these last few weeks?'

'Last week someone brought in a fragment of unicorn's horn.'

'No, I mean have you seen any new people at a meeting? Someone you never noticed before?'

Mr Cane shrugged. 'We often have eminent visitors.'

Aphra thought back to Mrs Adams's statement that Elias claimed to have found a powerful protector. This protector must have been the person Elias had arranged to meet. 'Has the Earl of Arlington ever attended one of your meetings?'

'Not that I know of,' Mr Cane said. 'But the Duke of Monmouth came as a guest only the week before last.'

It had never occurred to her that Monmouth might have been the powerful protector Elias had referred to, but it might explain his presence at the funeral.

'The week before last? That would have been the day after the funeral,' Aphra said.

'That's right.'

'You must have been surprised to see the duke again so soon.'

'Oh, no,' Mr Cane said. 'His visit had been arranged some weeks in advance so that certain experiments could be repeated in his honour, such as the mixing of chemicals to make different colours, cutting open a dead cormorant...' He rambled on and on, enthusiastically relating every detail of the various experiments performed for the duke, but Aphra wasn't listening. She was thinking back to Monmouth's odd behaviour at the funeral.

Elizabeth looked out the window, yawning.

'How go your rehearsals, Nelly?' the Duke of Buckingham asked as they strolled arm in arm through St James's Park.

'Very well,' she said. 'Mrs Decker will make an actress yet.'

Buckingham raised an eyebrow. 'Will she?'

'Oh, yes,' Nell told him. 'She behaves more like one every day. She complains her character would never say such and such a line, she accuses the other actors of destroying her concentration and only this morning she threw a tantrum.'

'Then she *is* making progress,' Buckingham said, steering Nell around a pile of fallen leaves.

'Definitely.'

'It is a shame about my wager with Rochester no longer being valid,' Buckingham mused.

Nell stopped dead in her tracks, pulling her arm away. 'What do you mean?'

'Rochester has left the country,' Buckingham said, 'and no one has heard a word from him these last two weeks. I assume this means the wager is off.'

'It means nothing of the kind!'

'But if Rochester is not here, then who am I to pay?' he asked, widening his bloodshot eyes in a laughable attempt at innocence.

'You may pay me,' Nell said. 'I can hold Rochester's winnings until his return.'

'Does that mean that if I win, I may come to you for payment?'

'I see your game now, George,' she said, laughing. 'But I promise you that circumstance will not arise. You have no chance of winning.'

'Don't I?' Buckingham asked, taking her arm again to resume their walk. 'As I recall the wager was not that Elizabeth Decker would make an acceptable actress, but that she make the *best* actress on the London stage. It's not the same thing at all, is it, Nell?'

Samuel Pepys pushed a file across his desk. 'Mr Cavell's records,' he told Aphra. 'They make depressing reading.'

'May I?' she said, reaching for the folder.

He shrugged. 'If you like. Though I can summarize the contents for you: Matthew Cavell was press-ganged on to a ship, and was wounded. He then went over to the Dutch.'

Aphra sat dumbstruck. Toby Rainbeard had been right.

'He was not the only one to do so,' Mr Pepys went on. 'Thousands of English and Scottish seamen deserted to serve with the Dutch fleet, though they were assured of hanging should they be captured. Certain Dutch ships were manned almost entirely by English crews. It was a question of money. The Dutch paid in cash; we paid in tickets. The Dutch fed their men; we starved ours. And those who were wounded or fell ill were abandoned.

'It was an abominable situation, Mrs Behn. I was then Clerk of the Acts for the Navy Board, and though I was aware of what was going on there was nothing I could do about it. There

253

was simply no money in the treasury. I remember days when the yard outside my office was filled with women sobbing for their husbands taken away by press-gangs, leaving them and their children to starve. I nearly cried myself for pity, but what could I do? There were so many of them. Too many for one man to do anything.

'One day I looked out the window and saw one of our seamen lying on the ground, dying for want of food. Because he was alone, I was able to help him. I sent him half a crown and ordered his ticket to be paid. He was one of the few to be so fortunate. In most cases, our tickets proved worthless.'

Aphra found Toby asleep at a table in the Blacksmith's Arms. He was wearing a torn green coat with tarnished metal buttons, several of them missing. Another hung by a single thread, ready to drop off at any minute. Lord, she thought, when will Arlington ever pay his agents a proper wage? 'Mr Rainbeard,' she said.

He opened his eyes, pulling a knife from his pocket. 'Oh, it's you,' he said. He put the knife away. 'You would be wise not to startle me like that again.'

'And you would be wise to tell me what is going on,' she hissed, sitting across from him at the table.

'I have already told you all I dare.'

'Tell me more,' she said. 'You keep saying that Matthew and Elias were traitors. I know Matthew changed sides during the first Dutch war, but that war ended nine years ago, and the most recent has been over for two. Why should his dealings with the Dutch concern Arlington now?'

He laughed. 'Am I right in thinking you have as little love for Lord Arlington as I do?'

'I hold his lordship in the highest regard,' she said carefully.

The old man nodded to show he understood. 'Then you may enjoy this, Mrs Behn. Do you remember a few years ago, when the Lord Chancellor's closet was robbed and the thieves paraded through Lincoln's Inn Fields displaying his mace and purse?'

She remembered it well. The thieves, led by a man named Thomas Sadler, marched in a mock Lord Chancellor's procession, applauded by crowds of mumpers and link boys. It had been a great humiliation for the Lord Chancellor, who happened to be the Earl of Arlington. But what did that have to do with Matthew Cavell?

'Do you recall how the thieves came to be arrested?' the old man asked her.

Sadler's landlady was cleaning his room when she found several small jewels scattered across the floor. She then opened the cupboard where Sadler had hidden the Lord Chancellor's jewelled mace and raised the alarm, thinking her tenant had stolen His Majesty's crown. Sadler and his confederates were arrested and hung at Tyburn. 'I still don't see what this has to do with Matthew Cavell,' she said.

Toby looked around to make sure no one was nearby. The tavern was empty, except for two men standing near the bar. 'A little over a month ago, an unsigned letter arrived at Whitehall Palace, delivered by General Post. The writer claimed to have found a certain item, which he described in such exact detail there could be no question as to its authenticity. He went on to say he would be in touch later regarding a price for its return, as he had other buyers. The letter was passed on to Lord Arlington, who immediately traced it to your friend.'

'But how? You said it was unsigned and delivered by General Post. It could have come from anywhere.'

Toby shook his head. 'Not anywhere. The item described in the letter was one of those stolen from the Lord Chancellor's closet. Arlington sent several guards to Sadler's old lodgings, where the landlady said she'd recently had a tenant named Matthew Cavell who had moved out the previous day.'

'Matthew found something in Sadler's room?'

Toby nodded.

'But I thought everything from that theft had been recovered.'

'Not everything,' Toby said, tapping his nose. 'Several important papers were taken that day. Sadler was questioned about them of course. As he couldn't read, he had no idea they might have any value, and said he'd burned them to warm his room. Though now it seems one survived the flames after all.'

'So all this is about a piece of paper?' Aphra said.

'Not just any piece of paper,' Toby whispered. 'One my Lord Arlington is most anxious to have returned.' He shrugged. 'Or destroyed.'

Aphra and Elizabeth were eating dinner when they heard someone knocking.

Aphra got up to answer the door. A man shoved a folded sheet of paper into her hand, bowed, then left without a word.

She unfolded the sheet and read the words:

Many eminent people have come to Doctor Alexander Bendo for the answers to many perplexing questions.

The doctor has a message especially for you.

Come to him tonight, at his lodgings in Tower Street, next to the sign of the Black Swan. He will expect you at eight. There will be no charge for this consultation.

Her first thought was to throw it on to the fire, but her curiosity was piqued by the promise of a message, especially one free of charge. She went back to the kitchen to tell Elizabeth she was going out for a while.

Chapter Thirty

A man in black hooded robes ushered Aphra into a small waiting room. The walls and ceiling were black; the only light came from a single candle flickering inside a human skull. About half a dozen people were waiting in the semidarkness.

'I have a letter from the doctor,' Aphra told the hooded man.

He gestured towards a chair, saying something in a language she didn't understand.

'I have an appointment for eight of the clock,' she said, trying to show him the letter.

The man pointed at the chair.

She gave up and sat down.

'It's no use. None of them speak English,' the woman next to her whispered.

A black curtain was thrust aside, briefly filling the room with a harsh orange glow. A hooded figure stood framed in the doorway, pointing at the woman next to Aphra.

The woman walked through and the curtain closed behind them, plunging the room back into darkness.

There was an awful smell of something burning, and a sound of evil, cackling laughter.

A man sitting across from her got to his feet and left.

Aphra briefly considered following him, but decided that as she had come this far she might as well wait to see what lay beyond the curtain.

One by one, the people ahead of her went through. Not one of them came out again.

Maybe this was not a good idea, she told herself, standing up to leave.

A voice called behind her, shouting harsh syllables that made no sense.

She turned to see the hooded figure beckoning her to follow. She walked through the curtain and was led down a long corridor, lined with doors. One of them was open, allowing her to see into the room beyond.

It appeared to be some kind of laboratory. The walls were lined with shelves holding all manner of bottles, tubes and jars. An iron cauldron hung suspended over a fire and a man with hunched shoulders and a wild expression stirred some noxious-smelling substance. Men in robes sat on stools at a number of high tables, some mixing brightly coloured liquids, others drying herbs and grinding them into powders, some extracting oils, all chattering in a language she didn't recognize.

She was ushered into a small office, the dark walls covered with an assortment of strange charts and framed certificates.

An old man sat behind a table, wearing a long green robe lined with fur. Around his neck was a magnificent medal, set with diamonds and pearls, hanging from a thick gold chain. His shaven head was covered by an elaborately embroidered antique cap fringed with fur. He stroked his long white beard, regarding her with deep-set eyes glittering beneath a pair of bushy white brows.

'I am so glad you could come,' he said, gesturing towards a seat. He spoke with a strange accent, unlike any she had ever heard.

She sat down across from him, looking at the various potions and powders on the table in front of her. A small scale sat at the man's elbow. 'Are these your medicines?' she asked him.

'You do not want medicine,' the man told her. 'Not this medicine, at any rate,' he added, no longer speaking with an accent.

Aphra pushed her chair back from the table. 'Who are you?'

'I am the grave, the wise, the just — not to mention modest and civil — Doctor Alexander Bendo. This robe I wear in memory of my master, Rabelais. This medal was a gift from the king of Cyprus for performing a cure upon his darling daughter, the Princess Aloephangia, whose portrait you see on the wall behind me. There is no distemper I cannot treat, no heart nor soul I cannot read, no future I cannot predict.'

Aphra looked at him wide-eyed, saying nothing.

He laughed, slapping the table in front of him. 'Zooks, Aphra. You still don't know me?'

She picked up a candle and bent forward, looking at him closely. His beard was false. The lines around his eyes were paint. 'Rochester?'

'Thomas,' he shouted. 'Have you locked the doors?'

'Yes, my lord,' a man's voice called back.

Rochester removed his hat and beard. 'Half the court has been here this last week, every one of them amazed by my intimate knowledge of their habits and desires.'

'And not one of them knew you? I can't believe you haven't been recognized.'

He winked, running his tongue around his lips. 'Shall I tell you a little secret, Aphra? It's not the first time I have gone unrecognized, even by my closest and dearest friends.'

'I recognized you just now,' Aphra said. 'I could see your beard was false.'

'Only because I allowed you to. You certainly didn't recognize me the other week, and we were standing this close.' He held up a thumb and forefinger, pressing them together.

'I don't know what you're talking about.'

'You must surely be a woman of rare tenderness and mercy,' he said in Fergus O'Bannion's voice, 'to greet a penniless stranger such as I as if he were a long lost friend.'

'Oh my God,' she said. 'That was never you!'

'After our discussion that morning, in which you expressed many worries and suspicions about the murders of your friends,

I thought I might be better placed to observe the true nature of those at the funeral if I were someone other than the Earl of Rochester. My only intention was to help you.'

'Then why did you not identify yourself to me?'

'I would have, but then I saw how Elizabeth, believing me to be absent, would so readily betray me.'

'What are you talking about?'

'I saw her with that Mr Cane.'

'You weevil,' Aphra said. 'Bevil Cane was only telling her about a play he's written, which he constantly talks about at great length to any who will listen.' Then she told him what had happened after he left, and about Nell's theory that she and Madam Gwyn had been given drops.

'Drops?' he repeated. He scratched his head, frowning. 'This worries me, Aphra.'

'You? Worried? I'm the one who should be worried, not you! I'm the one who has pawned nearly everything I own! I'm the one who is deeper in debt than ever, whose house has been broken into again, and who has found yet another murdered body! And if all that does not seem enough, Elizabeth has moved in with me!'

'Start again, from the beginning,' Rochester said calmly. 'And tell me everything.'

'I may be able to add another piece to this puzzle,' he said when she had finished. 'I had an interesting conversation with young Monmouth today.'

'Monmouth?'

Rochester nodded. 'He came here this afternoon dressed in a ridiculous disguise of workman's cap and leather apron. I looked at his palm and told him he had been recently touched by death, and that I saw him walking in a procession behind two coffins, which mightily impressed him. Then he asked if I could tell him about a woman. I asked if he wished to know whether some intrigue was worth pursuing, and he said no, he wished to know whether a certain woman was in possession of a lost item he wished to recover, and if not where could this item be found? I told him he must describe the woman, so my spirit guides may seek her out and watch her. He said she was vulgar, immodest and rarely sober. It was then I realized he must be referring to you.'

Aphra rose from her chair, clenching her fists. 'What?'

Rochester raised his hands in surrender. 'I am joking, Aphra. He told me her initials were A.B.'

Aphra sat down again. 'So what did you tell young Monmouth about this lost item?'

'I told him to come back tomorrow.'

Aphra took her place among the men in the laboratory, a large black hood pulled close around her face. 'We open the doors at three,' the one named Thomas Alcock told her. 'From that moment on, we speak only the ancient tongue of the Gibbers.'

'And what is the ancient tongue of the Gibbers?'

'Gibberish,' the man beside the cauldron said, laughing.

She asked him what was in the cauldron. He told her it was a mixture of asafoetida, soot and urine.

She was scraping dust from bricks when the Duke of Monmouth was led past the laboratory to his consultation with the wise and benevolent Doctor Bendo. Thomas Alcock tapped her on the shoulder, signalling her to follow him.

He opened the door to a cupboard, indicating she should get inside. He raised a finger to his lips to signal silence, then reached past her, removing a plug from the wall.

She pressed her eye against a small round hole, watching the duke enter Doctor Bendo's office, dressed in his workman's disguise. The table in front of Rochester was lined with skulls, and something was smouldering in a bowl. 'Have you performed the purification ritual?' Rochester asked him. 'Did you

261

stand beneath the sky at midnight, your naked body smeared with mud?'

'Yes, doctor.'

Aphra clamped a hand over her mouth, trying not to laugh.

'Good,' Rochester said, gesturing for Monmouth to sit down. 'I must caution you before we proceed. Necromancy is fraught with peril, and must not be approached lightly. Are you sure you wish to go through with this?'

'I am sure.'

'Then we shall begin.' Rochester placed his hands upon the table, taking several deep breaths. He shouted some nonsense syllables, then threw a handful of powder into the bowl, causing bright flames to leap into the air. He clutched at his heart and collapsed forward on to the table.

'Are you all right?' Monmouth asked him.

'He is here,' Rochester moaned, raising a hand to ward off an unseen attacker. 'I see his horrible visage before me, his throat slit from ear to ear!'

Monmouth gasped.

'He is angry,' Rochester said. 'Very angry.' He raised his head, cupping a hand to his ear. 'He says, "Why did you not protect me? You were meant to protect me!"'

'I only meant I would protect him from prison,' Monmouth protested.

'He is telling me you were to meet him ... Wait, it's coming to me. You were to meet him on a Thursday, outside Gresham College.'

The duke shivered.

'He had something for you ... He's holding something in front of him, trying to show me, but it isn't clear. What is it?'

'It's a document,' Monmouth said. 'A letter.'

'Ah yes, I see it now. A letter. I see the writing, but the words are unclear.'

Monmouth buried his head in his hands. 'I never knew what it said.'

Rochester turned towards the hole in the wall where Aphra was watching, mouthing the words: 'Now what?'

Aphra clenched her fists in frustration. Monmouth didn't know much more than her.

'But he told you something,' Rochester persisted, turning back to Monmouth. 'He told you it was important.'

'Yes.'

Rochester hesitated for a moment. Aphra could see that he was sweating. If he wasn't careful, he would lose Monmouth's trust. 'He was trying to sell you this letter, wasn't he?'

Monmouth began to look suspicious. 'Perhaps.'

'For a large amount.'

'Perhaps.'

'He told you the contents of this letter would make you king of England, didn't he?'

Monmouth's look of suspicion changed to one of amazement. 'How did you know?'

Aphra rested her forehead against the wall, relieved that Rochester had guessed right. 'The spirits,' Rochester said. 'The spirits tell me what I need to know. How did this man – ' He leaned to one side, cupping a hand to his ear again. 'Wait, he's telling me his name ... It sounds like he's saying "Elisha" ... No, I hear him more clearly now. He says his name is Elias. How did Elias first contact you?'

'I received an anonymous message from someone saying he had something which would be of great value to me.'

'He told you to ride your coach through Lincoln's Inn Fields, and he would find you?'

'Yes, that's it exactly,' the duke said breathlessly.

'Then what happened?'

'I was approached by a beggar. He said he had seen this letter and could obtain it for me for a price of five thousand pounds and the guarantee of my protection. I agreed to meet him again in three days' time.'

Rochester threw his head back, gasping. 'But he tells me he

263

was murdered in a woman's house of office, two days before your planned meeting. He saw you at his funeral. He says he floated above you, watching as you searched his pockets, but you did not find what you were looking for.'

Monmouth's mouth dropped open.

'Oh, he is vengeful and angry!' Rochester straightened up, looking Monmouth in the eye. 'He is asking me if you had anything to do with his death.'

'Oh, no! Never.'

'He wants me to ask if you know who killed him.'

'I have no idea.'

'He is giving me a list of names. He wants to know if you recognize any of them. Toby Rainbeard.'

Monmouth shook his head.

'Jan Grootvader? Mrs Adams? Josiah Mullen?'

'None of them.'

Rochester tapped his fingers on the table top. 'He has nothing more to say to you.'

'What about the letter?' Monmouth asked. 'Does he know where it is? Does the woman have it?'

'He says the woman doesn't have it and never did. He tells me if you wish to find the letter, you must first perform the purification ritual every night for the next three months.'

'Three months?'

Rochester shrugged. 'That's what he says.'

As Monmouth got up to leave, Rochester instructed him to ask the man tending the cauldron to fill him a large bottle, from which he was to drink twice a day.

Hortense Mancini and Anne of Sussex were walking arm in arm along the Stone Gallery when they came across Nell Gwyn, talking to the French ambassador.

'How goes Mrs Behn's play, Nelly?' Hortense asked her.

Nell told her it was going well enough, though there was one

264

scene that still worried her, in which Mistress Decker is supposed to fight a duel.

'And what is your worry?' Hortense asked her.

Nell rolled her eyes. 'She keeps dropping the sword!'

Hortense and Anne exchanged a glance. Hortense turned back to Nell, smiling. 'Perhaps we could help her.'

Chapter Thirty-one

A phra closed her front door behind her, alone at last. Elizabeth had gone straight to Nell's from rehearsal, to practise fencing with the Duchess of Mazarin. She wouldn't be back for hours. Hours of blessed peace and quiet.

Aphra went into the parlour to open the shutters and saw the latch was undone.

She froze, listening.

She didn't hear anything.

She glanced around the room. Everything seemed to be in order.

She told herself not to worry, she must have forgotten to secure the latch when she'd left for rehearsal that morning.

But she was certain she hadn't.

She grabbed hold of the poker beside the grate, and made her way around the house, searching every room, prodding every corner.

No sign of anyone.

She put down the poker and opened the window, sitting down to read the final act of Bevil Cane's play.

Half an hour later she put the finished manuscript aside. After nearly three weeks of promising, she'd finally done it. At last she could look the young man in the eye and tell him she'd liked his play.

What a relief.

She got up and went into the kitchen to find something to eat. She happened to glance out into the garden as she was reaching for a plate and saw something glistening in the sunlight.

She went outside to take a closer look, and found a metal button lying in the middle of the path.

She climbed the ladder to Toby Rainbeard's loft, determined to confront him.

He wasn't there.

The wardrobe had been left open. Her mouth dropped open at the sight of a long blue gown, exactly like those worn by the inmates of Gospel House.

A note had been left on the bed, written in a neat, precise hand: *'Six of the clock this evening. Mrs A's house.'*

It was nearly six now.

She hurried down the narrow St Giles alley where she had first met Toby Rainbeard, slowing her pace as she approached Mrs Adams's windowless little house. The door was closed.

She hid in a tiny space between two buildings, waiting to see who came out. After a while, she got tired of waiting. Who could Toby be with, to keep him such a long time? She crossed the alley to the door and pressed her ear against it, listening. Silence.

Maybe she was too late. Maybe they were gone.

She pushed the door open just a crack. There was no sound or movement within. She opened it wider, taking a tentative step into the dark interior. Her foot hit something soft.

She ran next door to Meldrick Bridger's house.

Aphra and Mr Bridger returned a moment later, Mr Bridger carrying a lantern. 'Oh, my soul,' Mr Bridger muttered, bending down over Toby's body.

He had been slashed to death much the same way as Elias and Mr Grootvader had been. Toby had tried to defend himself, of course. The cuts on his arms and face attested to that, as did the knife lying in the straw not far from his body. She knelt down to touch his cheek. The body was still warm.

She removed the glove from his left hand.

'I have to go,' she told Mr Bridger. 'I have some urgent business.'

She climbed into the room above the blacksmith's, and froze. There was someone in the loft already. A tall man stood with his back to her, hurriedly packing the contents of Toby's wardrobe into a trunk.

She'd come back to search the room, not confront Toby's killer. She carefully edged her way back to the ladder, keeping her eyes on the man's back.

Then he turned around. She gasped, recognizing him at once.

'I thought I would never see you again,' he said. 'I prayed I wouldn't.' He started walking towards her.

'Stay away from me,' she warned him.

He stopped, a curious look on his face. 'Don't you know me?'

'Of course I know you,' she said. 'We met only the other week, Mr Frost. At a funeral in Deptford.'

'Have I changed that much?' He removed his leather hat and brown wig and thick spectacles, placing them on the table.

Aphra stared at the man standing before her, his gaunt face ill and tired, his black hair streaked with grey.

'I see by your face that I have,' he said sadly. 'You, on the other hand, look just as I remember you from those long nights on board the *Guiana*.'

'No,' Aphra said. 'Matthew is dead! I buried him!'

'You buried a man named Josiah Mullen.'

'No, Toby Rainbeard was Josiah Mullen. I saw his little finger – '

'Josiah Mullen was an old sailor I found begging at Holborn,' Matthew interrupted.

Aphra stood clenching and unclenching her fists as the implications of what he was telling her began to sink in. 'I spent all that money to bury a stranger?'

'I'm sorry about that, Aphra. I would repay you if I could.' He gestured to a chair, indicating she sit down while he resumed his packing.

'Toby and I were partners from the beginning. I'd found a certain piece of paper – a letter – quite by accident, behind a cupboard in my lodgings, and instantly realized its value. I contacted several potential buyers, including Lord Arlington. When Toby learned Arlington knew my name but had no idea of my appearance, we paid Mullen to assume my identity while Toby assumed his. We offered the matron of Gospel House a share of our proceeds in exchange for hiding them. Toby had proof Mrs Barrow had been stealing from the almshouse funds for quite some time, which had some influence on her decision to help us. Toby handled negotiations from his bed at the almshouse while I remained here, with the letter. We concluded a deal with the Dutch on the day you encountered my brother in Lincoln's Inn Fields.

'Elias came to me immediately afterwards, saying he regretted having identified himself to you, but had been so surprised that he had spoken without thinking. And then you insisted he tell you where I was. Not daring to tell the truth, he had told you I was at the almshouse and now you were determined to go there. I left immediately for Gospel House, to inform Toby and Mullen that you were on the way.'

'Is that why Mullen was killed? Because you feared I would denounce him as an impostor?'

Matthew knelt down to search the drawers in the bottom of the wardrobe. 'My intention in going to Gospel House was merely to instruct Mullen in a few facts, in the hope he might convince you he was me, though ill and with much loss of memory. Now I wish I had never gone. If I'd only remained here, my brother would still be alive.'

'I don't understand.'

'Soon after I left Gospel House, Jan Grootvader agreed the sum to be paid and the arrangements for handing it over. But

Mr Mullen became upset, saying he had never realized we meant to betray our own country. He began shouting that he would go to the authorities, so loudly Toby was forced to ... silence him.' He shrugged, emptying the contents of the top drawer into his trunk. 'He gave Toby no choice and, besides, his usefulness was over. The Dutch had agreed to pay, and pay well. But while I was out, Elias stole the letter.'

He tossed the empty drawer aside and pulled out the next one. 'I now know he told you I was at Gospel House on purpose, in order to get me out of this room so he could steal the letter.' He looked up at Aphra, a tear glistening in the corner of one eye. 'I would have taken care of him, Aphra. I'd told him more than once that when this business was completed, I would do everything I could to restore him to something like his former position, though it would have to be abroad. But that was not good enough for him; he had to have every penny for himself.'

He shook his head. 'Grootvader was ready to pay, we could have had the money and been out of the country the very next morning. But Elias's greed was to be all our undoing.'

'I can almost understand why you killed him,' Aphra said.

'Killed him? No, never,' he protested. 'He was my brother!'

'If you didn't kill him, then who did?'

'I don't know. All I know is that everyone who comes into contact with that cursed letter dies!' He took a deep breath and resumed his search for anything of value, finding a ring which he tossed into the trunk.

'Toby didn't lie about me, you know. I am the traitor they believe me to be. But not without cause. Elias and I returned to England with nothing but the clothes on our backs. I was captured by a press-gang and forced on to a ship where I served without pay, living on bad meat and black bread crawling with maggots, wearing my one suit of clothes almost to rags. When I was wounded, they even took my clothes, abandoning me naked on a beach. Such experiences change a man, Aphra. Change him more than you might realize.'

Aphra's eyes filled with tears. 'I'm sorry.'

'It happened all the time,' he said. 'At least they will not hang me as a traitor now; they would never dare bring me to trial.'

'Why not?'

'Because of what I found, Aphra. What they wish to keep secret at all costs, for fear the people will rise up in revolt: that the King of England has made a pact with the devil himself.'

'What are you talking about?'

He shook his head, emptying another drawer into his trunk. 'It is better you do not know. The knowledge itself is dangerous.'

'That is what Mrs Adams said Elias told her.'

'And he was right. If they find me they will kill me for this knowledge.' He closed the trunk and stood up. 'Just as they killed the others, in secret with no benefit of trial.'

She slowly got to her feet, keeping her eyes on him as she moved behind her chair. 'Mullen refused to co-operate with you, Elias stole the letter from you, Grootvader attempted to retrieve it without paying you. All were murdered. And now Toby has met the same fate. Did he try to cheat you as well?'

Matthew stared at her. 'That is not wise, to accuse a man of murder to his face when there is no one to hear you over the constant clamour of a blacksmith's hammer. If your accusation was true, what would there be to stop him killing you as well, that very moment?'

She grabbed hold of the chair, raising it in front of her as a shield.

'But it is not true,' Matthew said, sinking into the other chair. 'I sent a note to Toby, asking him to meet me in St Giles. But when I arrived, he was already dead. I came here to take what I could, then escape. I never thought to find you here. All these years, I never meant us to meet again.

'Then Elias told me he saw you, and you were just as he remembered. And when Toby showed me the invitation to my own funeral, I couldn't stay away. I had to see you one last time, if only from a distance.'

'I don't understand you,' Aphra said, putting down the chair. 'Why did you once do me a great kindness only to determine we should never meet again?'

'You are referring to your father's funeral.'

She nodded.

He took a deep breath before he answered. 'That coffin wasn't empty. Within a day of arriving at my uncle's plantation, he and Elias had a terrible argument. I heard them shouting, and ran into the room to find my uncle lying in a pool of blood. Elias was my brother, Aphra. I had no choice but to protect him. My first thought was that the risk of discovery would be much greater if the body was buried on our property. That was when I had the idea of staging a funeral for your father.'

All these years she had thought of Matthew Cavell's action as selfless and generous, and he had only been using her to cover up a murder. 'You defiled my father's memory! The grave that should have been his, you defiled with the blood of your murdered uncle! Damn you!'

He stood, putting on his wig and hat. 'I never meant you or your dead father ill, you must believe me. But what could I do? He was my brother!' He bent to pick up his trunk. 'It broke my heart to think I would never see you again, but how could I face you after that? I could hardly ask you to be the wife of a murderer's brother.'

'Wife? What are you talking about?'

'I loved you, Aphra, with all my heart. But that was a long time ago, and there's nothing to be done about it now.' He walked over to the ladder, then turned back to look at her once more, a tear running down his cheek. 'I'm sorry I am not the man you thought you remembered.' He tied a length of rope around the trunk, then knelt to lower it to the ground below.

'What?' he said, dropping the rope. A blade thrust upwards through the hole in the floor, plunging into Matthew's stomach.

Aphra screamed. Matthew crumpled forward, clutching at his wound. A man's head rose through the opening. Matthew placed one hand on the floor and rolled on to his side, trying to drag himself away. 'No,' he gasped. 'No, please, no.'

Bevil Cane stepped up from the ladder, blood dripping from the tip of his sword. Then he stabbed Matthew through the chest.

'What have you done?' Aphra shrieked.

'Praise God you are all right,' Bevil said. 'I feared he'd already killed you!'

'No! No! He never meant to kill me!'

'But he killed all those others, Mrs Behn. Why should he treat you any differently?' He looked down at Matthew, twitching on the floor, red stains spreading across his clothes. He was making a horrible gurgling noise, just audible over the hammering in the shop below. 'What an annoying sound,' he said, slashing Matthew across the throat. Blood spurted on to the walls and ceiling, then Matthew was silent.

'Thank goodness I found you in time,' he said, turning to Aphra. 'Who knows what he might have done if I had not been here to rescue you?'

Aphra stepped backwards and found she was up against the edge of the table.

'Oh, Mrs Behn,' he said sadly. 'I thought you would be grateful I'd saved your life, not back away as if I had the plague.' He raised the sword, holding the tip to her throat. 'Where is it, Mrs Behn?'

'Where is what?' she asked, struggling to keep her voice calm.

'The letter, Mrs Behn. The letter.'

She decided there was no point in denying any knowledge of the letter while a blade was being held to her throat. 'I know a

273

letter of some kind exists,' she said. 'But I do not know where it is or what it is about. I have never even seen it.'

He shook his head. 'That isn't good enough. You are the only one left who could have it.'

'You've been through my house time after time, searching my desk and my shelves ... If I had it you would have found it by now.'

'But I've never searched *you*,' he said, lowering his sword to the ribbons at the front of her bodice. 'Maybe you've been carrying it on your person all this time. Unlace your bodice, please.'

Aphra reached up to untie her bodice, very slowly. 'Who do you work for, Mr Cane? Who pays enough for you to wear such fine clothes and carry such an expensive sword?'

He smiled. 'I am no traitor, Mrs Behn. Unlike your friend here, it was never my intention to expose secrets that might plunge this land into civil war. I am here to protect those secrets.'

'You work for Arlington?' she asked, amazed. 'I've never known him to pay more than a pittance.'

'Arlington? You jest! I receive a handsome allowance from the government of France, merely to report what I overhear in the household of Nelly Gwyn. At first it was only gossip about the most trivial matters, and then things started to get more interesting. I knew from the French ambassador that Arlington was looking for someone named Matthew Cavell in connection with a missing letter of great importance to both the governments of England and France, so imagine my surprise when I learned this man was a friend of yours and that you had met his brother in Lincoln's Inn Fields. Nell told her maid all about it when she stopped at home to change her clothes, the day you went looking for Elias.' He laughed. 'And then the maid told me. It was a simple matter to trace him to your house; you must have given your address to every mumper at Lincoln's Inn.'

Aphra suddenly remembered how she had come upon Bevil

Cane in her parlour on the night of the funeral, pushing her furniture back into its usual arrangement. She'd only met him for the first time that morning, but he didn't ask her where anything went. He already knew. 'It was you who killed Elias,' she said, cursing herself for not realizing it before.

'Do you know what he was doing when I found him? He was upstairs in your bedchamber eating from a bag of sugar sops. He tried to run, of course. He did not get far.'

'But he didn't have the letter,' Aphra said, trying to keep him talking.

'Alas no,' Bevil said. 'I searched Gospel House while we were there for the funeral, but could find nothing there, either.'

'So you put drops in the wine.'

'Only in the hope you might know something more than you were telling. I never expected you to collapse on to the floor and make the most shocking and wanton suggestions.' He smiled, licking his lips. 'Or have you forgotten that part?'

'But what about Madam Gwyn? Why did you give the drops to her?'

'She kept boasting she noticed things no one else saw, and I wanted to know if there was anything she hadn't mentioned. I never meant to make the old woman ill; I am very fond of her, you know.' He waved his sword in front of her chest. 'You are too slow, Mrs Behn.'

'It is my age, Mr Cane. My fingers are not as nimble as they once were.'

'Come, Mrs Behn,' he said. 'You are not that old.'

'I assume you also murdered Grootvader and Toby Rainbeard.'

'I watched the Dutchman break into your house, and then I followed him home. Then I followed Mr Rainbeard after *he* broke into your house. Your house is very easy to break into; you should do something about that.' He pressed the tip of his sword to her bodice. 'You are stalling, Mrs Behn.'

'No,' she protested, 'it is my fingers. They are stiff.' She lowered her hands, feigning exasperation. 'I beg you, do it for me, Mr Cane.'

He stepped forward, leering.

She braced herself against the table. 'You will need both hands, Bevil,' she murmured suggestively.

He smiled and put his sword back in his belt.

'Come closer,' she whispered.

He did.

She brought up her knee as hard as she could.

She leapt away from the table as he doubled over, cursing.

He drew his sword, holding it at arm's length in front of him, a look of hatred on his face.

She took several steps back, keeping her eye on the blade.

'There is no escape, nowhere to hide,' he said. 'Not even a house of office.'

She continued backing away, looking about in desperation for something – anything – she could use as a weapon. She tried to take another step, and found her back was against the wall.

To one side was the open wardrobe, to the other the window, too high and too small to offer any means of escape. The apron that served as a curtain flapped in a breeze only inches from her ear.

'Uh-oh,' Bevil taunted her, his eyes wide and unblinking. 'Nowhere else to go.'

She wondered if he had tormented Elias in the same way, revelling in the way he had him cornered.

'But you and I are on the same side!' she said. 'You may be paid by a different government, but our goals are the same. I do not wish to see this country torn apart by civil war any more than you. The men you killed were traitors, every one of them. No one at Whitehall would condemn you for their deaths; you have done His Majesty a favour by eliminating them. So what reason can you possibly have for killing me? Alive, I can help you. I can explain your actions to Lord Arlington, and see you are properly rewarded.'

He laughed.

She changed her tack. 'I can ensure your play is produced at Dorset Garden ... Did I tell you how much I enjoyed it? Quite honestly, Mr Cane, I have never read a more touching and affecting romance. It brought tears to my eyes. In fact, I had intended to discuss your manuscript with Mr Davenant first thing tomorrow, before rehearsal.'

'Had you really?'

'I have much influence with Mr Davenant, you know.'

'It is a pity you did not think to use it earlier,' he said coldly.

'Mr Cane,' Aphra said. 'Bevil. Haven't I always been your friend? What possible reason could you have for killing me?'

'None, I suppose.'

She breathed a sigh of relief.

'Other than I seem to have developed a taste for it. My blade is very sharp. See?' He lunged forward, slicing the apron beside her head in two.

She leapt aside, pressing herself against the side of the wardrobe. To her surprise, it moved. It wasn't solidly built at all; it leaned away from the wall at a startling angle, more than enough for her to fit a hand behind it.

Bevil began to laugh, toying with a piece of apron on the end of his sword. His face resembled some kind of hideous mask, lips pulled back from his teeth in a grotesque mockery of a grin, eyes wide and shining with madness.

'Mr Cane, I beg you.'

'Yes, Mrs Behn,' he said, 'beg me. I like the sound of it. You should have heard that filthy beggar in your house of office, how he begged and pleaded.' He took a step forward, raising his sword to her throat. 'It didn't do him any good, either.'

She slid her hand behind the wardrobe, pushing with all her might. It toppled forward, disintegrating into a mess of splintered wood as it crashed around Bevil's head. He swung his sword wildly, temporarily blinded by dust and blood and splinters.

She ducked past him, running towards the ladder that was her only possible means of escape.

He swung around, panting.

She stopped at the edge of the opening, knowing she had no chance of getting down the ladder in time. She turned to see him charging towards her, blood streaming down his forehead into his eyes, and then she stepped aside.

He plunged past her and disappeared from sight.

She knelt down, peering through the opening to the ground below. The ladder lay broken across the blacksmith's floor. Beside it Mr Cane lay motionless, his head and limbs twisted at odd angles.

She buried her head in her hands, weeping.

Once again, she found herself facing Lord Arlington across a desk.

'We have spoken to the French ambassador, and he has expressed his deep regret and shock at hearing of the young man's actions, of which he had no prior knowledge. He admits Mr Cane came to him shortly after entering Nell Gwyn's household, offering his services as a spy, but says the young man was politely informed the French do not spy on their English friends. He says Mr Cane must have been suffering from delusions.'

'And you believe him?' Aphra said.

'I should think the suggestion that Mr Cane was some kind of lunatic is unarguable, Mrs Behn. So it is hardly surprising he found employment in Mistress Gwyn's household; the orange girl has always been known for keeping bad company. Even so, he has done us a great service, not only eliminating several dangerous traitors, but saving us the cost of a trial.'

'He tried to murder me,' Aphra reminded him.

'Ah, yes, well...' he said, shrugging. 'You're quite recovered now, aren't you?'

'And what about the document that caused all this? You've never found it, have you?'

Arlington raised his eyebrows. 'Document? There was never any document, Mrs Behn. That was a lie concocted by Mr Cavell in an attempt to extort money from His Majesty's government. It makes me sad to think of the terrible fates suffered by those who were foolish enough to believe him. Good day to you, Mrs Behn,' he said, dismissing her, 'and good luck with your new entertainment.'

She sat where she was. 'My lord, I have had certain expenses these last few weeks, directly resulting from this business, as well as damage done to my house which is yet to be repaired.'

'That is nothing to do with me, Mrs Behn. Still,' he added magnanimously, 'you may send us an accounting if you wish.'

'Will it do any good?' she asked him.

He chuckled, turning his attention to something in one of his notebooks. 'Good day, Mrs Behn.'

She walked away from his office, steaming. Not only would there be not one penny of compensation, it seemed she was not even to receive a single word of thanks or even sympathy for what she'd been through.

She would never again allow herself to be dragged into intrigue of any description, she told herself.

Never again.

John Hoyle was waiting for her in the parlour. He leapt up to embrace her the moment she walked through the door. 'Oh, my poor darling! Sweet soul, I rushed over the minute I heard!'

'Elizabeth!' Aphra shouted towards the kitchen where the actress was lurking. 'How many times have I told you to let no one in while I am out?'

*

279

Madam Gwyn came to visit her that evening. 'I had to tell you how sorry I am, little duckling,' she said, her eyes even redder than usual.

'It is I who am sorry,' Aphra said, patting the old woman on the hand. 'I know how fond you were of him, and I think, in spite of everything, the affection he felt for you was genuine.'

'But it was all my fault,' Madam Gwyn said, sniffling.

'No, no, of course not.'

'You don't understand,' the old woman said. 'It was I who told Bevil you'd been asking about Toby Rainbeard, and it was I who told him to keep a close eye on you. I was afraid you might be getting yourself into danger.'

Chapter Thirty-two

The afternoon before the play was to open, Nell peered out from the king's bedchamber doorway, a blanket wrapped around her shoulders. A guard turned to look at her. 'Make the announcement immediately,' she told him. 'Lord Rochester has been forgiven.'

Hortense Mancini looked out one of the many windows of her apartment in Whitehall Palace. For the first time in weeks, she did not see the fishermen. Anne was right: the Duchess of Portsmouth had been trying to frighten her. And now Louise saw her ruse hadn't worked, she'd called her men off. Hortense sighed, relieved to think she had been worrying over nothing.

Behind her Elizabeth Decker was fencing with Anne, dressed in one of the costumes she would wear in tomorrow's performance: that of a young gallant. Hortense couldn't help thinking that in her man's garb she might easily be mistaken for Anne's sister, if not her twin.

'It is a shame Mrs Behn did not come with you,' Hortense said.

'She is too nervous about the play,' Elizabeth said, neatly dodging a thrust from Anne.

'And you are not?' Hortense asked her.

'Why should I be? I know my lines.'

'And that is all there is to it?' Hortense asked her, smiling. 'Just knowing your lines?'

'Oh, no,' Elizabeth said. 'You have to enter and exit at the

281

right moments, then speak with the right voice, making all the right faces. It's very hard work.'

The Duchess of Mazarin would not allow Elizabeth to take a hackney coach back to Whitefriars, insisting that it wasn't safe after dark and that her driver would take her home.

As Elizabeth was being escorted across the palace courtyard, she thought she caught a glimpse of someone darting into the shadows. She giggled, imagining she had interrupted some lovers' intrigue.

The duchess's black and gold coach pulled up in front of Aphra's house, and Elizabeth stepped out, still dressed in her gallant's costume. As she was turning her key in Aphra's door, she noticed another coach pulling to a stop in front of the house, but ignored it. Coaches were a common enough sight on the streets of London, even late at night.

She opened the door and stepped inside the hall.

'Elizabeth, is that you?' Mrs Behn called from upstairs.

'Yes, Mrs Behn, it's me.'

There was a knock on the door behind her. She turned around and opened the door to two men. 'Yes?' she said.

'That's her,' one of the men said, throwing a sack over her head.

Mr Davenant's reaction on hearing that the leading actress had been kidnapped was to instruct the stage-hands to change the set, today's performance would be yet another revival of *King Lear*.

'Wait!' Nell interrupted him. 'There is no need to cancel the play.'

'But Mistress Decker is not here,' he reminded her.

'Pray tell me who has spent every day this last month, coaching her line by line?'

Mr Davenant raised a hand to stop the stage-hands. 'You mean you will play the part, Nelly?'

'Who else?'

Aphra nudged her with her elbow. 'But the wager —'

'I pray you do not think me too boastful if I say it now seems we are certain to win it,' Nell said, winking.

'But Elizabeth isn't here.'

'Exactly,' Nell said. 'Though Elizabeth did finally reach a level of adequacy sufficient to keep her from being booed off the stage, we both know she could never reach the level required to make my dear Lord Buckingham part with any money. He would argue she was passable, but nothing more. I, on the other hand, intend to see him hand over every penny.'

'But you are not Elizabeth.'

'He's not going to know that, is he? Nor will anyone else in the audience. Have you forgotten you wrote a play where the heroine spends the entire action changing from one disguise to another? Now go sit down and stop worrying; I know the play backwards.'

Aphra sat in a box, trembling with nerves as a boy climbed a ladder to light the chandelier above the stage.

A row of girls positioned themselves at the front of the pit, baskets of oranges on their arms. Then the theatre doors opened and the audience began to pour in.

'Oranges!' the girls started shouting, 'Will you have any oranges?'

She tensed, watching a group of about a dozen fops with powdered faces file into the pit. They sat together in one corner, sneering at everyone else. They were going to be trouble. They were already talking loudly enough to drown out the cries of the orange girls, only pausing to sniff a nosegay or snort an occasional braying laugh.

She also noted to her dismay that the vizards were out in force today, openly plying their trade among the denizens of the pit. If the actors did not grab the audience's attention early on, these masked prostitutes would.

She looked around the upper levels; maybe there was some hope there. The upper gallery seemed to be full of journeymen and servants. That could be good – if they liked the jokes – or bad, if they decided they didn't care for a play without a lot of fighting. She told herself she should have added another duel.

The middle gallery and the other boxes were almost empty. The sort of person who sat in a box never arrived before the second act, and often waited until the third, so there was still some hope there. But the middle gallery was where respectable men sat when they'd brought their wives. And respectable men, she reflected, would never bring their wives to see a play written by an 'immodest' woman.

One of the fops in the pit got up to urinate in front of the stage, to much merriment from his companions. The orange girls left the front of the theatre and an actor walked on to the stage, unnoticed by the audience who kept on talking while he delivered the prologue.

Then the curtain opened, revealing a painted backdrop of a street. There was a momentary hush as two actors entered, one of them playing the heroine's father, complaining to a friend of his daughter's bad behaviour. The murmuring of the audience resumed, growing louder by the minute. One of the fops in the pit stood up to stretch, yawning loudly, again to much merriment from his companions.

Aphra sank her head into her hands.

Then Nell entered, dressed as a nun.

Rochester joined her in the box during the second act. 'How goes it?'

'John! I didn't think to see you here.'

'His Majesty has forgiven me, prompting my swift return from France,' he said, laughing. 'And how does Elizabeth?'

'Elizabeth?'

'Does she perform well?'

'Yes,' Aphra said weakly.

'Where am I?' Elizabeth demanded as the coach pulled to a stop. 'Where have you brought me?'

A rough pair of hands bundled her out of the coach. 'Home,' a man's voice told her. 'Where you belong.'

She was led a short distance, and then the sack was lifted from her head. 'Your wayward wife,' a voice proclaimed.

She raised a hand to shield her eyes, unaccustomed to the light after being kept under a sack all these hours, and stared about her, blinking in confusion.

She seemed to be in some kind of great hall, maybe even a castle. In front of her a man stood, gaping. 'Idiots!' he shouted. 'That is not my wife!'

Epilogue

Aphra leaned back on the settle in her parlour, thinking over the events of the last week, grateful her troubles were finally over.

Rochester had won his bet, and given her the two hundred and fifty pounds he'd promised. Enough to pay all her debts and have something left over to fix the bench in the house of office. The play was still running, despite the fact Elizabeth had been returned unharmed in time to take over her role from the second performance onwards. Elizabeth and Rochester had been reconciled and the earl had moved his mistress to new lodgings.

Aphra had also persuaded Rochester to pay Mrs Adams's debt, reminding him that twelve pounds was nothing to him and that if he refused she would tell the Duke of Monmouth the truth about Doctor Alexander Bendo.

Doctor Bendo's sudden appearance – and disappearance less than two weeks later – was still the topic of much gossip and speculation. They said the doctor and his assistants were demons raised by necromancy to walk the earth for a brief period before returning to the pit from whence they'd come, and everyone who had bought Bendo's medicines had since thrown them away for fear of witchcraft. She'd heard from Nell that Anne of Sussex had returned home to her husband, after her husband came to Whitehall personally to collect her.

Aphra had gone back to Gospel House one last time, managing to avoid Mrs Barrow long enough to present Virtue Hawkins with a knitted shawl to keep her warm through the coming winter.

And she and John Hoyle were speaking again. Nothing more, she told herself, despite Hoyle's insistence that the woman he'd been seen having dinner with was his aunt. Just speaking.

She stood up to survey the room, placing her hands on her hips. The whole house was in a dreadful state, dirty plates and mugs scattered everywhere, a wardrobe full of laundry.

Laundry, she thought. No wonder she had nothing to wear. All her clothes were crumpled into a heap at the bottom of the wardrobe. She had two options: wash them herself, or take them to a laundress and pay her to do them. She decided that now she had money again, she preferred the latter.

She started to go upstairs to collect her dirty clothes, then stopped, looking at the cloth draped across the little table near the entrance to the kitchen. She hadn't realized how filthy it had become, covered with melted wax and ash and wine stains. She lifted the cloth and saw a small sheet of paper, lying flat against the table top.

She picked it up and read the words:

My dear Arlington, the following clause has been added to our secret agreement at Dover: the King of England, being convinced of the truth of the Roman Catholic religion, is resolved to declare it, and to reconcile himself and his people with the Church of Rome as soon as the state of his country's affairs permit . . .

It went on to say that the King of France agreed to provide money and troops to assist in the execution of this design, though the number of troops was a matter for negotiation.

She looked down at the signature.

Charles.

So this was what they'd all been looking for. What they'd tipped over her bed and ripped the bench from her house of office for. What they'd scattered the contents of her desk and shelves across the floor for. What they'd lied, and killed, and died for.

And it had been underneath her tablecloth the whole time. Elias must have hidden it there before Mr Cane's arrival, intending to come back for it later.

She could imagine what Monmouth and his supporters in the Country Party would do if this were to fall into their hands. Or what the Dutch would have done. Or any number of foreign governments.

It didn't matter that the letter was years old, and the king had obviously never taken any steps to honour his promises to the French and probably never meant to; the fact that he had made them was enough. No wonder Matthew had spoken of a pact with the devil, and Bevil Cane of civil war. And no wonder Arlington had been so anxious first to have it back, then to deny it ever existed: it exposed him as a party to this double-dealing.

A dangerous document indeed, she thought as she stood by the fire, debating whether she should drop it into the flames or hold on to it as a kind of insurance.